MY BROTHER MY JUDGE

NEAL WOOTEN

ISBN 978-1-61225-119-6
1-61225-119-6

Library of Congress Control Number: 2012903596

Published in the United States
by Mirror Publishing
Milwaukee, WI 53214

Printed in the USA.

To my wife, Margarita

I would like to thank several people whose contributions were invaluable in keeping the storyline as authentic as possible.

Thank you to Virginia A. Davis
Virginia is a Harvard grad and partner with the Washington D.C. law firm of Katten Muchin Rosenman LLP.

Thank you to Irma Jacobs Tirro
Irma is a former Judicial Assistant in the Circuit Court, Brevard County, Florida, now retired.

Thank you to Sgt. Denise Whittaker
Denise is a 15 year Georgia and Alabama veteran law enforcement officer and former investigator.

Thank you to Jan Putnam Stevens
Jan is a retired educator having taught at several high schools, colleges, and five years with the Alabama Education Association.

Thank you to Major David Albrecht, Air Force
Major Albrecht is the Deputy of Program Control, Global Positioning System Satellite Acquisition.

Thank you to Nicolas Peruzzo
Nicolas is an artist from Uruguay, South America.

Thank you to an inmate of the Montgomery County Jail who wishes to remain anonymous.

"Although a system may cease to exist in the legal sense or as a structure of power, its values (or anti-values), its philosophy, its teachings remain in us. They rule our thinking, our conduct, our attitude to others. The situation is a demonic paradox: we have toppled the system but we still carry its genes."

"Do not be misled by the fact that you are at liberty and relatively free; that for the moment you are not under lock and key: you have simply been granted a reprieve."

— Ryszard Kapuściński, Polish journalist and writer

PROLOGUE

IT WAS ONE OF THOSE surreal moments. Trevor couldn't believe it was actually happening. The whole world stopped spinning as he wondered how he had gotten into the predicament he was in. His left eye was stinging from the impact, causing water to form in the corner, yet he could still see the other customers in the video store in his peripheral field of view. They were as stunned as he.

"Come on, Davis, you big fat coward. Hit me back."

Trevor didn't move. He had never been in a fight, not even as a kid, and he certainly never planned on it at age 30. He stared at his assailant. He knew him well; everyone in town did. William Traylor was a trouble maker and always had been. Trevor's eye fluttered as the moisture accumulated and threatened to tear.

"Are you going to cry?" William said.

Trevor's eye twitched again. It wasn't clear if it was from the pain or anger. Trevor was quick to lose his temper yet he still didn't respond. He looked William over as his mind played out the scenarios. Surely he could beat him. William was scrawny, a measly 140 pounds, which meant Trevor was almost twice his weight and several inches taller. But his heart was racing. Was it fear?

"You guys cut it out," the young clerk said. His voice was breaking up as if he was the one being threatened.

William danced around mockingly without a care in the world. He was enjoying the attention. "Come on, lard ass, let's go outside and finish this."

Trevor was about to walk away until he heard those words. He couldn't very well leave now or it would appear as if he was accepting the challenge. He didn't know what to do. He looked at William's greasy work-shirt and long, straight, blond, almost white hair. What was there to be afraid of? Was it the smell of alcohol? Was it the rumors he had heard about how many fights in which William had reportedly been involved? Was it the worry that William was concealing a weapon? Maybe a knife? Maybe a gun? Was it the worry that even if he did get into a fist fight with this person and won, it would never be over? Then it dawned on him; it was none of those things. It was the one thing that William possessed that Trevor did not—confidence. Trevor finally broke the stare-down and dropped his head.

"What's the matter, wimp?" William said. "Your big brother ain't here to protect you, is he?"

That hurt worse than the punch. What did Dustin have to do with this?

William laughed. "Forget it. Come on, babe."

Trevor watched him and his girlfriend, or so he assumed her to be, walk out the front door. He looked at the DVD in his hand but decided he wasn't in the mood anymore to watch a movie. As he placed it back on the shelf, he noticed that the five other customers were still fixated on him. They quickly looked away and continued their own movie searches as he scanned the room.

"Sorry about that, Tre," the clerk said.

Trevor didn't acknowledge. He walked out to his car and climbed into the driver's seat. He stared at his reflection in the rearview mirror. His eye was already red and somewhat swollen; no doubt a black eye in the making. He was angry at himself. No, he was humiliated. He replayed the events in his mind. Why had he done nothing? Surely getting beat up would not feel as badly as standing there like a fool.

The comment about his brother was literally adding insult to injury. He didn't need Dustin to protect him. So what if Dustin had more weightlifting trophies than Trevor cared to count. So what if Dustin could bench press a small village. So what if William Traylor, or most people, would dare not cross Dustin. So what if Trevor was not his brother. If Dustin had been here, it doesn't mean he would have lifted one finger to help, much less one fist. If anything, Dustin would have been cheering William on.

He started his car and left the valley, driving straight back home to Sand Mountain

MY BROTHER, MY JUDGE

CHAPTER

ONE

DUSTIN SMILED and turned off the riding mower as Frankie walked toward him carrying a bottled water from the cooler. Dustin took the offering and twisted the top. The seal was already broken. He never bought bottled water, only reused the containers and filled them using the filter on his home faucet. He turned up the bottle and drained the contents as the cold water ran down each side of his mouth and down his stout neck, providing a temporary reprieve from the Alabama heat.

It was hard to tell that Dustin even had a neck. It was very short and the muscles on each side, the trapezius muscles, were very pronounced, rising up almost to his ears. The grass clippings and dirt still adhered to his thick forearms as he handed the empty bottle back to Frankie.

"Thanks, partner," Dustin said.

Frankie smiled and took the empty back to the truck.

Dustin had been cutting lawns for a long time. That's how he met his wife. Sophia was the first female he ever hired and soon realized she was the hardest worker he ever hired. He soon promoted her to supervisor over a crew and later, to hear him jokingly tell it, promoted her to wife. This is when she usually interjects that it was clearly a demotion.

After Dustin and Sophia had been married for three years, it became apparent that they could not have children, although they never tried to find out why. They probably would have adopted but the fates were listening. Hannah, Sophia's younger sister, who was not married and had no boyfriend that anyone was aware of, became pregnant. Since she could not afford to raise a child on her own, Dustin accepted it as faith. He had been there the day Frankie was born and Frankie was his pride and joy. They spent so much time together. That's why Dustin had given him a summer job at the tender age of seven, retrieving water, gas, or hauling bags of grass clipping out to the curb. It provided Frankie with a little spending money and they could spend more time together.

When they finished with their last lawn for the day, they dropped off one of the lawn crew employees and then to Dustin's house. He backed the trailer in beside the house as always and began unhooking the trailer hitch and lights. Frankie carried trash out to the receptacles.

Sophia pulled in beside Dustin's truck and walked over to them. "How was your day, fellas?"

"Great," Frankie said.

"Hot," Dustin said.

"I believe you." Sophia looked at his sweat-soaked shirt. "Well it looks like you have figured out a way to get out of work—again. Does your mom or brother know you went up there yesterday?"

Dustin shook his head.

"You think it's over now?" Sophia said. "That guy's been picking on Tre for almost two weeks. You think he's just going to stop?"

"It'll stop; I guarantee it," Dustin said. "I'll bet you anything that Trevor brought this on himself. And what's with that stupid nickname? 'Tre' is not a shortened version of Trevor. The way he pronounces it makes him sound like a third."

"A third what?"

Dustin rolled his eyes, which he knew Sophia hated but it was an uncontrollable force of habit. "A third in generation terms. You know, like Charles Winchester the Third. Some people who are thirds go by 'Trey.'"

Sophia nodded but her eyes shifted upward.

"What are you thinking?" Dustin said.

"I'm trying to think if I've ever known anyone who went by Trey."

Dustin shook his head. "I got to take Frankie home. You want to come?"

"No, you guys go ahead. I'll start supper. I'll have to pick him up tomorrow and let him work with me since you'll be taking the next month off."

Dustin laughed. "Wasn't my plan. I've never gotten a jury duty summons before. I'm sure there's no way they will pick me but it would be neat to be a part of a trial."

"Why wouldn't they pick you?" Frankie said.

Sophia put her arm around Frankie. "Because they try to pick people with open minds, and your uncle is the most stubborn, hard-headed man on the planet."

Frankie laughed.

They got back into the truck and Dustin drove Frankie home.

The next morning, Dustin left Sophia to handle the lawn business and drove down to the county courthouse in Montgomery. It was a spring day and early in the morning but still a blistering 85 degrees, which was rough on Dustin since he had dressed in his Sunday attire. He went inside and to the courtroom where he had been instructed to go. He showed the guard his summons and was told to go in and sit down. There were a lot of people sitting in the first three pews, so he took a seat among them. The prosecutor and defense attorney, both males in their early 50s, were seated at the two tables in the front section and the judge was seated at his elevated station. Several more people filtered in and took a seat.

The judge was a large man with chubby cheeks. His hair was balding on top and he wore huge reading glasses. "Is everyone here?" he said.

The prosecutor counted heads and told the judge he thought that was everyone. The judge called roll and each person answered by saying "here."

The judge was completely expressionless as he explained what was going on. "You're all here because you received a summons to appear. We're going to move forward with Voir dire as we try to seat the jury. Each of you will be called up and asked questions. After we have 12 jurors and two alternates, this trial will begin."

Dustin looked around to see if anyone else was surprised. He didn't know they would be starting today.

They called the first person, Irene Adams. A handsome and well-dressed woman in her sixties was instructed to take one of the vacant chairs. She was given a Bible to place her left hand upon and told to raise her right hand.

"Do you swear to tell the truth, the whole truth, and nothing but the truth?" the judge said.

"Yes, Your Honor."

The prosecutor went first. "Have you ever been convicted of a violent crime?"

"No."

"Have you ever served time in prison or jail?"

"No."

"Do you believe in the death penalty?"

"Yes."

"Do you know anyone associated with this trial?"

"Yes, I know you and the judge."

The prosecutor motioned to the judge that he was satisfied and, to Dustin's surprise, the defense attorney did not offer a peremptory challenge. That was it, Ms. Adams was on the jury.

"Dustin Davis," the judge said.

Dustin took the seat next to Ms. Adams and performed the oath with his hand on the Bible. He was asked the same questions from the prosecutor and his answers were identical to Ms. Adams. But the defense attorney wanted to know more from Dustin.

"Mr. Davis, do you attend church?" the attorney said.

"Yes, sir."

"How often?"

"Three times a week," Dustin said.

"Mr. Davis, have you ever been the victim of a crime?" he said.

Dustin had to think. "Uh… I had the radio stolen out of my truck once."

"Were they caught?"

"No, sir."

"How did that make you feel?" the attorney said.

Dustin tried to remember. "Mostly upset that I had to spend money on another one."

The attorney wasn't satisfied with that answer. "If you had caught the guy breaking into your truck, what would you have done?"

"Called the police and probably asked him to stop," Dustin said.

As the defense attorney hesitated, the judge spoke up. "Mr. Davis, have you ever been in a fist fight?"

"Yes, sir," Dustin said. "Eleventh grade."

"And what was that about?"

Dustin was almost embarrassed to answer. "The Pythagorean Theorem."

"I beg your pardon."

"The Pythagorean Theorem, Your Honor," Dustin said again. "This guy on the math team with me was getting it confused with the Quadratic Formula, and he started to—"

The judge laughed and threw up his hands. "That's OK. I'm certain now I don't want to know."

Everyone in the room laughed.

The judge looked at the defense attorney. "Do you have

any more questions?"

"No," he said. "I'm satisfied."

The judge looked back at Dustin. "Remain seated right there, Mr. Math, you're on the jury."

Dustin couldn't believe it. He only tried to answer the questions honestly. He had hoped to get out of this thing but his math background seemed to have landed him right-square in the middle of it.

The morning continued in the same manner with each person taking the oath and answering questions. Oddly enough, when it was over, the prosecutor had used all his peremptory challenges to strike five women and the defense attorney had used his to strike five men. The jury ended up consisting of nine women and three guys, with two male alternates.

The judge told the jury what was expected of them and, as soon as that was over, the spectators were allowed to enter. The defendant was led to the table with his attorney and the opening statements were delivered.

After the opening statements, the court was adjourned until nine o'clock the next morning. The jurors were led to their deliberating room by the bailiff. He reiterated what the judge had said earlier—when they leave the courthouse, they aren't allowed to read the newspapers, watch the news, or anything that might influence their decision regarding the case. They are also not allowed to discuss the case until it was over, with anyone, including their families. The only task for today was to elect a foreman before going home.

Everyone sat in total silence after the bailiff left. One of the female jurors finally spoke. "OK, who wants to be foreman?" she said.

Silence.

Dustin raised his hand and everyone looked to him. He pointed to the first lady to be chosen. "Ms. Adams, I wanted to ask you a question if I could."

"OK," she said, somewhat puzzled.

"You said that you knew the judge and prosecutor. Can I ask how?" Dustin said.

All eyes were directed toward her.

"I worked as an administrator here for 30 years," she said. "I retired eight years ago."

Dustin smiled. "Then I would like to nominate you to be our foreman."

Heads began to nod, except for hers.

"Oh no, I wouldn't feel comfortable. But I have a suggestion," she said.

All the jurors continued to look at her.

She continued. "There is one here that seems to have a head for remembering details and a knack for asking the right questions. And it would seem this person is good at equations as well. I would like to nominate that person."

Dustin blushed as all the other jurors agreed and the ones on either side of him patted him on the shoulder.

"Are y'all sure?" Dustin said.

They all confirmed so Dustin reluctantly agreed as they got up and left for the night.

Dustin drove home wondering how he had driven to the courthouse this morning thinking he wouldn't even make the jury, but, not only was he indeed part of the jury, he had been elected foreman.

Sophia got a good laugh out of it as well.

CHAPTER

TWO

THE TRIAL LASTED a week and a half. The defendant was 21 years old, very tall at 6'5", thin and slouching with a deathly white complexion, with long, matted black hair. He seemed totally unconcerned with what was going on. Even in his cheap wool suit, he looked like a thug. He gave Dustin the impression that he was very cold-hearted, and therefore, capable of the crime he was being charged with—murder. The victim was a 63-year-old man who lived alone in a garage apartment at some type of old car business. Pictures and friends depicted the man as very frail with many health problems.

According to the prosecution, the defendant and his cohort broke into the older man's apartment because they thought he had drugs. When no drugs could be found, they decided to wait for him to come home. They got hungry and ate while waiting—cereal—and the box of cereal, bowls, flatware, glasses, and milk were all left on the table with the defendant and his partner's fingerprints all over them. The prosecutor presented pictures of the scene of the mess that had been created when the old man returned.

The most damning pieces of evidence were the baseball bat used to bludgeon the old man to death and the pictures of the apartment ceiling showing the bat's impression when the murderer brought the bat up with extreme force to hit the man on the back and side of the head, a total of 13 times.

The prosecutor showed that the defendant's partner-in-crime was not tall enough to make these impressions. The partner was short and, although not overweight, certainly not slim. While there were no fingerprints on the bat itself, and no blood found on any of the clothes of the defendant or in his car, his same partner provided the *coup de gras* with his testimony, ratting out his friend in delicate detail.

The victim's girlfriend, also in her early sixties, provided the most heart-wrenching testimony about what a great person her boyfriend was and swore he had never used or sold drugs.

The closing statements were delivered and the jury received final instructions from the judge.

"Take as much time as you need to deliberate. You must return a unanimous verdict for the defendant to be found guilty or not guilty. If the defendant is found to be guilty, you will hear more testimony before you decide on a sentence."

The bailiff escorted them to the deliberation room where they had voted Dustin to be the foreman. They all took their seats with Dustin sitting at the head of the table. A legal pad and pen was in front of each juror, as was a transcript of the trial. Dustin had not worn a jacket since the first day because, even though the courthouse had air conditioning, sitting in the confined area with the other jurors was just too hot for him. He rolled up his sleeves after sitting and loosened his tie.

All eyes turned to Dustin.

"OK," Dustin said, "I've been told that we should conduct a preliminary vote to see where everyone stands." Ms. Adams was sitting directly to his left, so he looked to her. "Let's start with you and go around the table."

Ms. Adams said, "Guilty."

It went on around the circle with everyone saying guilty until it reached the woman sitting to Dustin's right, the only elderly person on the jury, appearing to be around 80 years of age. When she said not guilty, you could feel the tension in the air as several jurors stared in disbelief.

"I vote guilty," Dustin said. "So we have 11-to-one for

guilty."

"How can you say that?" one male juror said.

"Are you crazy?" shouted a woman.

"Whoa," Dustin said, holding up both hands. "This isn't *12 Angry Men*—"

"I love that movie," said Ms. Adams, patting Dustin on the arm.

Dustin smiled. "Me too. The point is, we have no reason to get upset. The defendant hasn't done anything to any of us, and I'm sure this lady hasn't either." Then he looked at the lady to his right. "What's your name, dear?" he said.

"Kitty."

"Well, Ms. Kitty," Dustin said, "how about we do this?" He looked at the rest of the table. "Why don't I call on people and they can explain why they see it the way they do, and it will give you a chance to explain your views. Is everyone OK with that?"

Everyone nodded.

Dustin nodded to the male juror who first spoke out. "Let's start with you."

"OK," the guy said. "For me, it was the testimony of the detective. This dude has been in and out of trouble since he was born."

"But the defense objected to that and the judge told us to forget that testimony," Kitty said.

The juror shook his head. "You can't forget something like that."

Ms. Adams held up the transcript. "She's right. We have to concentrate on this crime only. If it's not in these documents, we can't discuss it or let it affect our decisions."

"I agree with that," Dustin said. "OK, how about you?" Dustin nodded to the female juror who shouted out earlier.

"For me it was the testimony of the other guy who was with the defendant. I mean, he saw everything and testified as an eyewitness to the entire thing." She looked at Kitty for a reply.

"But did you notice the words he was using?" Kitty said.

Everyone looked dumbfounded, even Dustin.

Ms. Adams began flipping through the transcript until she found the testimony. "Let me read it here." She put on her reading glasses and brought the paper up close to her face. "'We thought the guy was a drug dealer and needed a score. We entered the premises and searched the apartment but couldn't find any drugs. We decided to wait for him to make him show us where the drugs were hidden.'" Ms. Adams looked up as if wondering if she needed to read more.

"Is that what you mean, Ms. Kitty?" Dustin said.

"Yes," Kitty said. "Doesn't that seem odd to anyone else?"

Everyone shook their heads and a few "no's" were whispered.

Ms. Adams smiled at Ms. Kitty. "What are you trying to say?"

"Can you read the opening statement from the prosecutor regarding those same events," Kitty said, pointing to the transcript still in Ms. Adams' hands.

Ms. Adams flipped to the front and searched. "Uh…let's see. 'We will show that the defendant and his accomplice entered the premises and searched the apartment but couldn't find any drugs.'"

"I see what you're saying," Dustin said. "The defendant's partner did not appear to be an educated man. He would not have used those words. He wouldn't have said 'premises.' He would have said something like, 'We broke into the place.'"

Another female juror finally spoke. "So, you're saying he was coached?"

Dustin shrugged. "I think it's obvious that he made a deal to help his own charges and using the same exact words of the prosecutor does seem to suggest he was coached. The question is—does that make his testimony any less valid?"

They discussed it for a while but the consensus of opinion was that his testimony was still an accurate account of what had transpired.

After they had exhausted the subject, Dustin said, "Is there anyone who wants to change their vote?"

No one raised their hands, including Ms. Kitty.

Three hours later, they were still at a stalemate. They took a time-out when lunch was served and then continued. After another hour, the bailiff came to the room to inquire where they were and Dustin explained.

"I'll tell the judge," the bailiff said. He returned a few minutes later and led them back to the courtroom.

"Have you reached a verdict?" the judge said.

Dustin stood up and cleared his throat. "No, Your Honor, we have not." Dustin watched as the defendant smiled and twisted his head around to smile at family members seated behind him. It made Dustin sick to his stomach.

"Very well," the judge said. "As it's already late, let us resume deliberations at nine o'clock in the morning."

Dustin went home and, as they ate dinner, explained to Sophia what had happened without telling her any details of the case.

"A hung jury? That's all you can tell me?" Sophia said.

Dustin nodded.

"This is bothering you, isn't it?"

"Yes," Dustin said. "It really is. If you ask me, civilian courts need to operate more like military courts."

"What's the difference?" Sophia said.

Dustin took another bite then wiped the corners of his mouth. "Everything. A court martial follows the Uniform Code of Military Justice, which predates our constitution and even our country. Juries don't have to be unanimous and they vote secretly. We wouldn't be having a problem with a hung jury at all like we are now with this case. It would be over in 15 minutes."

Sophia frowned. "And that's a good thing?"

"Well, not for the defendant," Dustin said. "It's not about being good or bad but being efficient and just. In a civilian court, the burden of proof is on the prosecutor. In a military court, the burden of proof is on the defendant. He literally has to prove his innocence. That's the way it should be I think. I know that's hard to understand from the standpoint of someone who's never been in the military."

Maybe he was right since Sophia didn't ask anything else about it, even after they went to bed.

Dustin tried to get some sleep before delivering newspapers. That was another job he had before he and Sophia met. He was a bonded contractor for the Montgomery Advertiser, delivering newspapers to several neighboring towns each night for the home route people in those towns to pick up, bag, and distribute to the subscribers. If the press was on time, he worked from 2:00 a.m. until 5:00 a.m. Dustin was the youngest person ever to obtain such a contract position with the newspaper. It paid well but the hours were rough and the newspaper never took a day off. Anytime Dustin needed to get away, he had to hire a substitute to do his deliveries for him.

On his route, all he could think about was how to convince Ms. Kitty she was wrong, because as much as he liked her, and as much as what she said made sense, he was convinced the guy was guilty. He finally decided on his approach.

The next morning, the jurors took their places. Dustin came prepared. "I'd like to explain something I read online before we get started today if it's OK with y'all," Dustin said.

Everyone was in agreement.

Dustin began to recall the website's words. "I thought about what direction to go today and I was reminded of our instructions in the beginning. We were told that guilt must be proved beyond a reasonable doubt. I read this on the internet and it explained that the case being presented by the prosecution must be proven to the extent that there could be no reasonable doubt in the mind of a reasonable person that the defendant is guilty. There can still be doubt, but only to the extent that it would not affect a reasonable person's belief as to whether or not the defendant is guilty."

Ms. Adams smiled as everyone nodded in agreement.

"That means we can still have doubt," the same male juror said, "but we have to consider if it is reasonable that the defendant committed this crime. With all the testimony and evidence, it's very reasonable to me."

"But," Kitty said, "the only hard evidence at all only proves that the defendant was in the apartment. The only testimony provided was clearly bought with a promise of a lighter charge for the other person possibly involved. Even if the other guy didn't swing the bat, in this state he could still be charged with murder just for being there and still get the chair. I understand human nature. With the prospect of facing the death penalty himself, he would have said whatever the prosecution wanted him to say just to save his own hide."

Moans and whispers were heard throughout the small room. Dustin knew she had a point but it didn't change his views at all, or apparently any others. After two more hours without changing her mind, Dustin summoned the bailiff. When the bailiff took the note from Dustin, he looked at Dustin like he was a traitor. When the bailiff returned, he led them back into the courtroom.

"Have you reached a verdict?" the judge said.

"No, sir. We have not."

The judge was expressionless. "Then I declare a hung jury. These proceedings are over." He banged the gavel several times. "The jury is excused."

The defendant and his attorney rejoiced as if they had won a victory.

Dustin had little doubt that it would be tried again and

justice would eventually prevail. He followed the other jurors out of the courtroom and into the hall. Some went to the restrooms, some to the stairs. Dustin, Ms. Adams, Ms. Kitty, and three others went straight to the elevator. The bailiff was standing beside the elevator staring at them.

"You want to slide over so we can press the button?" Dustin said.

The bailiff didn't answer, only reached back and pressed the button himself. "What a day," the bailiff said as they waited for the elevator to open. "You know, we had a deputy on hand to walk y'all to your cars for safety, but I don't see that being necessary now."

No one said anything. Finally the doors opened and everyone filed in past the bailiff. Dustin let everyone go first and brought up the rear. When he reached the door, the bailiff grabbed his arm.

"Just so you know," the bailiff said, "the guy beat his cellmate half to death while he was awaiting trial. This was all a big waste of taxpayer money. We will just have to start over with another jury—a smarter jury."

Dustin looked down at the bailiff's hand, which only stretched around half of Dustin's 19-inch biceps. His face began to turn red as he looked up at the bailiff. "Let go of my arm."

The bailiff quickly obliged.

CHAPTER

THREE

WITHOUT TAKING HIS EYES off the computer screen, Trevor reached down beside his chair and fumbled through the open cardboard box of Mountain Dew Code Reds. It began with twelve but now only two remained; one after he managed to secure one in his large hand and bring it out. He snapped open the top and turned it up, consumed one-half of the room temperature liquid in one gulp, then placed the container on his desk next to his mouse pad.

Trevor leaned forward as he peered at the screen. He was tall and heavy and always slumped. His hair was long and unmanaged and his beard, which was several inches long, was untrimmed, running from his high cheeks to his lower neck. All he ever wore were black sweatpants and black shirts, either sweatshirts in the cooler months, or t-shirts like he wore now, which made his complexion seem even lighter.

Several boxes of comic books and baseball cards, plus at least six two-feet-high stacks of Dungeons & Dragons books lined the edge of the floor, making it clear to anyone who entered what Trevor's hobbies were. His desk was an oversized oak school teacher's desk, built around the beginning of the 1900s and had been a gift from his grandmother. It was so large Trevor never bothered to secure the top. It had to be taken apart to get through any standard doorway and since the top weighed almost 80 pounds, Trevor just let it sit on the frame in case he ever decided to move it again. He assumed that the best way to get it into a house was to conveniently build a house around it.

Two identical 21-inch monitors were perched atop the desk a few inches past his keyboard, spread just wide enough to have a natural spectrum desk lamp sitting between them.

The lamp had been a gift from his mother since she worried that he spent too much time in the basement. It's a matter of taste really; one man's dungeon is another man's damp, musky, dimly lit concrete cave. Trevor hid here most of the time and it showed. In contrast to Dustin, Trevor's skin stayed very white because he didn't care for sports, or working outdoors, or any event that took place outside. Computers were his world and he had taught himself how to do just about everything on a computer that could be done.

His office was in a room that Dustin had partitioned off years ago as a weight room when he moved back for a few months after being discharged from the Marine Corp. Trevor had a door and some cheap carpet added and moved in all his computer stuff after Dustin moved away. It had been his ever since. He practically lived down here, sometimes even sleeping in this room. His desk sat in the far corner of two block walls, which were painted white, behind his desk and to his left. On the wall behind him, which was sheetrock and also painted white, several original Star Wars posters were displayed, along with a custom light saber, the most expensive on the market.

Trevor checked his mother's bank account. Not there yet. He glanced down at the two thumb drives resting beside his keyboard, two programs he had designed for people he knew, one an anti-virus program and one an animation GIF file for a friend's company logo.

He checked his mother's account. Still nothing.

He clicked on the news to pass the time, read the first headline, and started laughing. It read "Man Awarded 750 Million Dollars in Fraud Case." Trevor read the story. An older man in south Alabama had contracted a small construction company to build a paved driveway. The estimate to do the job—$950.

According to the construction company's lawyer, a sink hole in the man's yard caused a portion of the driveway to collapse after the concrete was poured, resulting in several more hours of work as they had to fill in the hole, reset the forms, and get another truck out to pour more concrete. They added $300 to his bill. He sued. The jury awarded the man the $300 in actual damages, and 750 million dollars for pain and suffering.

"Unbelievable," Trevor said. "Why can I not find a construction company and jury like that?" He knew that the judge no doubt would decrease the sum substantially, but it was still crazy.

He checked his mother's account. Her paycheck had been deposited. He grabbed the two thumb drives and left the basement.

He drove off Sand Mountain and to the valley. As he drove through town, he passed the video store and cringed as he relived that ugly moment. He made two stops to drop off the two programs and collected $50 each. Then to his main destination—the comic book store. The store was in a small shopping center, which consisted of the comic book store and a beauty salon. Since the patrons of the latter business were always taking up all the parking spaces, Trevor parked on the curb and went inside.

"Hey, Tre, how's it going?" the owner said. The owner was much younger than Trevor.

"It is going well, my friend. Do you have my books?"

The owner grabbed a large box and set it on the counter. Trevor started going through them to make sure each one was there, every Spiderman, Thor, Avengers, Incredible Hulk, X-Men, and several older collectibles.

"What is the inflated price this month, mon frère?" Trevor said.

"A hundred fifty."

Trevor stared at the guy like he couldn't believe it. "Highway robbery." He handed him the $100 cash he had just collected and added his mother's debit card for the rest. After the transaction, he turned to leave.

"Hey," the owner said. "Whatever happened to that guy from the video store?"

Trevor stopped and turned around. "I do not concern myself with such shenanigans. My lawyer is handling it." That wasn't true, of course. Trevor did not have a lawyer and detested everything about them.

As he walked outside, there was a female patrol officer standing at the rear of his car writing a parking ticket. "Excuse me, woman. What do you think you are doing?"

The officer looked up and smiled. "I'm writing you a citation for parking here."

"Yes," Trevor said, "I can see that. What I wish to know is why."

She laughed and pointed to the sign directly beside Trevor's car. "Uh, because of that sign right there that says 'No Parking.'"

Trevor looked at the sign. "OK, at least I know you are not retarded since you can obviously read. However, it is your comprehension skills I question. Or maybe it is your eyesight. Do you not see that the other writing below those words you so eloquently read?"

The officer continued to write.

"Excuse me. I hate when people do not answer questions. You are surely learning impaired in some way, so let me read the entire sign to you. It reads 'No Parking' as you were so clever enough to notice, but then in smaller letters it reads 'Between Driveways.'" Trevor pointed with both his hands. "There is one driveway there and there is the other. My car is not parked between them. Therefore, I am not breaking the law."

The officer laughed again. "You're parked right beside the sign."

Trevor shook his head. "You cannot hold me responsible for where the Department of Transportation employee placed the sign. It was clearly an error on their part. Perhaps they have a program to employ mentally challenged people. I commend them for their efforts. I, too, believe that even the poor souls with limited capacities can be productive in society. But still, you cannot ignore the rest of the words on the sign to make it mean something it does not."

"There you go," she said, handing the ticket to Trevor.

Trevor was livid. He took out his cell phone and began to snap pictures of the sign. "My lawyer will take this up with the city. I can only hope you do not lose your job over this."

"That's very thoughtful," she said as she walked back toward her patrol car.

"Wait," Trevor said. He walked up to the officer who took a broad stance and placed her hand on her night stick as if wondering what he might do. "I could not help but notice that you are a very attractive woman. I also could not help but notice you are not wearing a wedding ring." Trevor waved the ticket in the air. "I am willing to forget this minor setback in our relationship since you think you are doing the right thing. I was wondering if you would you care to—"

"Ah shucks," said the officer. "You had me at 'learning impaired.'"

Trevor smiled. "So, we have a date?"

"Yes," she said tapping the ticket in Trevor's hand. "On or before June 2nd."

"June 2nd? Of this year?"

"Yep. Good old 2014."

Trevor's cheeks turned red. "That's only three weeks from now."

The officer just smiled and got into her car and rolled down the window. "You take care and try not to park there anymore."

"Oh do not worry," Trevor said. "Now that I know that the perfect English on that sign means absolutely nothing, I shall strive to lower my intelligence to your level for my life's duration. Perhaps one day you can give me a speeding ticket for driving five miles per hour below the speed limit. Who knows, maybe you can cite me for jaywalking when I am sitting in the park. I am surprised they even have judges in this town when they have you. Do the judges come to you for legal interpretations? Thank you for your lesson today; it was a real eye opener."

"Sure. It was the least I could do."

Trevor turned to walk to his car.

"Hey," the officer said.

Trevor stopped and turned around with anticipation.

"How's Dustin? Tell him Denise Goolesby says hello."

Trevor bit his lower lip as he glared at her then turned and walked away.

CHAPTER

~

FOUR

THE HEAT WAS almost unbearable, which added to the already dense air that swirled around inside the cab of the 2002 Dodge Ram pickup as it sped down I-59 with both windows down. The humid air of Dog Days in Alabama blowing in through the windows brought little appeasement and the sultriness of its impact felt like a heater blowing directly in your face as the air outside was as hot as the air inside the truck. Summer heat in the South is an entity, a living tangible force, and like water it surrounds and suffocates you.

"Mind your own business," Dustin said in a whisper as he watched the car pass.

Sophia looked in the direction of Dustin's stare. "What is it?"

"I'm tired of all the looks from the people in other cars. You would think they've never seen a vehicle with its windows down in the summer. They look shocked or have looks of pity like we're some kind of destitute vagrants." Dustin couldn't wait to get home and correct the problem. It had to be the compressor, or if luck holds, it simply needed recharging. Either way, Dustin had the tools to do the job. Deep down he was an irredeemable shade-tree mechanic stemming from an uncontrollable compulsion to save a dime.

He muttered under his breath, no doubt obscenities that would embarrass a sailor, as he adjusted the dials on the dash for the fifth time, as if somehow he had been so incompetent as to not have properly activated the air conditioning in the first four attempts. Still the hot air huffed through the slotted vents and, in a moment of utter annoyance, he walloped the dash above the controls with his massive clenched paw and it gave under the force of the encounter by fracturing into a three-inch-long crack in the outer shell.

He turned and directed a threatening glare at Sophia, a defying challenge almost daring her to speak, but she said nothing. She sat tacitly, her gaze fixed on the line of trees blurring by on the side of the interstate, the wind blowing her long black hair around her face forcibly making the strands dance like the heads of serpents, resembling a Latin Medusa, launching back and forth in complete disorder as it was bombarded by the full gush of hot air from the windows on both sides of the truck. Several seconds of silence passed before she spoke. "Why did you even come here? You could have taken care of this over the phone."

Dustin's gaze remained fixed on the road ahead. He knew she was right but he had no way of knowing before coming. He had repaired his mom's pump so many times in the past; he thought he could do it again and save some money. When her well was first dug, it was only 30 feet deep, so every drought clogged the submersible pump with Sand Mountain mud and he had pulled it out many times to clean it. Finally, a few years ago, he had paid to have it dug to 100 feet. But when his mom called a few days ago to say she had no water, in a habitual mode of progeny, he deserted his own weekend plans to drive the all-too-familiar three-hour excursion from Montgomery, Alabama, to where his mom lived atop Sand Mountain in the northeast corner of the state to make sure she had running water again. Only upon retracting the pump did he realize it was broken and needed to be replaced. Yes, he could have called his cousin, the one who installed the pump and dug the well in the first place, and it would have cost the same. But there was no way to know that at the time and few people were as thrifty as Dustin.

Dustin's face was almost beet-red making his deep blue eyes almost translucent, and seemed to emanate heat on its own. It wasn't clear how much of that was from working in the sun for the last two days and how much was motivated by his contentious hostility regarding the only person who could get him into this frame of mind. It wasn't the hours of sweat and toil, the long trip, or the money he dished out for a new pump that was now eating away at his gut and causing the abhorrent mood which now consumed him. It was the one thing that made him leave his mom's house in the same antagonistic demeanor on every visit.

"How much does Trevor weigh now, anyway?" Dustin said.

Sophia didn't answer. She apparently recognized a rhetorical question. And the truth was, Dustin probably weighed as much and was several inches shorter than his brother. But Dustin had been lifting weights since he first began playing football in junior high school, and even though he had a thick midsection, most of his weight was derived from massive arms, chest, and shoulders.

"It's bad enough he couldn't lift a finger to help me this weekend but he has a master's degree and has never had a job," Dustin said.

"Tre has a job."

Dustin turned his smirk toward Sophia. "Building computers and games for your slacker friends in your mom's basement does not constitute as a job."

Several seconds of silence passed as Sophia stared out the window and Dustin fumed.

"And you wanna know what really chaps my ass?" Dustin said. "Mom defends him not having a real job. This is the same woman who every summer from the time I was ten years old would dress me up in my one set of dress clothes, my one clip-on tie, and drive me around to the potato sheds to try to get a summer job, all the while explaining to me that a man without a job is not a real man."

Sophia looked at her husband and smiled. "Ah, the truth comes out."

"What the devil are you talking about?" Dustin said.

"That's the problem," she said. "It's not being your mom's favorite anymore that bothers you. I guess chasing pigs will only get you so far."

Dustin laughed. He knew all too well what this meant. When he was 12 years old, his dad decided that their 30 acres were going to waste and, without so much as a discussion, put the family in the pig business, with a flimsy electric fence no less. Dustin learned quickly that nothing short of hog wire, or perhaps the Great Wall of China, would keep a pig in the pasture, and it seemed like every few days they would get a call from neighbors up to a mile away informing them that some of their pigs were in their yard or garden. For years after that, any complaints from Trevor that he was getting unfair treatment, or that he was not getting the attention that Dustin received, quickly brought about a verbose and redundant defense based on those arduous pig-chasing exploits.

"Ah yes, the good old pig days. Fun times," Dustin said. "One of the best decisions my dad ever made."

"Are you serious? I thought you hated that."

Dustin turned his head fully to look at his wife. "Did you suddenly have a brain cloud and forget how to recognize sarcasm? Yes, I hated that. I hated everything about it."

Sophia laughed. "You knew I was gullible when you married me."

"No I didn't," Dustin said. "I thought you said 'Gulliver.' You know I've always wanted a boyfriend. You knew that when you married me."

"I'm glad you can joke about that," Sophia said, "because I sure can't talk to you seriously about it."

Dustin shook his head, ignoring the insult. "If Trevor had ever helped with the pigs, he might have learned some responsibility. And how did we end up with a liberal atheist in our family—or in the entire South for that matter? He thinks he's smarter than everyone; you notice how he talks down to people?"

"I think he is pretty smart. He knows a lot of trivia."

Dustin glanced again at his wife, a glance filled with disbelief, as if Sophia had just stabbed him in the back. "There's a huge difference in knowledge and intelligence. Being able to retain information has nothing to do with how smart someone is."

Sophia fumbled through her purse. She pulled out a folded sheet of paper and handed it to Dustin.

"What's this?" he said as he tried to unfold it with one hand.

"Tre gave that to me. It's an online I.Q. test he took and scored 181. He said genius is 140 so he's 41 points smarter than genius."

Dustin stopped unfolding and dropped it on the seat between them, which made Sophia have to grab it to keep it from blowing out the windows. "Anyone who spends as much time as he does sitting on his rear in front of a computer, and who has the time to waste to take these tests a hundred times, can score that. Plus, you don't even know if that's real. He could have easily manipulated that or created it from scratch."

"He told me an invention idea also that was pretty neat," Sophia said.

Dustin didn't even acknowledge but continued looking straight ahead. He had heard more of Trevor's invention ideas than he could count.

Sophia continued. "He sent this idea to the Department of Transportation. On every license plate, behind the paint, is a hidden bar code. Then the police can set up portable scanners anywhere they want, and even move them around every day to secret locations, and it will not only scan the speed of the vehicle, but the license number as well, and they can send a ticket in the mail. Like Tre said, it will increase revenue and decrease speeding."

Dustin glanced down at his speedometer and noticed he was going eight miles-per-hour over the speed limit. Looking at the side of the road, he imagined passing one of Trevor's scanners. His silence told his wife that it wasn't worthy of a comment.

The rest of the drive was fairly peaceful and they arrived around 7 p.m. at the small brick house they rented in Montgomery. He pulled into the driveway, which was really two worn tracks in the lawn. Sophia's small car occupied the actual concrete drive to the right of the artificial one. He parked in front of his lawn service trailer, which stayed parked beside the small house and carried the two Toro Zero-Turn mowers, four professional weed eaters, one push mower, and everything else needed for the job.

Sophia got out of the truck and started toward the door but Dustin stayed put. "Are you not coming in?" Sophia said.

"No," Dustin said. "I'm going to go to the gym for a while."

Sophia smiled. "OK, go work off some steam. I'll have supper ready when you get home." She waved as Dustin backed out of the driveway and drove to his gym.

Dustin's gym—not a fitness center—but a gym, was a real man's gym located in the rear of a small shopping center. There was no cardio equipment at all. The truth was, it was a hole-in-the-wall kind of place and that's usually how Dustin described it. It was for serious lifters, or at least people wanting to become a serious lifter, and it had a coded entry. Each month, as the members paid their dues, they received the new code for the next month. The vinyl letters on the outside of the door displayed the name, "Dustin's Gym," not his most creative moment. The gym had a small but devout membership, numbering about

70, but it provided an additional six or seven hundred dollars a
month to Dustin's income, and more importantly, provided him
with a free place to lift weights.

There were only five other people in the small concrete-
floored gym when he entered and he nodded to them as he
walked over to the bench press and began sliding the weights
onto the Olympic barbell. All five lifters stopped working out to
watch Dustin bench press. After his third set, when he racked
the barbell on the two uprights that reached up along each side
of the bench like black metal hands, he sat up on the end of the
bench, a circle of sweat underneath his collar like a bib.

Maybe Sophia was right. It wasn't his place to fix everything for his mom. It wasn't his house after all, although he had
pretty much built it. His dad had begun the construction when
Dustin was two years old but ran out of money. It remained a
foundation in the form of a partially above ground basement,
frame, and roof for many years, a hollow shell of a home that
mocked them for a decade and a half. When Dustin sold the
pigs, he finished the house, contracting out the kitchen cabinets, wiring, and plumbing, but doing everything else himself.
His mom and Trevor moved into it the week before he left for
the Marine Corp.

Dustin looked up as one of the younger guys walked over.
"How many reps was that?" the boy said.

He shook his head and shrugged. "I'm not sure." That
wasn't true. It was 19 reps and Dustin was a little upset for not
hitting 20.

"That's 315, right?" the boy said.

Dustin nodded. It wasn't worth the time to explain to the
kid that it was really 312.5 pounds. Dustin had been in enough
weight lifting competitions to know two official collars, each
weighing 1.25 pounds, were needed to complete the weight.

"How much do you bench?"

Dustin wasn't in the mood for weight-room banter, but

that was the most common question asked in his gym, or perhaps any gym. "I don't know. I don't lift heavy anymore."

The young guy looked back at the amount of weight on the bar and laughed.

Dustin really didn't lift heavy anymore, not by his standards, and he only worked out three times a week now instead of five. At 35 years of age, his body didn't quite handle the weight like before, at least not without his bones and joints complaining to him all night. But he continued to follow the program he had designed 15 years ago—work only one muscle group a day—the program that worked wonders for the people who stuck with it, people who wanted size and strength. He tried to explain to the people he trained that the muscles need rest to grow, not repetition. One of his best-selling gym-shirts was one that read, "I'm Not Resting, I'm Growing."

After the workout, Dustin felt better, more relaxed, and most importantly, he had forgotten about his brother—until next time.

CHAPTER

FIVE

DUSTIN COULDN'T SLEEP. He sat up and turned on the light.

"What's wrong?" Sophia said.

"My eyes are burning."

Sophia looked at his eyes. "Oh my goodness. They're so bloodshot. Working in that heat all weekend. I told you to take it easy."

"It's weird," Dustin said. "When we were kids, we played all day in the heat and never thought anything about it. Do we just get weaker as we get older?"

"I could tell you but you wouldn't believe me," Sophia said. "Global warming. It's actually hotter now."

"You're right. I don't believe you."

Sophia laughed and got out of bed. "Let me go cut some potatoes and place them over your eyes. That is supposed to draw out the heat."

Dustin didn't argue and was surprised to discover that it actually worked, enough that he could get to sleep anyway.

A few hours later, Dustin got out of bed and walked toward the bathroom with a slight limp, stemming from an injury in the form of torn ligaments and a damaged cartilage that had long been removed, souvenirs from his football days, which was always worse this time of morning.

The house was a two bedroom, one bath, brick house, about 800 square feet, where Dustin lived when he and Sophia met. Their plan was to save enough money to put down on a nice house, or perhaps even save until retirement when they would have enough to buy or build a nice house without having to finance any of it. They were very successful in saving thanks to Dustin's aversion to spending money. In fact, he was the cheapest person most people had ever known.

The press was not on time this night and Dustin didn't get back home until almost seven, only an hour before he would be getting up. Afraid that he would not wake up if he crawled back into bed, he decided to stay up. He sat at his wife's laptop, which was on the small imitation-wood computer desk that sat in front of the window in their small living room, and turned it on. As it illuminated the area, he noticed a folded sheet of paper beside the computer.

After unfolding the sheet of paper, Dustin stopped for a second and stared at it. It was the print off of the I.Q. test Trevor had given to Sophia. Noticing the web address on top of the page, Dustin looked around the room to make sure Sophia hadn't gotten up then typed in the address and read over the info that appeared on the screen. Feeling confident, he clicked on the tab that read "Begin," which initiated the timed I.Q. test.

1. Which number comes next? 7, 8, 10, 13, 17, ?

Dustin laughed as he realized how simple it was. It was clear that the numbers had increased by 1, then 2, then 3, then 4, making the last increase 5 and the last number 22. He entered his answer and the next question appeared.

2. Which number comes next?   4, 6, 10, 16, 26, ?

Dustin stared at the screen for a few seconds, somewhat perplexed that the last number listed wasn't 24. Was it a typo? The numbers increased by 2, then 4, then 6, then 10. Shouldn't the last increase have been 8 and the increase to find the missing number be 10? He remembered it was a timed test and decided to concentrate a little harder. Then it dawned on him; the numbers were being added together as they go (4+6=10 6+10=16 10+16=26). OK, still easy. Dustin typed in "42" and entered the info.

The next question got a little harder, as did the next 17. Some of the questions he found himself simply guessing. After he finished the last question, a spinning hourglass appeared as the total was accrued. Then it flashed up this info: "Congratulations! Your score is 169. You are a genius."

Dustin didn't notice anything other than the 169, the score that was 12 points lower than his brother's score. He scoffed as he turned off the computer, realizing that he didn't really have time to concentrate because he had too much to do. He was also tired and knew full well that his brother probably took the same test over and over or even faked the results. He crumpled the sheet of paper and tossed it in the trash.

～

TREVOR TRIED TO CONCENTRATE on his computer but the buzzing noise was driving him crazy. Robbie, one of his many Dungeons & Dragons buddies, was twirling Trevor's prized light saber through the air, his feet wide as he probably imagined himself as Luke or some other Jedi Knight defending the galaxy. Robbie was a short and thin guy, several years younger than Trevor, as were a lot of the guys who often congregated in the basement.

"This is awesome," Robbie said, making the light saber noise to the best of his ability as he continued to play Jedi. "I can't believe you have an authentic light saber."

Without looking back, Trevor shook his head. It wasn't worth it to explain there were no such things as "authentic" light sabers. But he did wish to convey some information. "My asinine friend, that authentic light saber you are so carelessly swinging about is an exceptional acquisition, which set me back to the tune of $600."

Robbie stopped and walked slowly over and returned the expensive toy to its perch. Then he walked back and peered over Trevor's shoulder, something Trevor hated, and looked at the computer screens. "What are you working on?"

"If you must know, it is an invention idea," Trevor said.

Robbie leaned closer. "What is it?"

Trevor tilted his head around to look at his young friend as if deciding if it was worth the trouble to explain. "It is a small electronic device that fits on your keychain and emits a radio signal so you can unlock your car doors."

Robbie laughed. "Dude, I hate to tell you but they've had that for years."

Trevor smiled. "You think? Thank you for the news update. But mine comes with several buttons which can be programmed for all the locks and alarms in your life. A different button can be programmed for every vehicle you have, and one can be programmed for your garage, one to turn on and off your house alarm, as well as open electronic deadbolts and locks, and one can even be programmed for rooms inside your home, or safes, storage facilities, you name it."

"Wow," Robbie said. "Man, when you die, all I want is the key to your closet. You have so many ideas."

Trevor rolled his eyes. He knew it was an attempt at a compliment but the implication was that he would never do anything with them in his own lifetime. He decided to see if he could really amaze Robbie. "Let me ask you this: would you like to see the greatest invention of all time?"

"Heck yeah."

Trevor opened a file and sat back and smiled as the animated gif file appeared on the screen.

Robbie stared for several seconds. It appeared to be an

underwater wheel, which resembled the old mill wheels usually built on the side of buildings from hundreds of years ago that used the running water from creeks or rivers to make them rotate. But this was all underwater. There were rods coming out of the center of the wheel on each side and then bending upward at ninety degrees, which turned two circular discs mounted on the sides of two large cylindrical objects. A pipe ran from the top of each cylinder up to the surface and out of the water a little way, and pipes ran out of the bottom of the cylinders and underneath the wheel. In the animation, bubbles were coming out of the lower pipes filling the compartments of the wheel, and, as the wheel turned, the bubbles rose and finally escaped to the surface.

"Wow," Robbie said again.

Trevor laughed. "You have no idea what it is, do you, my simple-minded friend?"

Robbie shrugged. "It's a cool animation. What is it?"

"That, my good boy, is the first real perpetual motion device," Trevor said.

Robbie shrugged again. "What's that?"

Trevor looked around in disbelief. "Are you kidding me? Perpetual motion? What most scientists say is impossible. It is a device that can run off its own power. See, as the wheel turns, it activates the two pumps on each side." Trevor placed his fingers on the screen to one of the cylinders. "That makes the pumps draw air from the surface and pump it down through the pipes and it is released underneath the wheel. The air naturally rises making the wheel turn, which activates the pumps. Once started, it will run indefinitely with no outside source of power."

Robbie stared with blank eyes. "And what good is that?"

Trevor shook his head. "Unbelievable. For one thing, my friend, you could build one in your backyard and provide the electricity to your home. Or more importantly, you could build these on the ocean floor anywhere in the world and deliver free energy to every third-world country, town, or village on the planet. It could effectively end poverty."

Robbie still stared with blank eyes. "Dude, you're going to be so rich someday," he said.

Trevor glanced around at the gloomy basement. He used to think that as well but he was a realist and knew better. "Well, not with this one. I would never make this invention public."

"Why not?" Robbie said.

"Are you kidding me? How do you think the huge power companies would react if someone invented something that would affect their pocketbooks? That is a billion-dollar-a-year industry. I would quickly become the target of an assassination plot, I assure you." Trevor loved a good conspiracy theory as much as anyone.

He heard the kitchen door open upstairs and Trevor realized his mother was home from work. Since the hosiery mills had closed down, she had been working as a cashier at a department store in the valley. Pots and pans could be heard clanging as Mrs. Davis went right to work on cooking as soon as she got home.

Robbie seemed to tire of the invention talk and took a seat on the other side of the room and started flipping through comic books.

Thirty minutes later, Mrs. Davis slowly descended the stairs into the basement carrying a basket of dirty clothes and made her way to the washer and dryer. She was a small woman, 63 years old, and her light brown hair had taken on a shade of gray. She adjusted her large glasses as she began to load the washer then paused and looked toward her son's office. She walked over and opened the door and looked around the room filled with so many boxes and books, but also with computers, parts, wires, several old Hot Pocket packages, and at least 50 empty soda cans.

"Hey, Miss Doreen."

She smiled at Robbie.

"Dinner ready?" Trevor said without looking up, his eyes still glued to the computer screen. When his mother didn't answer, he looked up and saw the sad expression on her face. "What in the world is the matter now, Mother?"

"Don't you think you could have helped Dustin at least a little bit this weekend? He did drive all the way up here to help us," Mrs. Davis said.

"Did you ask my brother to come?"

"No, but that doesn't matter. Y'all are family. Why must you always be mad at each other?"

Trevor huffed out an exaggerated exhale as he turned his attention back to the computer, signifying the conversation was futile and not one in which he wished to participate.

His mother persisted. "Talk to me. Just explain to me why you wouldn't help him."

Silence.

"Dustin is a good man. You both are," his mother said. "But Dustin had to grow up faster than most kids. He had it rough and just doesn't know any other way. He worked hard to build this house and he drove all the way up here just to help. Don't you think that deserves a little consideration?"

"No, Mother, I do not," Trevor said. "If you think that gives him the right to treat me like a dog, that is your prerogative. I have never accused you of being intelligent. Prejudice, however, I will give you. You know that man is a jerk. He always has been, especially when it comes to me. Just because I do not do everything the way he does makes my way wrong. Sometimes a person grows tired of being judged, Mother. And trying to help him do anything is an exercise in torture and futility." Trevor shook his head, and in a much more humble tone tried to explain. "Mother, do you remember all those stories you told me about how difficult it was helping our father do any project? You used to say to me that whenever he asked for your help, it was the worst possible thing that could happen and always ended with him getting angry because you could not do it right—whatever it was? You remember that feeling, Mother, the feeling of being worthless, useless, and humiliated?"

"Dustin is nowhere near as bad as your father was, I assure you."

Trevor sat motionless, his stance uncompromising.

Mrs. Davis stared directly into her youngest son's eyes, whose non-flinching return glare was relentless. Her somber expression let Trevor know she remembered.

Without waiting for her to answer, Trevor surmised. "That is what it is like trying to work with that man."

His mother lowered her head and stared at her feet for several seconds. She had no reply. She looked back up at Trevor who was still looking at her. She smiled a wry smile. "Supper's ready."

CHAPTER

SIX

DUSTIN AND SOPHIA walked out on the porch. They saw that everyone was here. Hannah, Frankie, and Mrs. Garza, Hannah and Sophia's mom, had come in Hannah's car, and Dustin's mom and Trevor were here as well. Trevor was holding Frankie in a headlock as they both walked toward the front porch. Frankie managed to wiggle free as they walked up the three steps onto the small concrete porch.

Trevor, without so much as a smile, extended his hand to Dustin. This was always the extent of their greeting. It was a nice day for Christmas in Montgomery, about 65 degrees, and Trevor had on short sleeves, which displayed the very large and elaborate tattoo on his forearm. Dustin squeezed his hand and then twisted his arm as he stared at the tattoo.

Trevor noticed Dustin staring at the tattoo and knew he would hear about it.

"That's new. Is that Merlin?" Dustin said.

Trevor ignored the question. It wasn't worth his time to explain to his brother that this was his D&D character. He had shown him the character many times but Dustin couldn't understand Dungeons & Dragons and usually scoffed at the idea of Trevor and his friends—grown men—playing a childish game, so he simply nodded.

"Ain't that cool?" Frankie said.

Dustin looked out in the yard. His mom and Mrs. Garza were conversing by the vehicles, each holding a dish. Hannah was walking past him and into the house, also carrying a covered dish. "No, it *ain't* cool. Why are you not helping the women bring in the food and presents?"

Frankie shrugged and turned to go out to the cars and help. Dustin followed as Trevor went on into the house and planted himself in front of the computer as if it were his own.

With the five of them, they managed to bring in all the food and presents in one trip. Dustin placed the presents under the small artificial tree in the living room and took a seat on the sofa. The food was spread out in the kitchen as the ladies began to set the table with plates and silverware.

Hannah walked into the living room and asked if anyone wanted a glass of eggnog. Dustin and Frankie, who were now seated on the sofa next to each other, shook their heads.

Trevor spoke up. "I will gladly have one."

Hannah did not acknowledge and returned to the kitchen and, after a few minutes, it became clear she was not coming back with the eggnog. Trevor gave up and turned back to the computer. Hannah and Trevor were the same age, so after Dustin and Sophia had been married a couple of years, it seemed only natural for Sophia to try to set them up together. They had gone on one date and that was all it had taken for them to be mortal enemies ever since. No one knew what happened that night and no one had ever asked.

Sophia walked in and brought Trevor a glass of eggnog.

Trevor looked over the computer desk with its particle board, ready-to-assemble, fake-finish construction. "I do believe this is new. Have you guys gotten a new computer desk? Let me guess, another fine acquisition from the prestigious Goodwill Industries?"

Sophia looked at Dustin, then back at Trevor, and smiled. "You know it." The fact was, it had come from Goodwill, as had most of the furniture in their home as well as a lot of their clothing.

Trevor chuckled.

Sophia slapped him playfully on the top of the head. "What's wrong with Goodwill?"

Trevor rubbed his head in an exaggerated manner as if she had hit him harder. "Not a thing, my dear sister-in-law. Not a thing. Why, I am a big fan of the organization myself. I take Mother to the new Goodwill Super Center back home all the time."

Dustin looked at Trevor as that phrase seemed to catch his attention.

"Super Center?" said Sophia. "What's that?"

Trevor explained. "It is a new giant Goodwill store, part of an experiment, I guess, before they open stores all across the country. It is patterned after the Super Walmarts. In fact, that is what people are calling them—Super Goodwills."

Both Dustin and Sophia looked on, apparently wanting to know more.

Trevor saw the anticipation in their faces and tried not to laugh. "Oh yes, they are quite popular. The allure is the fact that along with the normal gems you find there: clothes, toys, movies, and incredible computer desks, they also sell used food. Why just yesterday, Mother and I went and I found three cans of food for only a nickel each. I have no clue what is in them, but what a bargain."

Dustin laughed as he shook his head and leaned back into the sofa.

Trevor wasn't finished. "Yes siree—quite a store. I found a Granny Smith apple with only two bites out of it and Mother got into a fist fight with this old woman over a half-eaten meat-ball sub."

Dustin was laughing harder, maybe not so much at the silly story, but at Frankie who was now literally rolling on the floor laughing so hard he couldn't catch his breath.

Sophia was giggling pretty hard herself. "You are a nut."

Trevor turned back to the computer and continued surfing the internet.

As the laughter died back down, Dustin proved Trevor's earlier concerns. "I take it that tattoo was pretty expensive. Does that mean you finally got a job?"

Sophia noticed the tattoo. "Oh, that's nice."

Dustin glared at her.

"What? There's nothing wrong with a tattoo," Sophia said.

"There most certainly is," Dustin said. "It's plain as day right there in Leviticus. It says do not print any marks on your body."

Trevor spun around in his seat and faced Dustin. "Leviticus?"

Dustin said nothing.

"Leviticus?" Trevor repeated.

"Yes, Leviticus. That's a book in the Bible. But how could you possibly know that?" Dustin said.

Trevor opened his mouth and shook his head. "That is Old Testament, my dimwitted brother."

"And?"

Trevor stared at Dustin in disbelief. "What do you mean 'and'? The Old Testament does not apply anymore."

Dustin crossed his arms. "Of course it does."

Trevor looked back at Sophia to get her reaction, but she was expressionless. "So, you are telling me that the Old Testament, including the laws of Moses listed in Leviticus, are still valid today?" he said.

Dustin nodded.

"Really?" Trevor said. "It also says that a man should not shave his beard or eat pork. What do you say to that, Mr. Close Shave? Are you going to abstain from the ham or Mother's sausage balls this year or eat an entire hog like you normally do?"

Frankie giggled as Dustin's cheeks began to turn red.

"I'm amazed how well you know the Bible, Tre, I mean for an atheist," Sophia said.

Trevor broke his stare-down with Dustin and smiled at Sophia. "I think most atheists know the Bible well."

"It's a shame you don't study it for good reasons," Dustin said, "like learning the truth. It's a shame you study it just to find faults with people."

Trevor turned back to the computer. "It is a shame, brother, that you do not study it at all, only go to church and let someone tell you what it says. If you did, you might accidentally stumble across that section that says to judge not."

Dustin ignored the insult.

"So," Trevor said, "pray tell. Where is your computer?"

Dustin exhaled deeply. "We're just using Sophia's right now."

He looked at Sophia and decided to try the question on her. "Where is the computer I built for you guys?"

"Oh, we're going to get a new one after New Year's," she said.

Trevor looked at her and smiled. Then he looked over at Dustin as his smile disappeared. "Is this your feeble attempt at coded speak? Am I being intentionally demonized here? Both of you have effectively dodged the question—a very simple question I might add. The question again is where is the computer I built for you guys?"

"It crashed," Sophia said.

Trevor rolled his eyes to convey that also didn't answer the question.

"It's in the bedroom closet," Dustin said. "It doesn't work anymore so we're going to buy a new one."

Trevor shook his head. "All computers crash. It does not mean it does not work and you sure are not going to find a name-brand computer as good as that one. Quickly, bring it to me." Trevor knew Dustin didn't like being ordered around but if he could save their files and save them about a thousand dollars, he knew Dustin was game.

Dustin nudged Frankie to go with him. They went into the bedroom and came back with the computer. Dustin carried the tower and screen and Frankie brought the keyboard and mouse.

Trevor unhooked Sophia's laptop and connected the tower and screen. He took the keyboard from Frankie. "You are a good little gopher, my friend. That is your job with your uncle's dirty grass cutting business, is it not? You are a gopher?"

Frankie looked confused and looked up at Dustin.

"He's the best gopher I've ever hired," Dustin said with his arm around Frankie's shoulder.

Frankie smiled. It appeared he was oblivious to the intended insult, only happy that he had an actual title. He walked into the kitchen to inform his mom.

Trevor turned on the computer and watched as it tried to come on but froze. He looked back at Sophia and Dustin, who stood behind him watching over his shoulder. "Please inform me, good people, how often did you halfwits update the virus protection?" Seeing the blank stares answered his question.

"We did it pretty regularly," Dustin said. It wasn't very convincing.

Trevor smirked. "Of course you did, simpleton. It is like the old mattresses. Remember when the furniture stores told you they had to be flipped every six months. Most people did it the first time and then did not bother for the next seven years. When they notified the store that their mattress had a huge sunken spot in the middle, the stores always asked if they had flipped it every six months as the warranty states. Likewise, they would also lie and say they did it."

Dustin's cheeks turned red again. Trevor smiled on the inside, knowing he could punch his brother's buttons. As Trevor held the button in to turn off the computer, Sophia asked, "How often are we supposed to update it?"

"Thank you, honey. Finally a competent response. It

should be updated at least once a week, but even once a day would not hurt." Trevor pressed the button again to start the computer but this time he continually pressed one of the command keys above the numbers on the keyboard. The screen suddenly displayed a flashing cursor and Trevor began to type. The computer responded with more text and Trevor continued typing commands.

"You really think you can fix it?" Sophia said.

"My dear, I do not fix things; I repair them," Trevor said quite matter-of-factly as he continued to type. "The system is full of viruses so I just have to search them out and destroy them. Chances are, some of them have affected the operational programs and those will have to be deleted and reinstalled."

Sophia looked on as Dustin had returned to the sofa. "What is a virus?" she said.

"It is quite simple really," Trevor said. "A virus is nothing more than a program written by some fruitcake to either try to steal your information from your computer or simply shut it down. The virus protection is also a program designed to watch for known viruses so it can block them before they get into your system. And since the fruitcakes are coming up with new viruses every day, that is precisely why you have to update your protection constantly. It can only protect from viruses that have already been identified. Along with updating your protection, you should also avoid opening emails from people you do not know, visiting unverified websites, and ignore that poor guy from Nigeria who wants you to hold on to six million dollars for him."

"I have a question," Dustin said. Trevor and Sophia turned to look at Dustin, who was still on the sofa. Frankie had returned to sit by his uncle again. "If the operational system is infected as you claim, how can you get into the computer to 'repair' it?"

Trevor smiled. "That is almost an intelligent question. Did Frankie whisper that to you? Every system or program I design, I install a secret back door."

"Another program?" Sophia said.

"You are catching on, honey bunny. A back door is a hidden coded entry that only the programmer knows about so even a virus cannot find it. Once I go into the back door, which is what I have done here, I can run a systems check, install new software, or make any changes I want to make. In fact, all you had to do was call me and I could have done this from home."

Sophia patted Trevor on the shoulders.

"I didn't know that," Dustin said.

"I am not surprised," Trevor said. "Information like that is only available in universities." Trevor watched for Dustin's reaction but Dustin didn't reply. It was only the 500th insult Trevor had ever made regarding the fact that he had a college education and Dustin did not.

Dustin had wanted to go to college, especially having excelled in science and math and several of his high school teachers had urged him to continue his education, he just couldn't figure out a way to do it and still be able to help his mom financially. So, he decided to enlist in the Marines for the GI Bill. That way he could continue to draw a paycheck while earning money toward college. But after four years when he got out of the military, he never took the first class, and Trevor never let him forget.

Sophia went back into the kitchen to help prepare the meal. Dustin turned on the TV again.

Fifteen minutes later, Trevor had the computer up and running. "And there you go. All the viruses are gone. I have saved all your files. I have also cleaned off a lot of junk from your RAM and regular memory and I have also correlated all the operational files, which will make it run faster. It is as good as the day I built it."

Sophia walked back in and looked at the computer as Trevor was surfing the internet with ease. "I would have sworn that would never have worked again. You are a genius, Tre," she said.

"So true," Trevor said. "That is, after all, what it says on my business cards. Well, it would if I actually had business cards."

Sophia and Frankie laughed at Trevor's joke. Dustin continued to fix his eyes on the TV.

"So, darling, would you care to see something cool?" Trevor said, turning his head back to Sophia. As she nodded, he typed in a web address. The screen came on with an image of the earth from space and what appeared to be a flat round satellite. "I sent this idea to NASA," Trevor explained.

Sophia leaned over and squinted, trying to make out the image. "What is it?"

Trevor smiled, hoping she would ask. "It is an invention idea of mine. It is a mirror in space that can be programmed to open and point toward any coordinates in the U.S., or indeed the world."

"OK," Sophia said. Her eyes and tone explained she didn't understand what she was looking at, however.

Trevor picked up on that. "If there are any kind of emergencies at night, say a hurricane, tornado, flash flooding, escaped convicts, lost child, you name it, NASA could point the mirror at that area, open it up, and it would reflect the sunlight, hence making the area as bright as day. In fact, you would actually be able to see the sun in the sky just like in the daytime. That would make it easier for rescue workers, or whomever, to safely do what needed to be done."

"Oh my gosh! That's absolutely amazing. Dustin, are you seeing this?" Sophia turned to look at her husband.

"Yeah, that's clever," Dustin said in a monotone without diverting his eyes from the TV.

"It *is* clever. Seriously, check this out," Sophia said.

Dustin got up slowly and walked over and stood beside

his wife and looked over Trevor's shoulder at the screen.

Sophia leaned her head toward Dustin. "Think of the times that would come in handy and save lives—floods, tornadoes, and such."

Dustin nodded. "Or if a town was being attacked by vampires."

Trevor smiled, completely ignoring the sarcasm. "Now you are thinking, brother. Now you are thinking."

Dustin went back and sat down again. "Well I will say this; that does seem more likely to save lives than your scummy invention."

Sophia looked at Trevor for clarification, but he had the same puzzled look. "What's that?" she said.

Trevor shook his head. "Your guess, my dear, is as good as mine."

"Let me see if I can remember the specifics," Dustin said. "It was some stupid invention idea of yours several years ago. It had a name like 'scummy' or something. It was for breathing underwater."

Trevor rolled his eyes. "Moron. It was called SCUMBA. It is an acronym. It stands for Self-Contained Underwater Miniature Breathing Apparatus." He looked up at Sophia. "It is a portable compressed air canister about ten inches long and two inches in diameter, with a mouthpiece in the center. You could keep it in your car for emergencies or use it while snorkeling or if you wanted to explore the bottom of the creek or a pond. It would give you a few minutes of air so you could stay underwater longer. That is its purpose."

"Well, that's a good idea, too. Thank you so much for getting the computer up and going again. We should have called you in the first place." Sophia kissed Trevor on the check and went back to the kitchen.

"Yeah," Dustin said. "Thanks. Do we owe you anything?"

Trevor ignored the question. "It should last you another

three years, more if you actually display an ounce of common sense and update your virus protection on a regular basis."

Dustin nodded.

"You do understand what I am saying?" Trevor said. He knew Dustin hated when he acted this way, like what he was saying was over the head of the person to whom he was speaking.

"I said I got it," Dustin said.

"You sure, brother? You really do understand?"

"I got it!" Dustin said just under a shout. "Flip the damn mattress!"

CHAPTER

SEVEN

SOPHIA CALLED EVERYONE to the kitchen. Dustin sat at one end of the oval-shaped table, which normally remained a circle until they added the leaf to the center for company. Trevor sat on the opposite end, Sophia and Mrs. Davis sat on one side, and Hannah and her mom sat on the other. Frankie had a chair right beside Dustin.

Frankie was always right beside Dustin if possible and Dustin loved it. He knew that people mistakenly thought Frankie to be his son and that was fine with him. When Sophia was with them it completed the image. Sophia's mom and dad had moved to the U.S. from Mexico when she was just a baby and Hannah was born three years later here in the states. Hannah and her mom had the classic Mexican look, each only about five-feet tall, whereas Sophia was five-feet-six and had straighter hair and a slightly lighter complexion, though still olive in tone. Frankie, whom everyone suspected had a Caucasian father, was lighter still, but still had the thick black hair that he kept short around the sides, but the top, without needing gel at all, came to a stylish peak. He was a typical scrawny seven-year-old, full of life and laughter.

In stark contrast were his uncles. Dustin was five years older than Trevor but they looked remarkably alike; each had a wide body, yet Dustin's was more muscular, and each had dark hair and hairless torsos from their dad's Cherokee Indian heritage and deep blue eyes from their mom's Irish side. The noticeable difference was that Trevor was five-feet-ten, three full inches over Dustin, and of course the grooming. Dustin always stayed neatly shaved and kept his hair buzzed to almost a shadow, the sides around the ears already displaying a salt and pepper look, whereas Trevor rarely got a haircut and it appeared as though he was unaware of the invention of the razor. They did, however, share a great sense of humor and no one could tell them apart on the phone. In fact, Dustin could make people believe he was Trevor on the phone by using bigger words and faking a more unpleasant disposition.

After the Christmas meal was over, Hannah and her mom left to go home, leaving Frankie there, who had adjourned to the living room with his two uncles while Sophia and Mrs. Davis attended to dishes.

Dustin turned on the TV and flipped through the channels, coming to a stop on Court TV. He had been following a recent trial from Topeka, Kansas, where a man had allegedly killed his wife and dumped the body in a local reservoir.

"Waste of time. That man will surely get off on all charges," Trevor said as he turned away from the computer to look at the TV.

"You've been following this?" Dustin said.

"Yes, I have. I watch this channel all the time and follow all the major cases on the news and internet."

Dustin looked shocked as if he never knew he and his brother had this in common. "You got to be kidding, right? This guy is as guilty as sin. They have tons of evidence against him. He'll get life in prison—and he deserves it."

Trevor shook his head. "Silly man. The guy is Hispanic—

"LATINO!" Sophia yelled from the kitchen.

"OK, forgive me please... Latino. If you pay close attention, you will notice the jury. There are at least seven Latinos. It does not matter about the evidence, people will always vote along with their own prejudices," Trevor said.

Sophia had walked into the living room when she heard

the conversation. "Yep, nailed it, Tre. Us 'Hispanics' don't really cotton to the law." With a quick head tilt and evil eye directed at Trevor, she spun and went back into the kitchen.

"Will he really go to prison?" Frankie said.

Dustin patted him on the head. "As sure as we're sitting here."

"Not a chance, brother," Trevor said. "I can tell you without pause that the system is flawed. How many times have you heard or read about a judge refusing to recuse himself, or a jury that has been tampered with, or a runaway jury, or just jurors making a bad decision. I was just a kid when you made me watch the O.J. Simpson trial, brother, and you told me beyond a shadow of a doubt that he would be found guilty. And what happened?"

"OK," Dustin said, "O.J. was not found guilty. But the system is not flawed. It's the best system in the world."

"And what of the case you were recently on?" Trevor said. "Was it not flawed?"

"Not necessarily," Dustin said. "The guy could have been innocent."

Trevor shook his head.

"Besides," Dustin said, "how many times can you even name that a judge has not recused himself when he should have, or done anything unethical?"

Trevor smiled, up to the challenge. "You must be kidding. Let's start with Gable-Gate."

"What's that?" Dustin said.

Trevor rolled his eyes. "Wisconsin Justice Michael Gableman, just a few years ago, was being investigated for violating ethics rules, and then, while being investigated, he illegally received free services from a large law firm in Wisconsin who defended him. It was an ethics violation on top of an ethics violation. State law prohibits state officials from receiving anything for free, especially judges, because of the possibility that the person giving the gift might one day appear before them.

"Surely, brother, you remember when your favorite Supreme Court Justice, Antonin Scalia, refused to recuse himself in a case involving your favorite vice president, Dick Cheney, and he and good old Dick were hunting pals. That was in 2005.

"And please, let us not forget Supreme Court Justice Samuel Alito. During his 1990 confirmation hearings, the retard swore to senators he would recuse himself with any cases pertaining to his mutual fund operator, Vanguard, or cases involving his brokerage firm, Smith Barney. But he lied. He issued rulings in 1996 in a case with Smith Barney and in 2002 with a case involving Vanguard. Shall I continue?"

"How do you know what happened in 1996? You were only like ten years old," Dustin said.

Trevor shook his head. "For one thing, pea brain, ten years old for some people is a lot more advanced than most normal people's adult status. Besides, I am certain you are not aware of this, but let me explain—they document these events and a person who can read can easily learn about them."

"Still," Dustin said, "it's unusual. The system isn't flawed; people are flawed."

"And who, by chance, runs the system?" Trevor said.

Dustin shook his head. "It's still a rare thing. The system still works."

"What's a runway jury?" Frankie said.

Dustin patted him on the head. "It's 'runaway' jury. It's a jury that has been tampered with."

Trevor crossed his arms. "It is, in fact, not a jury that has been tampered with. Do try to read on occasion, brother. A runaway jury is one that has decided to act independently without utilizing the instructions from the court."

"Whatever," Dustin said. "This guy will still go to prison."

Trevor leaned forward, dropped his hands and rested them on his knees. "Perhaps you would care to make a wager. I am willing to bet you one thousand dollars that he will be completely exonerated."

"Do you have one thousand dollars?" Dustin said.

Trevor didn't answer, only continued to stare at Dustin.

Dustin shook his head. "Well, I don't."

"Really, Uncle Dustin?" Frankie looked up with his big brown eyes.

The truth was, Dustin and Sophia had been saving for a while and currently had over $28,000 in savings, but Dustin wasn't about to risk one penny of that. "Can't we just make this a gentleman's wager. Let's just say one dollar."

"An insult. 20!"

Dustin bit his lower lip. "OK, 20. I say the guy will be found guilty and gets life."

"You are on, brother," Trevor said, jumping out of the chair to walk over with his hand extended.

Dustin complied and shook on it.

His mom and Sophia had finished the dishes and came into the living room to join them. Frankie asked to play Santa. He handed out gifts to everyone, putting his in a pile beside him. Soon all presents were given to the rightful recipient and the floor was littered with torn wrapping paper.

Dustin opened one from Trevor. It was an electronic muscle stimulator.

"Oh my, brother. You do not even know what it is," Trevor said, seeing the look on Dustin's face.

"Oh, yeah," Dustin said. "Thanks."

Trevor nodded. "You are welcome. I know you are always complaining about sore muscles, among many, many other things, so I thought this would help."

"I'm sure it will. Very thoughtful," Dustin said.

Sophia was sitting beside Dustin and reading the box. "That was thoughtful, Tre. Let's try it out, Dustin."

Dustin gave her a quick look. "Not now, honey."

"If you do not like it, I have the receipt," Trevor said.

"I just don't want to try it now."

Everyone kept staring at Dustin, so he gave in. Sophia opened the box and pulled everything out. She hooked the power cord to the unit and handed the adapter end to Frankie. "Unplug the tree lights and plug this into the wall."

Mrs. Davis looked confused. "It runs off electricity?"

"Of course, Mother," Trevor said.

Sophia held the connectors. "Where do you want to try it?"

Dustin looked almost afraid. "Uh, just my forearm."

Dustin extended his arm and Sophia placed the four adhesive electrodes to his forearm, adjusted the controls to the lowest setting, and turned on the unit. Dustin jumped and jerked his arm back so fast it startled Sophia. One of the electrodes pulled loose and Dustin quickly swiped the other three off his arm.

"Whoa!" Frankie said.

Sophia tried to catch her breath, her hands at her chest. "What? What happened?"

"I don't know. . . uh, I don't. . . You just have to get used to it, I guess," Dustin said.

Trevor got up and walked over and dropped the receipt in Dustin's lap. "Merry Christmas, brother."

A few minutes later, Trevor decided it was time for him and his mother to head back to north Alabama. The sun was just starting to drift below the horizon as they said their good-byes and drove away. Both were tired from the day's events, but Trevor's thoughts were still festering over the gift.

"Ungrateful," he muttered.

"What?" his mother said.

"Dustin."

His mom seemed very sad. It had been such a wonderful day up until then. "I didn't know it was something that would shock him. Dustin is not a fan of electricity."

"It does not shock you, Mother," Trevor said. "It is not the electric chair. It provides a very mild current to stimulate your muscles. He was just being a jerk as always."

"You don't understand," his mother began. "Back when—"

"Oh, Lord, please let this be another pig story," Trevor said, his eyes lifted upward.

His mother tried again. "Back when we had the pigs—"

"Do you people not know of sarcasm?" Trevor said, looking upward again.

"Stop interrupting me," his mother said. "Back when we had the pigs, we heard a pig screaming one day way away from the house back where the fence ran deep into the woods. Dustin went to check it out and found one of the young pigs caught in the wires getting shocked by the electric fence. He managed to free the pig but got caught in the wires himself. It took him at least 15 minutes to get himself loose, all the while being shocked over and over. He was only 12 years old but it has affected him ever since. He's never been able to tolerate even the mildest electric current since."

Trevor stared straight ahead. He almost regretted his choice of gift and almost felt sorry for Dustin. Almost.

"Wuss!"

CHAPTER

EIGHT

TREVOR TURNED UP the aluminum can and drained the last of the carbonated liquid, crushed the container at the middle with his large mitt, then tossed it at a small, round trash receptacle on the floor a few feet from him. Although this can went into the target, the floor was littered with several crushed empties that had failed to hit the mark and lay there on the floor as evidence of either Trevor's lack of ability or lack of caring—or both. Trevor paid no attention to his accomplished shot, or his former failures, as his eyes were fixed on a dry erase board on the far wall of his office. The board had a cross-shape in red, with his name on top on one side and Dustin's on the other. Underneath the horizontal bar were eight single marks, seven on Dustin's side and one on Trevor's.

It had been six months since Christmas—six months since he and Dustin had bet on the outcome of the court case. Dustin had won and Trevor couldn't stand it. Their arguments over that case evolved into a more determined wager. The new deal was the first one to more accurately depict the outcome of ten televised court cases would be declared the winner. And it was the prize of the wager itself that had Trevor worried, a prize he wasn't sure he could own up to, or would even try. He hadn't, after all, paid the twenty dollars from the first bet. But this contest carried a much greater reward than a measly twenty bucks. The winner of this contest would be declared, by both brothers, as the more intelligent of the two.

He couldn't understand it. You couldn't turn on the TV

or the computer without hearing or reading some story about a failure of the judicial system. If it wasn't a judge not recusing himself, it was reports of a tampered jury or runaway jury, or of bribes, or just simply jury members voting their hearts and not going by the evidence. He knew the system was corrupt. But how could Dustin be winning if the system was as bad as he thought?

Trevor turned his eyes back to his computer and tried to concentrate on the system analysis program he was building for a friend. At least this made sense. There was no guessing here; just tell the computer what you want it to do and it does it, no questions asked. If only the contest was that simple.

Trevor stopped typing as his eyes shifted to one side and he tilted his head to look again at the board. Of course. Why hadn't he thought of it before? He could bring this game into his area of expertise. He rolled his chair away from the big desk and big computer he was working on and over to the opposite wall to a laptop that sat on a small computer desk. He pulled up the internet and typed "Ohio state laws" into the search and started reading through the lists of choices. The case they were watching now involved an Ohio State Trooper who had pulled a man over for speeding. Apparently suspecting the driver to be drinking, he had asked him to get out of the vehicle and proceeded to administer several sobriety tests. At some point, the motorist became outraged and a fight ensued with the trooper being struck several times. The man was charged with aggravated assault on a police officer, a 4th degree felony.

During the trial, the trooper admitted that the man had indeed not been drinking at all but defended his own actions of testing him. Also, several people had testified about this trooper's temper. He had at one time even been suspended for striking another officer. The defendant contended that the trooper started the fight and he was simply defending himself. There were no witnesses and the trooper's camera was supposedly on the fritz, so it was one's word against another.

Trevor had watched this case with intensity. It was in a small rural area and he could see in the eyes of the jurors that they believed the defendant. He wondered how many of them had heard their own stories about this trooper from people they knew. Trevor was convinced of the man's innocence and that was how he intended to vote. The trial had only one day left for closing arguments, at which point he was to call Dustin so they could exchange their predictions as to the outcome. As he glanced once again at the dry erase board, he knew he better come up with something besides what he planned to say—that the guy would be found not guilty.

He pulled up one of the websites for Ohio laws involving assault, which explained that aggravated assault carried a sentence of incarceration ranging from five months to 18 months, with fines not to exceed $5000. But this case also involved a police officer, so Trevor tried to find the laws on that. That proved a little more difficult. He found several cases involving where a police officer had been hit, either by a person or by a car. In one instance, the man had accidentally hit a police officer with his car and had gotten six years for it. Of course, he had been drinking. There was just too much information to try to put it all together.

Trevor pushed back in his chair and spun around as the chair rolled back across to the desk behind him where sat his main programming computer. He began to write a program that would allow him to type in the applicable laws from the state of Ohio and would also allow him to enter relevant cases. He knew the tricky part was not making the program simply apply the laws but to take into account testimony, evidence, and previous cases not only involving the same offense, but similarities such as this being the first offense for the defendant. It proved to be a daunting task. Trevor did not even budge when his mother called him for dinner. Later, Mrs. Davis brought him a plate, which he ate quickly, slid the plate aside, and continued working. He would glance at the clock periodically, grimace, and go back to it. Finally, after a dozen Code Reds and just before nine o'clock the next morning, he finished.

Closing arguments were scheduled at 11 a.m., which gave him two hours to get all the information keyed in and see if his program would predict the outcome. He was impressed with his own work but knew the program's only shortcoming was that it relied on a perfect system. He wouldn't be able to tell the computer about the emotions of the people in the courtroom. But he realized that was what he needed, a machine to think for him, a machine to think like Dustin. He could barely keep his eyes open as he slid the thumb drive with his new program into his laptop. A screen appeared with the words, "Enter Info." He began again to research Ohio state laws and entered each applicable law into the program. Then he searched several databases to find any former court cases involving the same offense, making sure to type in all the finer points of the cases and the outcomes.

He looked at the clock. 10:30. He continued adding as many cases as he could find. He finally stopped at 10:50.

"OK, here goes nothing." He hit "Enter" and the hourglass started spinning. He was so tired and suddenly realized he had been working for 15 straight hours on what was possibly the stupidest idea he had ever had. He wouldn't be surprised if the program didn't even work but rather came back with an advertisement for a car insurance company. His fears were laid to rest quickly as the hourglass only spun for about five seconds and the screen read: "Predicted Outcome. Defendant guilty. Two year sentence. Reduced to probation and a $1000 fine plus 40 hours of community service."

He stared at the screen. He had not programmed actual predictions, only to pull from other case outcomes, yet he still couldn't believe how official it read. He turned on the TV and watched the closing arguments unfold, each side giving their opinions on what the jury had heard and what their responsibilities now were. Trevor picked up his cell phone and called Dustin.

"Hello, brother, it is Tre."

"It's over?" Dustin said.

"Yes, it is, just now. What is your prediction?" Trevor wanted Dustin to go first.

"The guy's going to prison for striking a police officer. I say he's found guilty and gets five years. What do you say?" Dustin said.

Trevor cleared his throat. "I say defendant guilty. Two year sentence. Reduced to probation and a $1000 fine plus 40 hours of community service." He was reading it right off the screen.

There were a few seconds of silence before Dustin spoke. "You're going with guilty on this one?"

"Of course. You heard me," Trevor said.

"OK. I gotta get back to work. We'll see who is closer."

Trevor hung up the phone and stared at the screen again. Even if he didn't win, he was sure surprised at the program. He went upstairs and went to bed.

"I NEED YOU to wait outside," the doctor said, his right hand actually pressing against Dustin's chest. "He'll be fine. We've started an IV with Benadryl. Just wait over there and we'll come get you."

Dustin stood and watched for several seconds after the ER doors had closed behind the doctor then reluctantly walked over and took a seat in the waiting room where the doctor had motioned. As he sat down, his cell phone rang. It was Sophia.

"I got your message. What happened?" she said.

Dustin took a deep breath. "We were cutting grass on a

new account and there was a yellow jacket nest underground. Frankie got stung a couple of times—we all did—so I told him to wait in the truck until we killed them. After about ten minutes, he said his head was really itching. A few minutes after that his whole face was broken out in hives."

"Hives?" Sophia said.

"I don't know," Dustin said weakly. "It looked like mosquito bites. By the time I got him here to the hospital he was having trouble breathing. It was really freaking me out. The doctors say he's going to be fine but I am really shaken up." Dustin would never forgive himself if something bad happened to Frankie.

"I'm almost there," Sophia said.

Sophia walked in, found Dustin, and hugged him. They sat for about 30 minutes until the doctor finally came out and spoke to them.

"He's asleep now. Benadryl makes you drowsy. But he's fine," the doctor said.

Dustin breathed a sigh of relief.

"Can we see him, doctor?" Sophia said.

"In a few minutes. I would like to get some information first. Has he ever had a reaction to bee stings before?"

Dustin shook his head. "He got stung by a wasp a few years ago, but other than the sting area, didn't have a reaction like this."

"Well, that's common," the doctor said. "What happens is that bees are very good at adapting. We use pesticides to kill insects and bees become immune very quickly, and it becomes part of their DNA. What has happened over time is that bees are now using that against us so to speak."

Dustin looked at the doctor as if that story made no sense. "Will he have to take shots from now on if he gets stung?" he said.

"No, pills should be fine," the doctor said. "And you can

get them right over the counter. Just make sure to keep some available at all times, no matter where he goes."

The doctor led them back to the Emergency Room and Frankie was laying there smiling. He was allowed to get dressed and go home with them. Sophia sent Hannah a text to let her know everything was OK. After he was released, they drove away from the hospital, Frankie sitting between them as usual.

"Uncle Dustin," he said, "am I still going to be able to work for you?"

Dustin patted him on the shoulder. "Of course. We'll just have to keep an eye out for bees. And you have medicine now so it's no big deal. You want to keep working, don't you?"

Frankie looked down. "Yeah, but I'm a little afraid. Does that make me a coward?"

Dustin laughed. "No, it does not make you a coward; it makes you smart. That's your brain exercising common sense. You should be afraid. That's normal. Plenty of things happened to me when I was a kid that have made me afraid of things today."

"Really? Like what?" Frankie said.

Dustin smiled. "Pigs for one thing. I am still afraid of pigs today. Electricity also. And I'll tell you about another fear. One time when I was seven years old, Dad took us to visit his sister and her family in Loxley. It was close to the ocean, so we went on down and spent a day at the beach. It was my first time. I was amazed at how shallow the water was on the beach. I drifted way out on an air mattress then hopped off to walk back to shore. But it was way over my head and I almost drowned. Dad saved me but he was so upset. That's the last time we went to the beach. So, believe me, almost drowning in the Gulf of Mexico was a scary thing. That's why I'm afraid of—"

"Mexicans?" Sophia said.

Dustin and Frankie both laughed.

"Are you afraid of Mexicans, Uncle Dustin?"

Dustin looked at his wife and smiled. "Only one."

It was past 7:00 that evening when they got home after dropping Frankie off. Dustin had been afraid that Hannah might want Frankie to stop working with him after what happened, but she simply suggested everyone keep Benadryl from now on. Dustin was way ahead of her. He had stopped by the pharmacy and purchased five boxes, two for Hannah, two for him, and one for Frankie.

"Let me fix us some sandwiches," Sophia said as Dustin collapsed on the sofa. "The crews were able to finish up everything today so don't worry."

Dustin hadn't even thought about the crews or even about getting up to go to the newspaper in several hours. The phone rang and Dustin slowly slid his hand over to answer it. "Hello?"

"Hello, brother, it is Tre. I just heard about Frankie. Is he OK?"

"You just now heard about him?" Dustin said.

Trevor had just woken up from sleeping all day. "Can you not be belligerent and simply convey to me if Frankie is going to live?"

"I'm sorry. I'm just tired. Yes, he's fine," Dustin said. "We brought him home. He just has to keep Benadryl handy at all times now, just in case."

"That is excellent news. So, the doctor said he does not have to take shots?" Trevor said.

"That's what he said. He said it was because of all the pesticides we've been using."

There was a slight pause. "Pesticides? You use pesticides in your pedestrian lawn business?"

"No, not 'we' as in me, 'we' as in humans. He said bees get immune to it and then, when they sting us, we get it back," Dustin said.

Trevor scoffed. "The man, if it is a man, is retarded. Being allergic to bees has to do with the individual, not pesticides.

It is because of an overactive immune system. When someone like Frankie gets stung, the body, in a self-defense mode, begins releasing antihistamines throughout the entire system instead of simply concentrating solely on where the sting occurred. The reaction is due to that, not the actual bee sting, and certainly not because of pesticides."

"So, now you know more than the doctor?" Dustin said.

Trevor exhaled deeply. "Look brother, I am not calling to argue. I really wanted to know about Frankie. You know I love that little guy."

Dustin smiled. "Yeah, I know you do. I appreciate you calling. I was afraid you were calling to gloat."

"Gloat? About what?"

"The court case," Dustin said. "Didn't you see the outcome?"

"No, I have not watched TV at all today. They reached a verdict?"

Dustin chuckled. "You really don't know. Well, congratulations, you won another one. It's seven to two now. I guess I should worry."

"So, I was the closest?" Trevor said.

"No, not close," Dustin said. "You called it dead on."

CHAPTER

NINE

DUSTIN SIPPED his frozen margarita as he looked around the crowded restaurant. San Marcos was always crowded for Cinco de Mayo. This had become a tradition with Sophia's family every year since her dad started bringing them here when she was about 10 years old. Dustin had become part of the tradition when he and Sophia had gotten married and they had continued it after Sophia's dad died. Hannah had to work, so it was just Sophia and her mom, who occupied one side of the table, and Dustin and Frankie on the other side.

The waitress came by to take their order. "Are you guys ready?"

Dustin looked at Frankie. "You need another margarita?"

Frankie grinned really big and nodded.

The waitress smiled. "I might have to see your ID. How old are you?"

"Nine," Frankie said.

"Oh shoot," the waitress said, "you have to be ten."

After everyone gave their order and she walked away, Frankie said, "Are you Mexican, Uncle Dustin?"

Dustin laughed. "Only by marriage."

Frankie looked confused. "Am I Mexican?"

Sophia smiled. "Yes you are, dear."

"Was my dad Mexican?"

No one knew what to say. The fact is, no one knew.

"Of course," Dustin said. "How else could you turn out to be such a fine specimen of a Mexican gentleman?"

Frankie laughed then said, "What's a specimen?"

Everyone laughed. "That means you're a fine example," Sophia said.

Sophia looked at Dustin. "I'm just glad you're in a great mood today."

Dustin looked confused. "Why wouldn't I be? Have I been in a bad mood lately?"

Sophia smiled. "No, not really. But I know you were bummed out that Tre won the contest."

Dustin shook his head. "Yeah, I still don't know how he came back from behind like that."

"So, who's the smartest one now?" Sophia said.

Dustin held up his fist to Sophia, which he did often in a fake gesture.

"Come on, say it. Who's smarter?" she said again.

Dustin exhaled deeply. "OK. In accordance to the bet, I have to say that Trevor is smarter. You happy?"

"Yes," she said as she took her husband's hand. "I am very happy."

THE DRY ERASE BOARD still displayed the final score, ten to eight, although the game had ended weeks earlier. Trevor had tried to get Dustin to bet again on a new contest, but Dustin had simply conceded and explained he had no wish to go again and certainly not for money.

The phone rang and, as usual, Trevor let his mother answer upstairs.

"Tre?" she called out.

Trevor picked up the phone and waited for his mother to hang up. "Yes?"

"Is this Trevor Davis?" the voice said.

That sounded official. He had told his mother about creditors calling and to say he wasn't there or didn't even live there anymore. "Who, by chance, wants to know?"

"My name is Marion Palmer. I'm an attorney in Gadsden."

An attorney? This must be a really delinquent debt. "And?"

"And my son owns the comic book store there and he said you're a regular. He told me about your computer program regarding court cases and I wanted to ask about it," Mr. Palmer said.

Trevor breathed a sigh of relief. "Sure. It is a phenomenal program to be sure with an impressive track record. What do you want to know?"

"Can you predict outcomes of cases in the state of Alabama?" he said.

"Yes, of course." One of Trevor's many victories had come from a case in Alabama, so he already had it programmed with most of the information. Trevor knew where this conversation was going. He knew this attorney was hoping to use his program to test one of his own cases. Trevor's eyes gleamed as he realized an opportunity for cash had presented itself. Now he needed to be wise. Should he ask for $50 or would that scare him off? Maybe $30 would be best.

"If it's possible," Mr. Palmer said, "I'd like to use your program to test the possible outcome of one of our cases. We're pretty much through the meat of the trial and I don't think it's looking good for our client. We're not sure we want it to even reach the jury, but your program might be able to shed more light on our case. I'll pay you $500."

Silence.

"Hello?" the attorney said.

Trevor swallowed hard. "Yes, I think we can work that out for you. Uh… I need to know what kind of case it is so I can formulate the program to your specific needs. If you can email me that information, I will send you an invoice via your email address and then we will get started."

"Great," Mr. Palmer said. "Will you send me the program?"

"No, sir, I will not do that," Trevor said. Actually, he would have done that until someone offered that much money to use it. Now his mind was working overtime wondering how much a program like this could be worth. "I will have to key all the information in here and let you know the outcome."

And that's what happened. After the attorney paid the $500, Trevor designed the program to work for his particular case, which Trevor was surprised to learn was a murder case. The attorney's client was a wealthy businessman accused of killing his partner. Once Trevor configured the program, he entered all the information provided by the attorney regarding evidence and testimony from the trial. Trevor had a bad feeling about this case as he typed in the last of the data and punched the "Enter" key. Like every time before, it only thought for a few seconds before displaying the results. Trevor grimaced as he read: "Predicted outcome: Defendant Guilty. Sentence: Death."

Trevor worried about calling the attorney to give him this information, but then realized the man was not paying for good news but honest insight. He dialed the number and conveyed the results to the attorney. Much to Trevor's surprise, he was very appreciative.

"Thanks so much," Mr. Palmer said. "It was what we had feared, but that reinforces our position. I do believe we need to think about a plea bargain. Thanks again, Mr. Davis. That's a truly unique program you have there. You might want to consider marketing it somehow."

When Trevor got off the phone, he looked at his reflection in one of the disconnected computer screens and smiled. Mr. Davis? Yes, it must be an important program if it can turn a hippie into a Mister.

The next day, Trevor went to the comic book store, paid up his account, and picked up all the new copies the owner had ordered and stored for him, with money from the owner's dad no less. That took up half the money. Trevor blew the other half on eBay buying Star Wars memorabilia.

The revelation that this program could be useful to attorneys stemmed a deep-seated desire in Trevor's heart to take it further. He began to implement his new idea. The first step was to take one of his computers and convert it into a server. This would save him money as he wouldn't have to pay another company a monthly hosting fee. He had already chosen an available web address, www.testyourcase.com, and had begun designing the art for the home page. It should be very appealing to private law firms, if he could only make them aware of it. It wasn't like putting up a flyer in the comic book store would do it. All day long he worked on his new project then worked all night. He slept the next day and started again. In a few days, he had it all worked out and the site up and running. It was perfect, a sure winner. The problem was, he was going to have to be able to advertise it. But how? He had blown all the money he just made and he knew his mother didn't have it. He picked up the phone and dialed.

"Hello?" Dustin said.

"Hey, it is Tre."

"What's up? Is everything OK?"

"Yes. I just needed to ask you something," Trevor said.

"What?"

Trevor was almost afraid to say it. "I have this great business idea—"

"Oh great," Dustin said.

Trevor waited, not sure whether to continue.

"I'm working," Dustin said as an excuse.

"You are always working, brother. Listen. You want to know how I beat you at the court contest?"

That seemed to get Dustin's attention.

Trevor continued. "It was quite genius, really. I created a program that can predict the outcome. A lawyer just paid me $500 to use it. I can build a website, target 50 states, and market it to law firms. Lord knows they can afford to use it."

Dustin paused for a few seconds. "Why would they use it? Why did the one lawyer use it?"

"You are not paying attention, as usual. He used it to test the strength of his own case. That is valuable insight. It can show them where their weaknesses are and give them an idea of the likely outcome if the trial continues," Trevor said.

Dustin rubbed his eyes. "Just get to the point."

"Very well. I need to borrow some money, about $2000."

Dustin shook his head. "You don't know what borrow means. I thought you had a thousand dollars. That's what you said when you wanted to bet on the first outcome. In fact, I never even got my twenty dollars from that bet."

"To what twenty dollars are you referring?" Trevor said.

"You know very well what twenty dollars. That's what you wanted to bet."

"I do not know what you are talking about, brother. I remember you saying it was a gentleman's bet and not for money."

"I don't get you," Dustin said. "Do you really not remember or just claim you don't to get out of paying?"

"I shall pay you back with interest. This is a sure deal," Trevor said.

"Everything is always a sure deal with you, but I know otherwise. I'm sorry; I can't give you $2000."

"OK," Trevor said. "Just loan me $500. I can purchase advertising with that and get started."

Dustin shook his head. "You just said a lawyer paid you $500. So, if that's all you need, then you're already set."

"I do not have that anymore," Trevor said. "I helped Mother catch up some of her bills and buy groceries."

There was a long pause. "I'm sorry, I can't help you," Dustin said.

Trevor hung up. He sat and stared at his website and new business idea. He wasn't surprised that Dustin had turned him down, but he wasn't sure how to get the website off the ground. He had tweaked the program several times over the last year and it was pretty much perfect. He knew he could personalize it to fit any case profile for an accurate prediction. But without funds, he couldn't advertise it to the extent he would need to do. But that wouldn't stop him; he knew it was a great idea. That would just have to work itself out later. For now, the important thing was being ready for business. Trevor already had a business license and Paypal account under the title, "Computer Demigod," but had never actually filed taxes under the name. He thought this business would fit well within that same concept.

After Trevor designed the website, he looked at the home page with pride. It depicted an image he had invented and designed himself—a set of justice scales with a box on the right that read "evidence," and a box on the left with a question mark. The subsequent pages explained about the business and near perfect record for predicting the outcome of criminal cases.

It was complete, now to figure out a way to let the world know about it with a zero budget. He emailed the attorney, Marion Palmer, and gave him the info, hoping he might use it again or help spread the word. He didn't. If he could just get one customer, at $500, it would cover enough to take out a banner ad on one of the most influential law sites on the web. He began to wish he had not spent the $500 that Marion Palmer had paid him on comic books and collectibles, but you know what they say about hindsight. That money was gone and now he had to figure out how to get that first customer.

CHAPTER

TEN

HANNAH AND HER newest boyfriend were at Dustin and Sophia's house and all were gathered around the small dining room as Sophia placed the cake on the table. Dustin, who rarely used his creative skills, had always decorated Frankie's cakes since he turned one. Many years they consisted of a design that was correlated with taxes, since Frankie's birthday was April 15th, and Dustin often referred to Frankie as Hannah's little deduction. Last year, at Frankie's ninth birthday party, the cake displayed a very large yellow-and-black cartoon bee.

"Why are we waiting?" said Hannah's new boyfriend.

"Granny and Uncle Tre are coming," Frankie said, who was already seated in front of the cake, which was decorated in a baseball theme this year, a sport he had just discovered and fell in love with.

Sophia walked in from the front porch holding her cell phone. "Trevor just turned off I-65 onto I-85 so he'll be here in about ten minutes. It's just him; Granny Doreen had to work."

"That's your mother and brother?" the boyfriend said looking at Dustin.

Dustin nodded, mainly because he couldn't remember this guy's name. Hannah had had so many boyfriends over the years, most for only a month or so, and most she treated like it was a long term relationship by doing things like bringing them to family events. Dustin had given up trying to keep up with them. He was polite and hospitable to all of them, but he kept it as informal and impersonal as possible.

"He's the rich one?" the boyfriend said.

Dustin looked hard at Hannah, who simply shrugged off his blatant glare. "I wouldn't say rich, but he does OK."

A few minutes later, Trevor pulled into the yard along the driveway and parked his new 4X4 Ford F150 right alongside Dustin's 14 year old two-wheel-drive Dodge Ram. The contrast was stark. Dustin's mom had told him about Trevor's new truck, but to see it in person was something else. He tried not to stare.

Frankie was less obvious, running out to hug his uncle and immediately wanting to sit behind the wheel of the beautiful truck. Trevor left Frankie in the truck and walked over to Dustin for his normal less-than-cordial handshake.

"What'd that set you back a month?" Dustin said, without even looking at the truck.

"Not to worry, brother, it is a lease," Trevor said. "It is only $650 a month."

Dustin shook his head. "Only?" he said. That was the same as Dustin and Sophia's rent. But his mom had told him that Trevor's website had finally taken off and he was now pulling in about $6000 a month. So the lease payment didn't seem like so much compared to that, especially considering Trevor still lived with their mom and had no other bills that he knew of.

"Hey, Tre, glad you could make it. Sorry your mom had to work," Hannah said.

Dustin's mouth dropped open as he turned slowly to see Hannah standing on the porch and smiling. He watched as Trevor went up and hugged her as if they had always been best friends. He guessed it was true that money changed people, or maybe more accurately, it changed people around you. Trevor hadn't changed at all. He was still a rude hippie to Dustin; the money just made him a bit more unbearable. The strange thing was, Dustin made more, but he worked hard for it and saved as much as he could. He had a lot of bills and preferred not to spend on what he considered frivolous things. In other words, no matter how beautiful Trevor's new truck was, he would drive his old Dodge pickup until the wheels fell off.

"Come on, knucklehead," Dustin said motioning to Frankie, who still sat behind the wheel of the truck pretending to drive. "Let's have that party."

After singing "Happy Birthday," the cake was cut and everyone sat around the table and inside the living room and ate. Then it came time for Frankie's favorite part—the presents. He opened the one from his grandmother first. Sophia's mom had stayed home because she wasn't feeling well. Then he had two presents left to open: the one from Uncle Trevor and the one from Dustin and Sophia. Trevor handed him the one from Dustin and Sophia, which was noticeable, making Dustin wince as he wondered why he had done that.

"Wait," Hannah said. "Me and Glenn got you a present but I have to get it from the car." She walked out the front door while the boyfriend, whose name was apparently Glenn, stood there with a toothy smile. A minute later, Hannah came back in carrying a box. "Close your eyes," she said.

Frankie obeyed.

Hannah sat the box on the floor at Frankie's feet and instructed him to open his eyes.

Frankie reached down and opened the box. "Oh, wow." He pulled out the scrawniest, ugliest puppy Dustin had ever seen. It had patchy white fur, short stubby legs, and its bottom teeth stuck out. "What's his name?" Frankie said.

"It's a her," Hannah said. "Her name is Sadie, but you can change it if you want."

"No, I like Sadie." Frankie was rubbing his nose against the dog's nose.

Dustin was appalled. He knew Frankie was too young to care for a pet, and Hannah was far from what he called a responsible person. He feared this little ugly mutt would not be well cared for, and would most likely be gone not long after. . .

Grant. . . no, Greg. . . or whatever the new boyfriend's name was.

"Has it had its first shots, like Parvo?" Dustin said.

The boyfriend laughed. "No, she's healthy."

"Does she come with papers?" Sophia asked.

The boyfriend laughed again.

"No," Dustin said, "but she's going to need some before she goes on the floor."

Frankie set the puppy down and continued petting her.

"OK, now ours," Sophia said.

Frankie opened the gift. It was a man's wallet. "Oh wow." He stood up and tucked it in his back pocket and sat back down, his face displaying a grin.

Trevor smiled and nodded. "That was nice."

Dustin wasn't sure if Trevor was being sincere or sarcastic, but decided it wasn't important. "You might want to look inside that wallet, young man."

Frankie's eyes opened wide as he jumped out of the seat and reached back to retrieve the wallet. His entire body twisted as he tried to free it from his small back pocket. Everyone was laughing at his hysterics. He finally got it out, opened it, and pulled two tickets from the money area. "Holy Smokes!"

"What is it?" Hannah said.

Frankie held up the two tickets and panned them around so everyone could see that they were for a monster truck rally.

Hannah laughed. "Oh goodness. You have turned my boy into a complete redneck. When is this?"

Frankie read off one of the tickets. "May 6th at the Garret Coliseum. All right. That's not too long from now. Thanks, Uncle Dustin and Aunt Sophia."

"You're welcome, sweetie," Sophia said with a grin.

"OK, little buddy, now this one," said Trevor, handing Frankie the last gift, the one marked from him and his mother.

Frankie quickly ripped the wrapping paper away to reveal a plain cardboard box about five inches square and an inch thick.

He opened it and pulled out a small, flat black object, slightly larger than a cell phone. Frankie looked confused as did everyone else.

Hannah's boyfriend broke the stillness. "Son-of-a… Is that what I think it is?"

Hannah noticed the logo on the side. "What's 'Flair?'"

"Are you kidding me?" her boyfriend said.

Frankie pressed the 'on' button and the screen lit up with the same logo. It was indeed a Flair, the latest device in the hand-held electronic arena. It had full time internet and phone service, provided directly from a satellite, so you were never without a signal as long as you were on this planet. The back panel was a heat sensor, and as long as it was at least 90 degrees Fahrenheit, it activated the built-in charger, so keeping it in your pocket kept it ready to go. And one of the cooler features was that it came with a small device that could be placed on the back of any TV, and push the right button and your Flair screen was now projected onto that TV. You could literally pull it out of your pocket and quickly get internet updates or check your email during commercial breaks of your favorite show. The reason everyone around the table knew this, even Hannah once she thought about it, was because of the maker's own extensive advertising campaign. The commercials, billboards, and magazine ads were everywhere and non-stop. It also came with a price tag of just over $1000.

"Tre, that's too expensive. You shouldn't have spent that much." Sophia looked at Dustin.

Dustin was torn between Frankie's amazement and Sophia's reluctance. "I agree. That was way too much."

"That's all you're going to say?" Sophia said. "Well, I'm not going to be the lone spoilsport."

Frankie got up, leaving all his other presents on the table, including the wallet that he had not returned to his back pocket, and Sadie, who he had left on the floor by his chair, and ran into the living room to try it out on the TV. "How does it work, Uncle Tre?"

Trevor took the little piece out of the box, which was only about the size of a match box and had connections for a cable line or the three-color video wire, and walked into the living room, unscrewed the cable line going into the TV, and reattached it to the box, which he then inserted onto the TV.

Frankie pressed the 'Screen" function and his screen appeared on the TV. Everyone gathered around to watch, except Trevor, who took his normal seat in front of the computer and, without so much as asking permission, began surfing the net.

Hannah's boyfriend, who seemed to be taken with Trevor, walked up and peered over Trevor's shoulder. "What's your business, dude?"

Trevor pulled up the website and began explaining in detail the premise behind the business. He diligently discussed every facet of the company with Hannah's boyfriend as if he were going to test him on it.

Dustin tried to shut it out. He couldn't believe Trevor was spending so much time talking to a person whose name he didn't even care to remember, a person who, if history repeats itself, they would never see after this day.

"You're a genius," the boyfriend said after Trevor finished.

"That is an accurate depiction, and what my business cards say," Trevor said. "Well, they would if I had business cards."

Dustin grimaced, wondering how many times he could tell that tired old line.

Hannah said, "I can have you some made if you need them."

Once again, Dustin's bottom jaw dropped.

The boyfriend continued to ask questions. "Did you start making money right away with it?"

"No, actually I did not," Trevor said. "It took a few months to catch on. I was broke after setting up the business and could not afford to advertise. No one I knew was willing to take a chance on me."

Dustin looked up expecting Trevor to be staring or even pointing at him, but he wasn't. He got up and went into the kitchen to check on Sadie, who had fallen asleep on the floor, right next to her poop. Dustin took some napkins and began cleaning. He picked her up, carried her back into the living room, sat back on the couch, and she fell asleep in his lap.

Trevor continued. "Eventually, I had some moron lawyer order the service, then I could afford to advertise a little, then I had another and another, and so on. I do not even advertise that much anymore because most law firms know about me now."

"'Why do you say 'moron lawyer'?" the boyfriend said.

"Because they did not know what they were doing. They sent me all this information about a current trial case, but it was not really systematic or methodical like an attorney's files should be. It was almost like they were making it up as they went. But I put together a prediction for them and that is what got the ball rolling."

Sophia, who was standing in the entrance to the kitchen and listening to Trevor's story, looked down at the floor when he called the first customer a moron. She lifted her eyes and smiled lovingly at Dustin. It was subtle, but one other person in the room noticed.

Dustin realized Trevor was staring at him and wondered in Sophia's expression had tipped him off. He looked back at Sophia and smiled. Even though he had thought it was a bad idea and wouldn't openly support Trevor's business endeavor, he couldn't sit back and not help at all. Dustin was, in fact, the first moronic lawyer.

The boyfriend was asking more questions but they appeared to be falling on deaf ears as Trevor watched Dustin and Sophia for several more seconds. He turned back to the computer. "Son-of-a-gun," he whispered.

CHAPTER

ELEVEN

IT WAS FOUR DAYS before Thanksgiving and Trevor was sitting at the kitchen table at his mother's house looking over house designs. He had made the decision to build a home on the same 30 acres where his mother lived, just a hundred yards away. He had been approved at the bank to build a home up to $150,000 but he couldn't stop looking at the ones for $200,000 or more. Perhaps the bank would approve more. Either way, he was going to make the announcement on Thanksgiving Day when Dustin, Sophia, and Frankie had planned on coming to north Alabama this year. His mother was out playing Bingo, a regular Sunday event for her, when the doorbell rang to the front entrance.

Trevor walked over, opened the door, and found two men standing there in black suits with black ties, wearing sunglasses. One had neatly parted light hair with a handsome face. He almost resembled a young Robert Redford. The taller guy was an ugly cuss with dark hair in a buzz cut and a large scar across the bridge of his nose. He seemed to be upset. It was around noon, so Trevor figured they were church folks out and about. "I gave at the office, whatever you are pushing."

"Trevor Davis?" the smaller guy said.

"Who wants to know?" Trevor said.

"U.S. Government." The smaller guy pulled out a badge.

Trevor's mind rushed to think what he had done to warrant the attention of the government. He took the badge and examined it. "Homeland Security?"

The guy smiled as he took back the badge and returned it

to his inside jacket pocket. "May we come in?"

Trevor ignored the question and looked at the taller guy. "And your badge, Slick?"

The man stood motionless. No one moved for several seconds, so Trevor began to close the door.

"Whoa," the smaller guy said as he blocked the door. "We're getting off on the wrong foot here. We're here for something good. I'm Agent Daniels and this is Agent Marks."

Once again, Trevor ignored the smaller guy and looked at the taller guy. "And your badge, Slick?"

Agent Daniels nodded to Agent Marks who then reached into his pocket and handed Trevor his badge, which was identical to the first one.

"Homeland Security?" Trevor repeated. "So, what exactly does that mean? That is about as vague as you can get. There are what, 20,000 departments that fall under that ridiculous organization now? Who exactly do you guys work for?"

Agent Marks finally spoke and in a rough sounding voice. "Let's just say we work for that department no one likes to talk about."

Trevor scoffed. "That certainly narrows it down, does it not? I cannot believe that you two are so stupid to go around announcing it. Come on in, I guess."

They followed Trevor into the living room where, when prompted, they took a seat on the sofa. Trevor sat in a recliner next to them.

"So, what is this about?" Trevor said.

Agent Daniels continued to be the spokesperson. "It's about your website, test your case dot com."

"What about it? It is perfectly legal."

"Of course," Daniels said. "We love it. We want to offer you a job to build us a similar program, only on a grander scale."

Trevor continued to survey the duo without so much as a smile. There was something about them that didn't seem right, especially the one called Marks. "What would the government want with a program like this?"

Marks spoke for the second time. "That's not your concern."

"Look," Daniels said. "This is a great opportunity here. The job should take at least a year and the government is willing to pay you twenty thousand a month, plus a bonus of one million dollars when completed. You'll live on site and have absolutely no expenses during that time either."

Trevor still didn't change his expression. It was a great offer, but he didn't like these two so he offered his rebuttal. "Forty thousand a month and two million upon completion."

Marks moved so fast for a tall guy that Trevor didn't even have time to flinch. In a flash, he was out of his seat and had both his hands on the arms of the recliner with his face just inches from Trevor's. His jacket was now open and his holstered pistol was clearly visible. He spoke looking directly into Trevor's eyes, but it was clear he was not speaking to him. "Let's just take the program and whatever else we need and erase everything else. We don't need him."

Trevor was terrified but never let it show. "Is this your idea of good cop, bad cop, Slick? If you could do it without me, you would not be talking with me. Two things I know: One— if the U.S. government can spend a billion dollars on trying to figure out how grasshoppers mate, they can afford my price. Two—retards like you guys are paid from the neck down and cannot make decisions on your own. So, get on your little phone and call the one who thinks for you and tell them the price is now sixty thousand a month and six million upon completion."

Daniels laughed then looked up at Marks. "Sit down!" Then he got up and walked toward the front door. "I'll be right back."

Marks sat back down. He stared at Trevor with an evil look that Trevor had never witnessed but wouldn't back down.

Neither would break the stare until Daniels returned.

A few moments later, Daniels came back in and sat down. "OK, here's the final offer. And by final," he said, glancing over at Marks who still stared at Trevor, "I mean final. The government will pay you fifty thousand per month and four million upon completion. Or... we take the program and hire our own programmers. Either way, the website shuts down today."

"I assume I am going to get that in writing," Trevor said.

Daniels smiled. "Of course. But here's the thing you need to know before you even get the contract. This is considered classified, top secret, a black op so to speak, and is strictly on the QT. You cannot tell a soul about it or it will void the agreement—or worse. Someone will be in contact with you tomorrow to discuss the arrangements."

Classified? Top secret? Black op? Trevor chuckled. Maybe Daniels just liked the sound of his own voice. Maybe that's why he was verbose, redundant, and repetitive.

Daniels got up and Marks followed.

"Thanks, Trevor. Look forward to working with you." Daniels extended his hand and Trevor accepted, although he felt as if he had just made a deal with the devil.

Marks did not offer a handshake as the two men exited through the front door.

After Trevor watched them drive away, he fell back into the recliner and his hands started shaking. He couldn't believe what had just happened. Was it real? Had two secret agents just paid him a visit? Had one of them just indirectly threatened to kill him? More importantly, had they just offered to pay him 4.6 million dollars for designing a program that basically was already designed?

He wanted to pick up the phone and call everyone, but that was one thing he knew he could not do. He went to his office so he could change the home page of his web site to read "This site is no longer available," just in case they checked it later. He would take the entire site down once he knew for sure this was real.

EVERYONE SAT AROUND and ate their Thanksgiving meal in almost silence. It seemed to be a good atmosphere, but Trevor was uncharacteristically silent. He wore his black shirt and sweatpants and kept his face toward his plate. Frankie and Dustin made small talk, as did Dustin's mom, but most of the time was simply filled with the sound of forks scraping plates and napkins rustling.

"How long are you staying?" Mrs. Davis said.

"We're going to go back Saturday afternoon," Dustin said as he got up and placed his empty plate in the sink.

Frankie handed him his plate, also. Within a few minutes, everyone had followed. As they all resumed their seats in silence, it was clear something was amiss. This was normally the time for family stories or for Dustin and Trevor to argue, but without Trevor leading the way, it didn't seem to want to start.

"So, you sold the gym?" Trevor finally said.

Dustin nodded. "Yeah, it was just getting to be too much for an old man like me."

Frankie spoke up. "Uncle Tre, where's your new truck?"

All eyes looked at Trevor as if they hadn't even realized it wasn't out front.

"I turned it in yesterday," Trevor said.

Dustin seemed shocked. "Really? What did you get now?"

"Nothing."

"Nothing?" Dustin repeated.

Sophia finally spoke. "Tre, is everything all right? Is the website still doing OK?"

"I shut it down," Trevor said.

"You what!??" Dustin said loud enough to make Frankie

and his mom jump.

Trevor looked around the room at the bewildered faces. "I have an announcement and I guess now is the perfect time to make it." He thought back to Monday when the woman, another agent as secretive as the first two, had shown up at the house while his mother was at work. She had brought the contract and told him the things he needed to bring and gave him a plane ticket for Friday. She also gave him a lot of fake documents and the story to tell friends and family, which is what he was trying to recall now to make sure he said it correctly. "I have been offered a job by a large game company."

Silence. Everyone just stared without even blinking.

"Anyway, that is why I closed down the website. I will not have time to keep that going," Trevor said.

Dustin spoke first. "This job will pay more than the website then?"

Trevor couldn't help but smile. "Yes, considerably."

Silence.

"Congratulations," Sophia said. "Can you give us some details?"

"Not a lot, honey," Trevor said. "Unfortunately, they have so many privacy issues. I never knew how competitive the gaming industry was. I am not allowed to tell you the name of the company or the name of the game I will be helping design, but I can tell you it is in Washington D.C. and I have to leave tomorrow."

"Tomorrow?" his mother said. "I thought you were going to announce your plans to build a new house. When did all this come about?"

"Just recently. I am sorry I could not tell you about it," Trevor said.

"I don't understand." Dustin looked at his mom then back at Trevor. "Since when do you design games and how did they find you?"

"I can program anything, brother. You of all people should know that. I have sent several game design plans to several different game manufacturers."

That seemed to make sense to everyone, including Dustin. Trevor was always sending ideas to companies. It just seemed odd that one had actually worked.

"Congratulations," Dustin said.

CHAPTER

TWELVE

DUSTIN AND SOPHIA took Trevor to the Huntsville International Airport, all the while Dustin complaining that Trevor should have taught him how to do the business instead of just shutting it down. Trevor, of course, couldn't tell him the real reason behind shutting it down, so just kept saying he never thought about it.

From Huntsville, he flew directly to Washington D.C. and was met at the airport by a driver, who then drove him to a large white building somewhere in a less-desirable part of town, far from the hustle and bustle of downtown.

As the driver turned into the entrance for the underground parking, he was stopped by two armed guards. One walked over to the driver's side as the driver rolled down his window and showed him his ID. He looked to the back seat at Trevor then stood up and motioned them onward.

The driver stopped beside an entrance door and explained to Trevor to ring the bell beside the door. Trevor got out and took his suitcase from the trunk. As soon as he closed the trunk, the driver made a u-turn and headed back the way he had come.

Trevor rang the bell and, after a few seconds, a very stern-looking woman opened the door. She was wearing a long black skirt and a black jacket over a white button-up. Her hair was pulled back so tight that it looked like her eyebrows were two inches higher than they should be. She seemed to be in her mid-fifties, but her hair was completely dark and her face had more wrinkles than Trevor had ever seen on even a much older woman.

"Trevor Davis?"

Trevor nodded.

"This way." The woman never smiled or offered any greeting, simply turned and walked away. Trevor quickly followed carrying his suitcase.

They only went about 20 feet to a door on the right. The woman entered and Trevor followed. Inside the room was another woman with the same clothes and hairstyle, and only slightly different facial features, but with exactly the same demeanor. The room had several monitors, all monitoring scenes outside the building except one that was focused on the outside of the door where Trevor had just rang the bell.

"Put your case up here," the second woman said, pointing to the table.

Trevor complied and the two women began going through every single item and examining it thoroughly: toothbrush, socks, underwear, everything. They meticulously caressed their fingers through every inch of every object.

After 45 minutes of that, the second woman looked at Trevor and said, "Take off your clothes."

Trevor acted calm as if he had been expecting the next phase, which he certainly had not. He took off his shoes, socks, jacket, shirt, and pants, and handed them to the women, who stood like old witches around the kettle reaching out with their skeleton-like fingers. Trevor stood there in his boxers, hoping that was going to be the end of it.

"Come on," the second woman said, motioning toward the boxers.

Trevor slid his boxers off and stood there naked, his hands cupped in front of him. Only then did he notice that it wasn't particularly warm in the room, and the floor was stone tile, which added to the effect. As the women picked through his clothes like vultures, his teeth began to chatter. Thank goodness it can't get any worse.

Snap! The rubber glove popped as the second woman released the band after sliding her fingers in. "Turn around and bend over."

"What?" Trevor said through chattering teeth. "No drink first?"

The woman did not seem amused, so Trevor assumed the position for his first ever, and hopefully last, cavity search. When that was over, the first woman picked up a phone and spoke softly then they both sat at the table and peered over at the monitors as if they were broadcasting their favorite soaps. Trevor stood there with his hands still cupped in front of his privates.

The door opened and another similarly dressed woman appeared, only noticeably younger and almost attractive. "What are you doing? Put on your clothes."

"Thanks, ladies," Trevor said to the first two, who ignored him. He put on his clothes and followed the new woman out the door and down the hall.

"So, do you have a name?" Trevor said.

The woman kept walking without so much as acknowledging the question. Trevor took the cue and didn't speak himself. She led him to an elevator and entered, whereupon she took a key and placed it in the slot to activate the control panel. They took that several flights up and Trevor followed her out and down another hallway, which had identical white doors ten feet apart on either wall. She stopped at one door, opened it, and went inside and turned on the light.

Trevor walked in and couldn't believe his eyes. It was a room about ten feet square. It was obvious that it had been an office at one point. You could still make out the areas where the desk, chair, and file cabinet had been from the only bright areas in the carpet, which seemed to have been installed when the building was constructed. Only two items made up the entire contents of the room: a twin-sized bed and a small three-drawer chest.

"You have got to be kidding me," Trevor said.

The woman was expressionless. "This is your personal room."

"Great," Trevor said. "So, my bedroom is the only room not locked in this building? Where is the bathroom?"

"At the end of the hall," the woman said.

Trevor couldn't believe it. "I have to share?"

"No, you're the only one in this hall. It's all yours. Now leave your stuff here; we have to get to orientation."

Trevor followed her as she walked down the hall in the same direction they had taken to the room. As they passed an open entrance on the left, she pointed and explained that was the bathroom. Trevor walked in, looked around, and couldn't believe what he saw. It was indeed a bathroom, a community bathroom. It looked like the main men's room from his high school. It had three urinals, three sinks, and two stalls. There wasn't a shower. Trevor opened the first stall door and saw a standard commode, but when he opened the second, he saw the genius for whom he worked. The commode had been removed and a drain was in its place. Two pipes came directly out of the wall about six feet high, one hot and one cold he suspected, and each had an outdoor garden hose spigot attached. Trevor shook his head in amusement and walked out. He smiled at the woman. "I do not know how we are both going to fit into that shower, sugar."

She turned and walked away. He followed as they turned left down another corridor and she came to another obscure white door and went inside. It was a small conference room and there were four others already seated at the table, three males and one female, and all seemed to be several years younger than Trevor. She motioned for Trevor to take a seat then walked to the front of the table.

"OK, everyone's here and we all know why we're here.

You have been contracted by the U.S. government to design and build the most comprehensive computer program in the area of judicial law. This undertaking should take at least a year in which time you are being paid quite adequately. You will be provided with a complete set of specs for this job when you get to your work stations. Everything you need is on this floor. You are not permitted to leave this floor for any reason, other than death. If you get sick we will bring a doctor to you. You will be allowed to write out grocery items and those will be picked up for you. You each have a private bathroom and there is a bathroom outside your work area. There is a kitchen where you will eat all meals. No food is allowed in the work area or your rooms. You are allowed one phone call per week to call home and that call will be closely monitored."

Trevor looked around the table at the others, who were all listening intensely. The three guys looked like they would have fit in with his crowd. If he'd seen them at the comic book store, he wouldn't have thought anything. The female, on the other hand, was someone he would have noticed. She was Indian with a dark complexion, a slender build, beautiful black hair that was perfectly straight and came down to about her waist, with a beautiful face and almost black eyes. She was the only one dressed in professional clothes, wearing black dress pants and a half-sleeve, suit-style blouse. She turned and looked at Trevor as he realized he had been staring and quickly looked away.

"OK," the woman said, "let me introduce you to each other." She pointed to the two guys on the left. "This is John Grohberg and Ralph Kowaski. They are your data entry guys and probably the fastest typists in the country."

The guys stood up and nodded to everyone. Trevor was impressed. For some reason, he would have thought women to be faster typists. He was still a two-finger typist himself.

"And this is Radhika Kaur who is our legal expert," the woman said.

The beautiful young woman stood and nodded to each side and quickly sat back down. Trevor tried to say the name phonetically in his mind in hopes not to forget it. *Rod – a – ka. Rod – it – ca.* Then he realized that if he just took the "e" off "erotica," he had it down pat. He could certainly remember it that way.

"This is Bradley Bradford. He's the backup programmer."

The guy beside Trevor stood and nodded. He was short and dumpy like the other two guys but with a thick head of brown curly hair.

Then the woman pointed to Trevor. "And this is our team leader, Trevor Davis."

Team leader? Trevor liked the sound of that. He was glad he had decided to shave as he stood and nodded to everyone who was staring at him, including Radhika. After, they were all led to the kitchen.

"We have stocked the fridge and cabinets with basic food," the woman said. "However, there is a notepad on the fridge for you to write down whatever normal foods you like to eat, and we'll have them brought to you here. If you have something specific you requested, you might want to write your name on it. We're all adults here and I don't want to hear complaints about someone stealing your food."

Everyone looked around at each other as if pondering if anyone there might actually do that.

Next the woman led them to a laundry room, also converted from an empty office or bathroom, and then their work area. Like the bedroom and the kitchen, there were no windows. Trevor concluded that the entire area must be within the center of the building. But this room was fairly large. There was a long table in the middle with simple wooden chairs only on the right side as you faced into the room. Across the room on the opposite side was a table along the wall with five huge monitors and keyboards, each with its own mouse. Identical gray desk chairs sat in front of each. The actual computer towers were nowhere to be seen, but Trevor could see the cables from the monitors ran straight through the wall.

"Have a seat and the director will be here shortly. Are there any questions?" the woman said.

Radhika raised her hand. "Is there a gym or someplace to exercise?"

"Yeah," the two data entry guys agreed, which made Trevor smile since each of them were as out of shape as he.

The woman looked at the guys also in disbelief, then back at Radhika. "No."

"What about sunshine?" Trevor said.

Everyone turned to look at Trevor.

"What about it?" the woman said.

Trevor looked at everyone else for a little support. "Well, honey bunches, all the places you have shown us where we are 'allowed' to go, have no windows. You cannot expect people to go a year without seeing the sky or sunshine. It is not even healthy or productive. We will not be able to do our jobs effectively if we never have access to fresh air or sunshine."

"He's right," Radhika said.

"Yeah, he's right," the others echoed.

The woman looked confused as if this is something she had never even considered and wasn't sure how to respond. "I'll see what I can do," she said and turned and went out the door.

The five new hires just stood around a few seconds as if they didn't know what to do next. Finally, Trevor spoke. "Well, thank goodness that was not weird."

As he took a seat, the others did the same.

"What's weird," said Bradley, the other programmer, "was that naked greeting at the entrance."

They all laughed, except Radhika who seemed to blush.

"I'm Bradley." Bradley put his hand out to Radhika. It seemed he was wasting no time to zero in on the one female, who shook his hand and said her name as well. That prompted everyone to introduce themselves, for even though they had done so in the conference room, it was less than formal and each one seemed to realize that if they were going to be stuck together for a year or more, they should get to know each other.

"It's all a little scary for me—not what I expected for sure," Radhika said as the others nodded.

"Oh heck, Radhika," Trevor said, "this woman with no name and even the gorgeous ladies who provided the free cavity search are not nearly as bad as Scarface."

The guys laughed but all faces quickly went from amused to confused. "Who's Scarface?" asked John.

Trevor looked at all the blank faces. "You guys were not visited by this scary agent named Marks?"

More blank faces. "Are you kidding around?" Ralph said.

Trevor realized that he was the only one recruited the way he was. Of course, it was his program after all. "So, how did you guys get this job?"

Each took turns explaining and most of the explanations were all similar. The guys had all applied for a job with the government and each had been contacted on Monday and offered the contract position. Each added the contract stipulated total secrecy, but still none of them had an idea it was going to be like this. Radhika, on the other hand, was already a practicing attorney with a local law firm in D.C. and her firm had been contracted to provide a legal expert for this endeavor. Trevor wanted to ask them about their pay but he knew that speaking of that was also forbidden by the contract, and he was afraid that the others might be on a fairly normal salary compared to his paycheck.

Radhika looked at Trevor with those beautiful black eyes resting behind the small frame glasses. She was the only one of the group with eyeglasses. "I want to hear more about Scarface."

The others nodded.

"Oh, he is nobody," Trevor said. "But, just in case you ever do see a guy here with a scar across the top part of his nose, do not mess with him. He is grumpy."

Before they could acknowledge, a middle-aged man came in the door. He was six-feet tall, African-American, and wearing a black suit and tie of course. He was carrying five professionally printed manuals and set one down in front of each of them, then stood erect across the table. He began to speak, almost like a parent disciplining a child, and his eyes shifted from one person to the next, then back, as he spoke. "I'm Agent Franks. These are your objective manuals. You will read and learn them tonight. Tomorrow you will be in this room at 0700, not one minute after. We have a lot of work to do, gentlemen. It's now 1830 hours. Go to the kitchen and eat dinner, then to your rooms to learn this book back and front. I'll see you first thing in the morning."

That was it. He abruptly turned and walked out as quickly as he had entered. Everyone looked at each other then slowly got up and made their way back to the kitchen. Radhika complained about there only being sandwich stuff but Trevor was fine with that. That's basically what he lived on. Well, that and pepperoni pizza Hot Pockets.

The kitchen seemed to be the only place they could actually converse freely. Trevor learned where everyone was from and that everyone was single. Although that seemed like an odd coincidence, he was glad to know that about Radhika. All the guys were.

Afterward, everyone went back to their own rooms. Trevor changed into some sweats since he had decided to dress up with a pair of holey jeans for his first day, and sat on the edge of the bed and tried to read through the manual. Although the temperature was fine, the room was hardly comfortable. He couldn't believe they hadn't at least provided a desk with a lamp. The manual read like it had been put together quickly and the language was very repetitive. But the context was clear. They were wanting to build a program and install it into a super computer that would not only contain the data of every law in every state, city, and town, but one that would update automatically every time a new federal, state, or local law went into effect, or was changed or taken off the books. Now Trevor understood why they had two data entry guys and wondered if that was enough.

About halfway through, Trevor couldn't keep his eyes open. He did what he used to do in high school. He flipped through the book, picking up a little info here and there, and then read the ending. Then he lay down on the little bed with the flat pillow and tried to sleep, although his mind was not making it easy. He tried to just focus on the money and not the thoughts that kept creeping into his conscience, the thoughts making him wonder why in the world the government would want such a system.

He was glad at least that he had his own room and no one was around him. He finally drifted off to sleep and began to snore loudly.

CHAPTER

~

THIRTEEN

AFTER A MONTH, everyone had settled into their routines. Trevor sat at the first station with Bradley beside him at the next station. Their first priority was to take Trevor's program and build from there, beginning with making it automatically upload and apply all laws that John was busy keying in at the station on the far end, and all precedence cases Ralph was busy keying in at the station to John's left. Radhika sat in the middle and her job was to monitor the progress and make sure the laws and cases were not only being keyed in and updated correctly, but to make sure each simulation they ran applied the laws and precedence cases in the proper way.

It was tedious work but Trevor enjoyed it for the most part. Seeing his program evolve through this group effort into a more spectacular design was exciting. Plus, getting to see Radhika every day didn't hurt either. They seemed to click right away and he spent every break and every weekend trying to get to know her better. About the only thing that bothered Trevor, other than the attitudes of all the agents, was Bradley. Bradley's job was to help Trevor design and create the special functions of the program. Bradley proved himself to be very knowledgeable in the HTML language and was very helpful to that end. Trevor was even impressed with his experience and resourcefulness. But something about him rubbed Trevor the wrong way. He was always checking to see what Trevor was working on, almost demanding to know what he was doing every step of the way. It was getting on Trevor's nerves. Of course, since he was always hitting on Radhika and trying to muscle in on her and Trevor whenever they were conversing didn't help matters either.

"What are you doing now?" Bradley said while looking over Trevor's shoulder.

Trevor did not look back. He still hated someone staring over his shoulder. "Working."

"I can see that. But what are you working on?"

Trevor stopped typing. "The same thing you're supposed to be working on. I'm trying to configure the programming to assimilate the data from John and Ralph to accurately process each new influx of information."

Bradley continued to stay behind him for several minutes as Trevor became more agitated. Finally, he returned to his seat. This had become a common occurrence. It seemed to Trevor that Bradley was making sure he knew every single step Trevor was taking and every single command he was implementing into the program. Trevor had pointed out to him many times that his job was not to oversee the production, but to assist in it.

This continued every day. One morning when Trevor came into the workroom, there were two agents he had seen two times before, at least he assumed they were agents. They were never introduced at all. Each time Franks had explained they were here to monitor the progress and each time they were less than impressed—at least, that's what they claimed.

It seemed to Trevor that they wanted a super computer that would not only store every single law in the country, not only update every new or old law as it changed, but a system that would literally give instantaneous results of every kind of criminal and civil court case imaginable.

But this morning was different. Franks told everyone to go back to their rooms, or to the kitchen, or wherever they wanted to go, but Trevor was instructed to stay behind. After the others left, the two agents approached Trevor.

"Run this case," one of the men said, holding a folder out

to Trevor.

Trevor took the information from the folder and looked it over. It was not complete. "OK, I cannot run this."

"You better be able to," the man said. "That's what you're being paid to do."

Trevor shook his head. "This has not been to trial. I can only give you a prediction once it has gone to trial and has been through most of the process. But this has not been to trial so there is too much missing."

The two unnamed men looked furious. "What do you mean?"

Trevor ignored their harsh looks. It was nothing he hadn't already gotten accustomed to. "What part did you not understand? Are you asking which missing parts am I referring to, or was there an actual word in that sentence that baffled you?"

"Just do your job and run the damn case," the same man said.

These guys reminded him of Agent Daniels and Agent Marks; one always had to do all the talking. "Let me explain and I will strive to use small words. All you have given me is a police report, some evidence, and several depositions. This is not a court case. It has not yet even been to court."

The same man continued to speak as the other and Franks looked on as if Trevor had impregnated their daughters. "That's right. That's what the computer needs to evaluate."

Trevor shook his head. "You do not seem to grasp the concept here. A judge would have to decide what evidence is admissible, and a deposition is performed from only one side. We do not have the benefit of a cross examination, which has totally different rules. For one thing, a lawyer is allowed to lead the witness in a cross examination. We do not know what objections the opposing team might provoke, nor do we know how the judge would rule on such objections. We do not know what testimony might be stricken and instructed that the jury ignore.

Those are the things needed to complete a test of a case for this system."

The man stared directly into Trevor's eyes. "What do you think we're paying you for? That's what the system needs to be able to do. We don't need a computer expert to tell us the outcome of a case that's already been tried."

Trevor shook his head. "You are not listening. There are certain things a judge has to make decisions about. These are judgment calls. Do you not understand the premise? Judgment calls, hence the word, judge."

"It's you who don't understand the premise," the man said. "We want to remove human error completely. Judges are human, or didn't you realize that? A judge's decisions are supposed to be based on law, not his feelings or personal agenda."

"I do understand that part, and even agree," Trevor said. "But a judge still has to apply what he knows of the law to interpret these decisions."

The man smiled, but not a polite smile, more like a devious smile. "That's what your program has to be able to do—interpret and apply the laws."

Trevor stared at him in disbelief. "For a computer to do all of that, it would have to be able to think."

Blank stares.

"A computer cannot think, fellows. That is called AI," Trevor said.

More blank stares.

Trevor felt like he was talking to first graders. "Artificial Intelligence. That is not possible, at least not in this millennium. Of course, without possessing any normal intelligence, you guys have no way to know that."

The man leaned in and tapped the folder. "Then you cannot fulfill your contract. Is that what you're telling us?"

Trevor sat there for several seconds. "No. I just have to rethink the matrix. Next time we meet, it will be up to specs."

"It better be." The man snatched the folder from his hand and the two walked out.

That put things in perspective for Trevor. He knew what they were asking was not possible, but he had to figure a way to make the program emulate the human decisions made during an actual trial. Starting from that day, things got a whole lot harder, but he went to work from that point knowing what he had to do.

He had a meeting with Bradley and Radhika to explain the new direction. The weeks passed as he read every HTML book available and had to learn on the job to invent never-before-used computer program commands to manipulate the system. It was difficult work and proved to be more demanding than he ever imagined. Many times, while the others went on break or to lunch, Trevor stayed behind as he wrote and rewrote commands for his program to do what they wanted it to do. To that end, he was successful.

A month later the two men returned. Franks nodded to the others who took the cue and got up to leave the room.

Bradley stopped at the door. "Do you guys need me to stay? I've built this program as much as he has," he said.

That would have been fine with Trevor, but it apparently wasn't fine with the unnamed men.

"Get the hell out of here!"

As Bradley quickly exited, Trevor smiled at the one man who continued to do the talking. Looking at the quiet one, he said, "Does that one speak?"

They paid no attention to the question and the man handed him another manila folder. "Run this."

Trevor took the folder. "You guys really need to work on your people skills. I guess it is not your fault, though. You did not get a chance to choose your parents." As they ignored the insult again, Trevor opened the folder and noticed it was the exact same case they had given to him before. Trevor was more confident this time as he keyed in the information. An hourglass appeared and began to spin. Within a few seconds, the results appeared on the screen. Trevor got up so they could have a closer look.

The two men leaned over Trevor's computer chair and stared at the screen.

Trevor walked over and sat at the table in the middle of the room. He watched as Franks leaned in and the three of them whispered amongst themselves. He really didn't care what they were saying.

They all stood up and the unnamed man, the one with the ability to speak, stuffed the paperwork back into the folder. The two men walked out without a word, nod, or even a glance at Trevor.

"OK," Franks said. "They think we're getting closer. You can retrieve the others."

CHAPTER

~

FOURTEEN

IT WAS VALENTINE'S DAY and Dustin had gotten the call that morning that his mom had been involved in a car accident and had been taken to the hospital. He had called the guy who substitutes his newspaper route as he and Sophia drove directly from Montgomery to Erlanger Hospital in Chattanooga, Tennessee, where his mom was already in surgery. Apparently, she had been on her way to work that morning, but when she neared the end of the short dirt road that led to her house, she mistakenly hit the gas pedal instead of the brakes, propelling the car across the paved street and into the edge of the woods. It was not a serious accident, but the doctor explained that she had Osteogenesis imperfecta, a disease that makes the bones very brittle, a new diagnosis, and the impact of the wreck had literally broken her lower back.

After she was taken from recovery to an ICU room, they were able to go in to see her. She was still out of it a little from the medication but smiled as they entered. She looked tired and her gray hair was thick, wild, and moist, adhering to the pillow. Dustin and Sophia smiled back and stood beside her bed.

"I understand you're going to have problems at the airport from now on," Dustin said to keep the mood light.

His mom smiled. "Yes, that's what they tell me. Four metal pins. How's Frankie?"

Dustin smiled. "Growing like a weed."

"How's his puppy dog?" Mrs. Davis said.

Dustin didn't reply but Sophia did. "Don't get Dustin

started."

"Why? What's wrong?"

"He stays too upset over it," Sophia said. "He goes by there several times a week just to check on poor Sadie. Tell her, Dustin."

Dustin shook his head. "They keep her chained up in the backyard and her chain gets tangled and sometimes when I go by there, she can't even reach the water dish, which doesn't matter most of the time since it's hardly ever got water in it. It's horrible, Mom."

"Dustin keeps her up-to-date on shots and vet visits and Hannah did let him take her to be spayed," Sophia said.

Mrs. Davis frowned.

But right now, that wasn't what was bothering Dustin. Seeing his mom in the hospital bed was bothering him and it showed on his face.

His mom reached over and squeezed his hand. "Don't worry. You're not going to have to hold me down."

Dustin smiled.

"What does that mean?" Sophia said.

Mrs. Davis looked at Sophia then back at Dustin. "You haven't told her about your dad?"

Dustin said nothing.

"No," Sophia said. "I don't know this one."

Mrs. Davis patted Dustin's hand. "When Robert had his stroke, Dustin was what, 12 years old?"

"Thirteen," Dustin said.

Mrs. Davis continued. "Robert had been taken to UAB Hospital in Birmingham, so we left Trevor with my mother and drove down. He was unconscious when we got to see him. We tried to get a room at the hospital's hotel, but it was full, so we stayed in the waiting room all night. At three o'clock that morning, a nurse came into the room to wake us and we thought we knew for certain why they would be coming to get us at that hour, but it wasn't what we had feared. The nurse took us to see the doctor who said they can't sedate a stroke victim and it was common for the patient to wake up during the night and not know where they are and panic. That's what happened with Dustin's father. He had regained consciousness and, in a state of confusion, as they were trying to restrain him, had literally thrown two female nurses across the room, which injured them both. Then the doctor told us what he wanted—he needed Dustin to try to hold his father all night until morning, and try to talk to him in hopes he would recognize the voice and calm him somewhat."

Dustin was expressionless but Sophia's eyes were already tearing up.

"Dustin lay out over the top of his father all night," Mrs. Davis said. "We tried to communicate with him but I don't think he even knew who we were. Dustin held him by his biceps as he fought to get out of bed all night. It couldn't have been easy. Robert was the most powerful man I have ever known and holding him down took all of Dustin's strength and will. By daylight, his dad had finally drifted off to sleep and we went back to the waiting room. Dustin was worn out and fell fast asleep. But they came back an hour later to inform us that Robert had passed away."

"That had to be rough," Sophia said.

Dustin was still expressionless. He never spoke to Sophia about all the bad memories he had from childhood. He knew his mom had told Sophia plenty of stories about how hard a man his dad was to live with, but Dustin didn't care to dwell on such things. About the only thing he ever told his wife was how he remembered the sound it made when his dad whipped his belt off, the friction of the leather against denim, and the unmistakable auditory effect it created, which sent fear to Dustin's heart faster than anything else could.

"Has anyone called Tre?" Sophia said.

"You can't call Tre," Mrs. Davis said.

Dustin was staring at his mom trying to understand her statement. "What do you mean?"

His mom slowly moved her head from left to right, as if trying to shake her head. "You can't call him. He is allowed to call every Sunday morning at nine o'clock. That's all."

Dustin looked at Sophia who had the same expression of disbelief. What kind of game company could control its employees like that?

"You need to be there this Sunday for his call so he will know what happened. Please, Dustin, for me," Mrs. Davis said.

Dustin agreed he would. He knew he would probably be around for the next four days at least. He still had to go get her car out of the woods and get it home.

When visiting hours were over, Dustin and Sophia stayed all night in the waiting room. They had eaten dinner at the hospital cafeteria and then went back to the waiting room. Luckily there were no other people in that waiting room overnight so Dustin's snoring didn't seem to bother anyone.

The next morning, they were standing outside the door at 8 a.m. sharp awaiting the next visiting period. After another visit, where his mom reinforced her wish that Dustin be there to take Trevor's call, they walked out of the ICU to go get some breakfast. But the doctor stopped them and asked if he could have a word. They walked out into the hallway and the doctor explained what was going on.

"Your mother's surgery went well and I think she will heal fine, as long as she doesn't put any stress on it for several months. She cannot go back to work—ever. I hope that's not a problem for her financially, but she's already a year past retirement age, so I hope it's not a big deal. She's also going to need at least a month of physical therapy. We have a facility here just for that."

"Someone will have to bring her here every day?" Dustin

said.

"No, you don't understand," said the doctor. "She will need to stay here during that time. And even after that she will need to make regular visits, but for the first month, she needs to stay here."

Dustin was actually a little relieved. With Trevor gone, he wasn't sure who he could ask to drive her back and forth to Chattanooga, a one-hour drive each way from her home on Sand Mountain.

"The problem is…"

Dustin and Sophia both looked at the doctor with surprise at those words.

"…her insurance only pays for the hospital visit and surgery."

Dustin wasn't sure how to phrase the next question. "What happens if she doesn't do the physical therapy and just goes home from the hospital?"

It wasn't the best way to phrase it.

"Dustin!" Sophia said. "What my husband means to ask is—how much will the month of physical therapy cost?"

"I'm not really sure but I'll have someone give you those figures," the doctor said.

"You have an idea, I'm sure," Dustin said.

The doctor nodded. "Probably around $400 a day."

"Twelve thousand dollars!" Dustin said quickly.

The doctor had to think for a few seconds before agreeing. "This is just my recommendation, guys. I have to go. I'll have someone give you some specifics."

As the doctor turned and walked away, Sophia looked at Dustin.

"I know," said Dustin, almost defending his earlier question. But in the back of his mind, he was hoping Trevor could help.

RADHIKA WAS SITTING beside Trevor in the break area that had been set up for them. It had a few dumbbells, an exercise bike, and a stepper. Trevor had logged many hours on the exercise bike. It wasn't to get fit; he actually hated exercise. But it was the best way to spend time near Radhika, who hit the stepper for an hour every day without fail. From the bike he could converse with her and watch her without it being so obvious. He loved to watch her thin muscular body at work, her toned calf muscles flexing with each step. He had learned that she had been on the swim team in college and was, in fact, a total jock, participating in marathons, rock climbing, kayaking, you name it.

The most important thing about the break area, however, was it had a sliding glass door with a small balcony so they could see the sunshine and breathe some fresh air. Their work day wasn't over yet, this was just one of their two daily breaks. John and Ralph, the two data entry guys, were somewhere else and Bradley was on the balcony smoking, which he did every chance he got.

"How does someone continue to do something that they know will kill them?"

Trevor looked out the glass door to where Radhika was motioning with her head. "I do not know, just human nature I guess. I cannot really say anything. I do not smoke, but goodness knows I have not kept up a great diet, and heart disease kills more people than anything else in this country."

"You've lost some weight, though, since being here," Radhika said.

Trevor smiled. He knew he had but wasn't sure if anyone else had noticed.

"I see you eating pretty healthy in the kitchen all the time."

Trevor nodded. "Well, I did not eat this way at home. I ate everything bad for me I could get my hands on. I still cannot stay away from my Hot Pockets. But to be honest, I was embarrassed to write down my normal foods when I saw the healthy foods you always wrote down. Plus, I never had anything inspire me at home like someone does here."

"You are a sweet guy," Radhika said with a smile.

"No, I am not," Trevor said matter-of-factly. "The truth is, I can be a jerk when I put my mind to it."

Radhika patted Trevor on the hand. "I'll take honesty over sweetness any day."

Trevor liked that response. He really liked Radhika but wasn't sure if he could tell her; he wasn't sure if she liked him or was just a friendly person. He saw how she was with the others, just as friendly and joyful, but there did seem to be a little difference in how she acted with him. Everyone got along fine. Trevor enjoyed the company of John and Ralph, who thought Trevor was the coolest guy they had ever met. The only one that occasionally rubbed Trevor the wrong way was Bradley, who was constantly hitting on Radhika and trying to be too aggressive at work and trying to take charge. Since Trevor and he were the actual programmers, Bradley tried to make it competitive, always wanting to know what Trevor was doing. Trevor had even at one time suspected that Bradley was a plant to monitor the group, but had eventually dismissed that idea as paranoia.

"So, are you ready for your phone call tomorrow?" Trevor said. He realized it was a stupid question as soon as he said it, but he was hoping to find out if she had a special someone she called every week.

"Isn't that ridiculous?" she said. "When they said the calls would be monitored, I assumed they meant electronically."

Trevor laughed. "I know. The first time they led me to the phone and just sat there and stared at me, I did not know what was going on. It was one of the same women from the office by the entrance. I asked her, 'What, do you want another cavity search?'"

They both laughed so loud that Bradley stopped staring at the traffic below and looked back inside.

"So," Trevor said, deciding to go for the kill, "who do you call every week?"

Radhika seemed to know why he was asking but apparently was not going to make it easy on him. "My boyfriend. He's a linebacker for the New York Giants."

"Ah, I see. So you call your mom and dad, huh?" Trevor said.

She was busted. "Yes, that's exactly who I call. What about you?"

Trevor nodded. "My mother."

Well, they had that over with, so now they both knew. The problem was, neither knew what to do with that knowledge and it created an awkward silence. Trevor knew he better say something—anything—before the moment passed.

"Do you have brothers or sisters?"

Radhika shook her head. "Nope. I'm an only child. Do you?"

Dustin's image came to Trevor's mind. "Unfortunately, I have one idiotic brother."

"Let me guess; he's a jerk, too?" Radhika said.

Trevor had to think for several seconds before answering. "No. He is actually a great guy. Heck, he is perfect. That is the problem."

Radhika nodded but said nothing. Instead, she asked an unrelated question. "Why did you take this job?"

"The money. I was doing OK as it was, but this offered more. And you?" Trevor said.

She nodded. "The same. I am employed at a law firm here in town and they have the contract with the government. I get paid 60% of that, including the bonus. Plus, I have a lot of bills."

Trevor was impressed. "They are paying off your student loans?"

Radhika laughed. "You got me. You're very smart."

They noticed the time and got up to go back to work.

They called to Bradley to make sure he knew as well.

The rest of the work week went by and Sunday morning Trevor got up to go stand outside the office with apparently the one phone on their entire floor, at least the only one they knew of. The woman from the monitor room, the one who had let Trevor in the very first day, always showed up at nine o'clock sharp to let them each in one-by-one to make their weekly 15 minute phone call.

When Trevor's turn came, he walked in, sat at the desk, and winked at the woman, something he did every Sunday morning. And just like every other Sunday morning, she continued to stare at him with no expression. This morning, however, Trevor was in for a bit of a shock.

"Brother, is that you? Are you visiting Mother?" Trevor said as the phone call was answered.

Dustin began to explain about the wreck and the surgery and that their mother was doing OK. He began to tell what the doctor had said about the physical therapy when Trevor cut him off.

"I only have 15 minutes."

"That's a bunch of crap," Dustin said. "No game company can be that strict. You stay on as long as you need to."

Trevor looked across at Ms. Grumpy, as he called her. "I cannot. Just get to the point."

Dustin explained about the twelve thousand dollars needed for physical therapy. "Can you pay half?"

"Not right now," Trevor said. "I mean I have it, but no way to get it to you. If you can pay it, I shall pay you back when I get home."

Dustin hung up the phone.

Trevor got up and went back to his room. He had been the last one to make his call so no one was in the hallway as he exited. He was glad. He was sure they would be able to tell by his expression that something was wrong. He hated that he could not help. He now had enough money in his account that he could easily pay this for his mother and Dustin, but he knew without a doubt that this was not a valid reason to break the ridiculous protocol thrust upon them by the strangest people he had ever met. He hated being here. Other than the people he worked with, he hated everything about it.

CHAPTER

FIFTEEN

SOPHIA WALKED INTO the house after getting home from running one of the lawn crews. Dustin was just hanging up the phone and his face was red. "What's wrong?" she said.

"I'm going to get Sadie." Dustin grabbed his keys and headed for the door.

"Wait," Sophia said. "Is Hannah going to let you just take her?"

Dustin stopped and turned to face his wife. "It's not her choice. Sadie's at the pound."

Sophia shook her head. "Oh no."

Dustin drove to the Montgomery Humane Society and went inside. He explained to the clerk what he was doing and they called another employee.

"Hi, my name is Charlene," the young woman said, extending her hand.

Dustin shook her hand and introduced himself, then told her the story of why he was there.

The woman smiled. "I'm glad someone cares, but I'm not sure what I can do. Sadie is a special case. She has not been well cared for at all. She's very undernourished, and she is afraid of people. She just sits in the back of her cage and won't come out for anyone."

Dustin felt horrible. "I used to go by and check on her all the time. My mom had a wreck recently so we have been spending a lot of time in north Alabama. But I assure you, if you let me take her today, she will be loved from now on. I will pay whatever fee there is."

The woman smiled. "I tell you what, why don't we go back and see her? I'd like to see how she reacts."

Dustin agreed and followed the woman to the back area, where she led him to Sadie's cage.

"Hello, Sadie," the woman said in a soft tone.

Sadie didn't flinch, just remained lying on her side.

Dustin stared at her and couldn't believe the shape she was in. Her ribs were very prominent as if she hadn't eaten in a while. He swallowed hard. "Hey, Sadie."

Much to the woman's surprise, and to Dustin's, Sadie jumped up and ran as fast as her stubby legs would carry her, over to the gate where Dustin was squatting, and began to lick his hands through the chain-link fence.

The woman smiled as a tear rolled down from one eye. "Yes, I think you should take Sadie home now."

FOUR MONTHS HAD PASSED since his mother's wreck and she was home and doing much better. Trevor had gone four consecutive Sundays with no phone call. He had called home each time but his mother wasn't home yet, and no one else was there to answer. Or if Dustin was there, he never picked up. When he finally did get her on the phone, she gave him the update. Dustin and Sophia had paid for her therapy. They also had cleaned out the garage to remove any tripping hazards, and added guard rails to the steps going into the kitchen. Dustin had also, at the suggestion of the physical therapist, replaced the commode in her bathroom with a taller one made for handicap people, and added guard rails and a shower seat to assist her getting on and off the commode and in and out of the tub.

Although his mother now was getting along fine and Sophia wasn't having to stay there full time like she had been doing,

Trevor was still ready to return home. But there was still at least five months to go, and of course the last payday was the only one that mattered. When things got almost unbearable, it was the thought of the four million dollar bonus that kept him going. It was tedious work, work that had long since lost its amusement. The program he was designing was far removed from the program he had designed for himself.

He walked into the work area one morning and something seemed odd. It was agent Franks; he wasn't there. He sat at the monitor where he normally worked and looked around the room. Everyone looked confused. Franks was always there before everyone else and always there when everyone left.

Franks finally walked in and was obviously not in a good mood. "Everyone take a seat at the table."

What happened next almost took Trevor's breath away. Agents Daniels and Marks entered the room. Radhika stared at the scar on the bridge of his nose then looked over to Trevor.

Trevor was expressionless.

Agent Marks smiled at Trevor. "Hey, partner. Remember us?"

"How could I forget? Knick and Knack, my two favorite retards," Trevor said.

Agent Marks stopped smiling.

Agent Franks was not smiling either. "OK, people, listen up. We have a serious problem and these gentlemen are here to address it." He nodded to Daniels.

Daniels remained calm as always and pulled a small piece of paper out of his jacket. "We found this in the hall."

All five of them looked confused.

Daniels continued. "This has information written on it, information about what we're doing here. It's not written as part of what your job actually is, but more as if it were describing what we're doing. Someone in this room is trying to leak classified information to someone outside and we are going to find out who it is."

Trevor shook his head as if this was a setup. "*We* do not even know what we are doing in here."

"You're the number one suspect, wise ass," Marks said with a pleasurable smirk on his face.

"Of course," Trevor said. "Did I mention the word 're-tard'?"

Marks glared at Trevor. "I'm keeping my eye on you."

Trevor laughed. "Oh, I know you are. I can feel you undressing me with those baby blues. I sure will be glad when you get a boyfriend."

Marks' cheeks became red as his jaw muscles flexed.

Daniels ignored the back-and-forth between Marks and Trevor. "Just know we're going to be watching everyone very closely from now on."

Trevor looked up at the cameras in each corner of the ceiling and chuckled. How could they possibly watch them any more than they already did?

Later that day at lunch, everyone sat together at the same small table.

"That's him, isn't it? That's the guy you mentioned the first day here." Radhika's words were barely above a whisper.

Trevor spoke normally. "Yes."

"He gives me the creeps," Ralph said.

Trevor nodded. He understood. But he didn't understand how someone could even try to get information to the outside. Then it dawned on him—the break room had the balcony. But no one really went out on it since it was still too chilly outside to enjoy it, except.... He noticed the rectangular pack bulging from Bradley's shirt pocket. Bradley went out there several times a day to smoke.

Bradley seemed to sense Trevor was looking at him so he got up and excused himself to go to the bathroom.

Trevor decided to conduct a test. "John, is it you?"

John's eyes got real big and his jaw dropped. "Are you serious?"

Trevor laughed. "No, I am just messing with you."

John exhaled and wiped his forehead in an exaggerated display of relief.

The four of them talked about other things and, a few minutes later, Bradley came back in and sat down again. When there was a break in the conversation, Trevor continued the experiment.

"Bradley, is it you?"

Bradley shot a dead-stone glare Trevor's way. "You're the suspect, remember?"

"He was just messing with you, dude," Ralph said.

"Yeah, he did it with us, too," John said.

Trevor smiled and nodded, but he wasn't just messing around. He was conducting an experiment in human nature and Bradley had just failed. Radhika seemed to pick up on it, too.

The next few days were tense as Marks, Daniels, and even the two women from the monitor room seemed to be lurking about at all times. It was hard getting any work done with people constantly looking over your shoulder. Finally, after a few days, it started to subside, with usually only Franks sitting in the work area like it had always been. After a week, they didn't see Marks or Daniels again. Trevor figured they had put a scare into everyone and that was probably their only goal.

One morning, Trevor was working at his station reading one of the many HTML books in the work area, the books that covered every known area of programming. They were not allowed internet access so everything came from books or reports brought to them by Franks.

Ralph looked over to Trevor. "Hey, I'm starting on your home state of Alabama."

"Oh great," Trevor said, tilting his head over to look at Ralph. "That should be fun. Might be the only state with laws more antiquated than Mississippi."

As Ralph laughed and returned his gaze to his monitor, Trevor noticed Bradley slide his hand over a thumb drive sitting beside his own keyboard. It was probably nothing but Trevor continued to watch and when Bradley brought his hand away from the keyboard, the thumb drive was not there. Then Bradley put the same hand into his shirt pocket and pulled out his pack of cigarettes and sniffed them as if he was having a nicotine attack and needed a boost. He placed the pack back in his pocket and Trevor couldn't see the thumb drive anywhere. He glanced up at one of the cameras and quickly looked back at his screen, realizing how stupid a move that was. But had something just happened that he thought had just happened? Had he witnessed Bradley stealing? He wondered what to do but decided he wouldn't do anything. He was no big fan of Bradley's, but he was less of a fan of his employer. Trevor couldn't imagine what value this could be since he still couldn't understand the purpose for this thing they were building.

At lunch, he heated up a Hot Pocket and took his normal seat beside Radhika.

"Where's your salad?" she said.

"I needed this today," Trevor said.

She looked at him closely. "What's the matter, Tre?"

"Oh you know, just so much to do." He looked around and only saw four of them in the kitchen. "Where is Bradley?"

Without looking up from her salad, she said, "He said he needed a cigarette and went to the break room."

Trevor stared at his Hot Pocket. "I thought he preferred to smoke after eating."

Radhika simply shrugged her shoulders and continued eating. She had not noticed how tense Trevor was.

Trevor, however, was very tense. He didn't like what he had witnessed. He didn't want anything to mess up this deal. He tried to focus on work but couldn't get the thoughts out of his head. Even when he went to bed that night, he kept thinking about it. Although he had gotten used to the little bed and small bedroom, it took a while for him to get to sleep this night.

Suddenly, Trevor jolted awake. He looked at the clock—2:47 a.m. He sat up wondering what had awoken him. After a few minutes, he didn't hear anything and assumed he had dreamed it. He decided to go to the bathroom while he was up, so he got out of bed and walked out the door. He rubbed his eyes as he walked down the dimly lit corridor to his bathroom then went inside and up to his favorite urinal. When he finished, he walked over to his favorite sink and washed his hands and started to leave. Stopping at the door, he turned back and paused. His thoughts were no longer on Bradley, but Radhika. He smiled as he thought about how beautiful she was and the thoughts of continuing their acquaintance after this rotten job was over. He knew now he might continue thinking about her after he got back to bed so he walked back in and grabbed a towel.

As he turned to go back toward his bedroom, he heard a slight noice, a cushioned impact like friction of two materials making contact. He walked back past the bathroom entrance to where the corridor turned left and peeked around the corner. About six doors down, he could barely make out Agent Daniels unlocking one of the identical white doors. As he opened it and walked inside, Trevor couldn't believe what he saw next. It was Bradley, with Agent Marks, Scarface himself, standing behind him with one hand on his shoulder, motioning him toward the door. They disappeared into the doorway and the door closed on its own.

In Trevor's mind, the way Marks was positioned behind Bradley, he could almost imagine a gun in his back. Not hearing any sounds coming from the door, Trevor slowly walked toward it and placed his head up against the white painted wood. It opened several inches. He realized it had not closed entirely, which meant it hadn't relocked. Inside, he could see a dimly lit stairwell. He eased open the door and walked inside. He could hear the footsteps below, so he peered over the railing and saw the trio go down five flights then enter another door. Trevor knew they were on the fourth floor—that could be determined by the balcony at the break room—so he surmised this must be the basement.

He stood there several seconds trying to decide if he should follow them or go back to bed. He never considered himself a courageous person, but not knowing what was going on was killing him. It felt like there was a jackhammer inside his chest as he walked quietly down the stairs and eased open the door. It was indeed the basement. He could hear the voice of Daniels farther into the basement so he went toward the voice. There were pipes and ductwork running everywhere and the floor was littered with debris. He watched the floor carefully as not to step on or kick anything, guiding his socked feet carefully along the cold concrete. He had no idea what these guys were capable of if they discovered him.

Then he saw them. Bradley was sitting in a chair underneath a hanging light bulb, the kind that had a string to turn it on. Both men were standing in front of him, one to each side. Daniels was still doing the talking. Trevor realized he was probably visible to them if they turned around, so he tried to find a place to hide. The lone light bulb was providing the only light in the area, so the perimeter was mostly shadows. He eased himself between two large ventilation ducts, an area that was completely dark. He didn't try to stick his head out; he just listened.

"I'm going to ask you one more time," Daniels said, his voice now a tone that Trevor had never heard. "Who are you working for?"

Trevor couldn't hear Bradley's answer, but it apparently wasn't the right one as he then heard the sound of impacts, the unmistakable sound of a fist hitting a face. He also heard Bradley moaning.

"OK, that's enough," Daniels said after several blows.

Trevor knew that meant that Scarface was administering the punishment. That was no surprise; he knew the man was a sadist. The curiosity got to him and Trevor decided to peek out and take a look. Bad mistake. His right arm nudged the duct-work and it collapsed inward ever so slightly. But it was enough to make a noise.

"What was that?"

Trevor wasn't even sure which of the agents had spoken as he gritted his teeth. He was so angry with himself. The metal of the ductwork was still compressed, so he couldn't move his arm at all or it would make another noise as it popped back out. But that might be a moot point. He may have already given himself away. Suddenly he froze, not even the blink of an eye, as Marks appeared in his sight only about ten feet away, his pistol drawn. Trevor closed his eyes and tried to think how to pray. He wished he had listened to Dustin and gone to church then maybe someone up there would be willing to listen to him, because now, indeed, would certainly be the time for a miracle.

He got it.

As Marks passed by another large ventilation duct, the heat kicked on and the ductwork made a slight popping noise. Marks relaxed. "It's nothing," he said as he returned to the inter-rogation.

As Marks holstered his pistol, Bradley, who had not been restrained in any way, and who must have thought the situation beyond hope, suddenly jumped up and began to run away. A single gunshot was heard and it made Trevor flinch. He could immediately smell the discharge of gunpowder in the air but he wasn't sure of the outcome.

"Damn it, I didn't want him dead," Daniels said. Several seconds of silence passed. "All right, we got to get some people in here to clean this up, and I mean the whole thing."

After they left, Trevor stayed motionless for at least 15 minutes, afraid to come out. Then he thought about the people coming to "clean this up," and didn't want to be here when they arrived either. He finally came out of his hiding place as the ventilation duct popped back out into its natural form. He turned and saw the motionless lump on the floor still halfway in the light. He couldn't move for several seconds as the image mesmerized him into a sullen trance. Of all the surreal moments he had experienced here, nothing could ever top this. This was murder, the thing reserved for movies or newspaper stories about people you don't know. Trevor suddenly realized his legs were shaking, so he turned and walked quickly back to the stairwell, counting the floors as he ascended to know which door to use since they all looked alike and none of them were marked. He eased the door open and peered outside into the corridor. There was no one there, so he quickly walked back to his own hallway and toward his bedroom. He grabbed the towel off the floor where he had left it and quickly went to his room. He crawled into bed and stared at the door all night, half expecting to be paid a visit.

When his alarm went off at 6:00, he was still staring at the door. He got up and tried to make sure not to do anything differently. He took a shower and got dressed and went to the work area. It was a few minutes before 7 a.m. and the other three were already there. He took his seat and began to work. He could feel the cameras boring a hole into his thoughts. At one minute after, he looked around the room. "Uh oh. Someone overslept."

"Yeah, where's Bradley?" Ralph said.

"Bradley is gone." Franks' words were loud so everyone could hear. "He had a family emergency and had to go home. His contract is now cancelled, so he won't be returning. You'll just have to do without him for the duration."

"Well, is he not the lucky one?" Trevor's words almost nauseated himself. He knew very well that Bradley was far from lucky, but he needed to keep up the front. "At least he will not have to deal with you clowns anymore."

Franks ignored Trevor's barbs, as he always did.

Trevor went back to work, but things were different from that point. Trevor had trouble sleeping and often had night-mares. Every time he had to go to the bathroom at night was an exercise in terror as walking down the dark passageway made him very uneasy. He had never noticed how many shadows adorned the corners and doorways of the hallway, and often they seemed to take on a life of their own.

CHAPTER

SIXTEEN

THIRTEEN MONTHS after he arrived at the mysterious building on the outskirts of Washington D.C., it was finally over. He sat with the other three in the kitchen as they talked about what they were going to do when they got home.

Franks entered the kitchen, the first time they had ever seen him anywhere but inside the work area. "Davis, come with me."

Trevor followed him to the work area but they stood in the hall outside the door.

"You've done a good job," Franks said.

Franks' words surprised Trevor. He had never heard one compliment from the guy in over a year. "Thanks."

Franks nodded, still with no expression. "They just need for you to give them a final demonstration and this one will be in the books."

To Trevor's surprise, Franks opened the door next to the work area and motioned for him to go inside. Trevor walked into another room, which looked identical to the work area, but was set up much differently. There was a computer, or so he believed it to be, but it was much larger than any modern day computer he had ever seen. In fact, it looked more like a computer from the 50s. It was almost a perfect cube, five feet in each direction, with several lights along the top edge. One side consisted of twelve identical fans mounted flush against the unit, all running, he surmised to keep the gigantic motherboard cool. He stared at it for a few moments until Franks nudged him and motioned for him to go on around it into the room.

Trevor walked around and noticed a table in front of the machine with a monitor, keyboard and mouse. The room was set up with folding chairs, which were filled with about ten people, most of whom he had never seen. In the next to back row, there were four familiar faces: Daniels, Marks, and the two unnamed agents. The room was dimly lit in the back and there were two people sitting behind those four agents that Trevor couldn't quite see. That seemed to be intentional.

"You've done a good job, son."

Daniels' words made Trevor sick to his stomach. "High praise indeed coming from someone of your limited stature."

The room was filled with chuckles.

For the next two hours, Trevor ran sample scenarios of every kind of criminal and civil cases, all based on police reports, evidence, and depositions only, each time the outcome impressed everyone in the room, which often erupted in whispers after a verdict was displayed, or even applause. When it was over, the four people sitting up front got up and shook Trevor's hand. Trevor didn't know who these people were, but they certainly had better manners than anyone else he had worked with here. Marks, Daniels, and the other two stayed seated, as if still trying to conceal the two men behind them. But Trevor's eyes had adjusted to the dim light and he could make out the facial features of one of the men. He was tall, thin, middleaged, with salt-and-pepper hair, and had the narrowest chin Trevor had ever seen. It almost came to a point.

Franks came back in and led Trevor back to the kitchen. "You can let everyone know it went well. You can get packed. There is a driver waiting to take you guys to the airport and you have a ticket to the airport you each flew in from."

Trevor walked up beside Franks and kept pace with him. "And?"

Franks smiled, the first smile Trevor had seen from him.

"You can tell everyone their bonuses have been deposited in their accounts." He then looked at Trevor and added, "Even yours."

As he walked back into the kitchen, all eyes were on him. Trevor gave them a thumbs-up, explained all went well, and all bonuses had been paid, and more importantly, they were going home. Everyone hugged each other as if they had just survived a year at sea in shark-infested waters.

"I hope my dogs remember me," Ralph said. "What are you guys going to do when you get home?"

"I'm going to sleep in my king size bed for a month," John said.

"Trevor?"

Trevor looked at Ralph and tried to think. "The truth is, I do not really know. One thing is, I will probably try to find a place to get those cavity searches."

Everyone laughed.

Ralph Looked at Radhika. "What about you?"

"The Y," Radhika said. "They have the best swimming pool in town. I'm going to do laps until I forget about this place."

"You love the water, don't you?" John said.

Radhika nodded half-heartedly. "I'm more at home in the water."

Trevor believed she needed to forget about this place. Ever since the Bradley incident, Radhika had withdrawn somewhat and Trevor's workload had increased, so Trevor had never advanced their relationship. He wanted to, but never pushed it, sensing she was worried. Sleeping in an unlocked room probably didn't help matters. Ralph and John had accepted the story about Bradley, but Radhika seemed to sense something was wrong.

After they hugged, Trevor gave her his cell number. She smiled and thanked him and put it in her purse. He was hoping she would return the favor, but she did not.

An hour later, Trevor was on a plane headed for Huntsville. He felt odd sitting and looking out the window at the clouds. He wasn't sure what the feeling was until it dawned on him—he felt relaxed, a feeling he had not felt in a long time. It was over and he had over 4.65 million dollars in the bank. He wanted to smile but he couldn't help thinking about Bradley and feeling guilty for knowing he would never tell a soul about this. He had just spent the last 13 months building a program that was all about justice, yet he was refusing to see justice prevail in this case. The fact was, he was afraid. He wasn't sure if these agents were above the law, but he knew now beyond a shadow of a doubt that they were dangerous. He wanted no part of it. He just wanted to get on with his life.

When he arrived at the airport in Huntsville, he got a haircut and a shave. He had begun keeping his hair cut pretty short during the stay in Washington since they only brought in a barber about once every two months. Trevor also picked out a new t-shirt, since his old ones were very loose on him. He had convinced them to pick him up some new sweat pants as he had lost almost 60 pounds since arriving on the job, and his old ones would barely stay on him.

Trevor didn't even realize it was the day after New Year's Day until he signed for the rental car. He had spoken to his mother the previous Sunday and knew he had missed Christmas, but he had no calendars at work and had gotten used to not knowing. It occurred to him that he had not once written the date 2018, much less 2019.

It was already after 4:00 p.m. when he left the airport. It was only 70 miles to home, the place where he had been dying to go for a long time. Yet, now his emotions were mixed and, for some reason, he turned south on I-65 instead. Almost in a hyp-notic state of mind, three hours later he arrived in Montgomery and drove the all-too-familiar route to his brother's house.

Trevor smiled as he saw his brother's old pickup truck still in the driveway. In fact, nothing seemed to have changed at all, except a new chain-link fence that extended around the back-yard. He walked up on the porch and rang the doorbell.

"Yes?" Sophia said. "Can I help you?"

That prompted Dustin to get off the sofa and walk to the door to see who was there. Sadie, who always stayed right by Dustin's side, got off the sofa and walked with him

"Yes, honey bunny, you may first help me by inviting me in," Trevor said.

"Oh my gosh! Tre?!" Sophia threw her arms around Trevor and then grabbed his hand. "Come in. Come in."

Dustin extended his hand with a huge smile. "Holy Moly! Look at you. Mom didn't tell us you were home."

"She does not know. I just got in today and drove here first," Trevor said.

Dustin looked puzzled. "Well, you look great. Did you join the military? Is that where you've been?"

Trevor convinced them again that it was a game company he had been working for, a lie that he had told so many times that it seemed to burn his tongue. He used to not mind telling a fib. In fact, he was a true artist. But now it turned his stomach. He sat in the chair in front of the computer as Sophia sat in the recliner and Dustin and Sadie took their place on the sofa.

"Oh my goodness," Trevor said. "Is that—"

"Yep," Dustin said, petting Sadie on the head. "She's our girl now."

"Your girl, you mean," Sophia said. "She doesn't have anything to do with anyone else."

Trevor laughed. "That explains the new fence."

Sophia nodded. "So, it's all over now?" she said.

Trevor looked at Sophia and nodded. "Yes, thank good-ness. They were not pleasant people to work for." Then he looked directly at Dustin. "I am sorry for how strict they were. I wish it could have been different. But thank you for taking care of Mother."

Dustin seemed perplexed at the change in Trevor. He looked dumbfounded as he stared at his younger brother. "What happened in the last year?"

"Thank you for taking care of Mother," Trevor repeated.

Dustin snapped out of his trance. "Sure. What else would I do?"

Trevor smiled and nodded. "That is true, brother. What else *would* you do?"

"Are you hungry?" Sophia said. "I can heat up some spaghetti."

"No, thank you. I try not to eat a lot of fats and sugar," Trevor said.

Dustin threw up his hands in jest. "OK, that's it. Who are you and what have you done with my brother?"

They all laughed. But what transpired next really seemed to confuse them.

"I just wanted to come down here to see you guys and let you know I am home," Trevor said.

There were several seconds of silence as Dustin and Sophia stared at each other. "Are you all right?" Dustin said.

Trevor wasn't sure if he was. He wasn't even sure why he drove all the way to Montgomery instead of going home. "Yes, I am fine."

"You sure you don't want to spend the night?" Sophia said.

Trevor smiled. "No, I think I am ready to go home now."

CHAPTER

~

SEVENTEEN

"WHAT'S THE MATTER?" Sophia said.

Dustin looked around Frankie and over at her for a second then back to the road as they continued northward on the interstate. It was a beautiful morning in September, the day before Trevor's wedding. "What do you mean?"

"You seem distracted. You're not upset that Tre didn't choose you to be a groomsmen or his best man, are you?"

"Upset? No. Surprised? No," Dustin said. "He's always favored his slacker friends to family."

"What's a slacker?" Frankie said.

Sophia gave Dustin her "stop being a bad influence" stare. "A word we won't be repeating," she said.

Frankie nodded his understanding. "I'm glad Uncle Tre's finally getting married."

Dustin smiled and patted him on the leg. "That's 'cause you're a knucklehead. It didn't take long after coming home with a nice bank account."

Frankie laughed but Sophia frowned over Dustin's insinuation that money was what led to someone wanting to marry Trevor. It was around noon as they turned onto the dirt road leading to his mom's house. As they pulled into her drive, they could finally see what they had only heard about.

"Wow!" Frankie's mouth was wide open.

So was Sophia's. "I second that. So, that's what a $500,000 home looks like."

Dustin shook his head. "Please, you guys are going to get

drool on the seats." But even Dustin was amazed at the sight of Trevor's new house, which had only been completed for a few weeks, and sat in an area cleared out of the woods about 100 yards behind his mom's house. It was huge, seven bedrooms in all and five full baths. Trevor had emailed them the design, but it paled in comparison to seeing the finished product. It looked like a small castle.

Dustin got out and grabbed Frankie's suitcase from the back of the old Dodge pickup and handed it to him as Frankie also slid out the driver's side. Then he grabbed his and Sophia's suitcase and they walked into the garage to the kitchen entrance of his mom's house. She greeted them at the door.

"Hey, Granny Doreen," Frankie said as he went up the steps first and hugged Mrs. Davis.

"Oh my goodness. Look at you," Mrs. Davis said. "You're taller than your uncle now, aren't you?"

Frankie grinned. He wasn't quite as tall as Dustin yet, but he was very close, and still scrawny as a rail. They carried their suitcases to their perspective rooms, went back into the kitchen, and sat around the table.

The door opened and Trevor came in. He had been working out pretty regularly and had maintained his weight loss, and even firmed up quite a bit. "Hey. I thought that was you guys," he said.

Frankie got up, met Trevor halfway across the floor, and threw his arms around his waist. "Hey, Uncle Tre."

Trevor smiled and rubbed his head. "Wow, you are taller than your uncle now, are you not?'

Frankie laughed.

Sophia hugged Trevor next. "Congratulations, Tre. We're so happy for you."

"Thanks, honey bunny."

"Yeah," Dustin said. "We're real happy for you."

Trevor nodded and extended his hand. "Well come on, let

me show you my house."

They followed Trevor out and walked the distance from their mom's home to his new house. The dirt drive became a paved drive about 100 feet from the house and looped around into a circle in the front. Fresh sod lay between the driveway and a stunning sidewalk, which extended from the front entrance, curved around each side, and went all the way to the backyard. Inside the curved areas were neatly planted shrubs and flowers.

A man appeared at the left side of the large home carrying a roll of cable. He got everyone's attention. He wore camouflage pants and a black tank top.

Trevor noticed everyone staring. "That is Juan Carlos. He is installing a security system for me." Trevor waved in his direction and called out. "Juan, come here and meet some of my family." Trevor then turned back to the group, leaned in, and whispered. "He is an ex-SEAL and merc, so do not make him angry."

Before they could respond to that, Juan walked up to them. He was six feet tall and slim but very muscular. His biceps and triceps were disproportional to his slender frame. He seemed to be in his mid 30's but the scars along his arms and shoulders, along with the weathered face, gave him the appearance of an older man. His skin was bronze and his head was shaved on the sides with a round thick patch on top, the way Dustin had seen many of his military friends wear. His knuckles were even scarred from many fights. On his side was a holstered pistol. He did not smile at all but looked at Trevor. "What's up, boss?"

Trevor nodded toward the others. "I wanted you to meet some of my family. This is my brother, Dustin, his wife, Sophia, and this little snail darter is Frankie. Guys, this is Juan Carlos Lemos."

Dustin took his hand when Juan offered it. He had always remembered what his dad had taught him about having a firm handshake, and a lot of people grimaced in pain when Dustin shook their hand. Dustin had at one time bench pressed nearly 500 pounds and had several weight-lifting trophies. But arm wrestling was his main love and he had even more trophies in that arena. But as Dustin squeezed his thick fingers around Juan's hand, he assumed that Juan's dad must have taught him the same thing as he returned the grip as good as he got. As the seconds passed, it became clear this was no ordinary handshake.

Sophia's brow lowered. Then she noticed the long indentions in her husband's forearm as the muscles contracted into ridges and she shook her head.

"So, where you from, Juan?" Dustin said as he tried to squeeze harder.

Juan tried to squeeze harder as well. "Chicago."

"I mean originally."

Juan didn't break the stare and like Dustin, spoke in a normal voice as to not let it look like he was straining. "Chicago."

Trevor seemed to be enjoying the contest. "Juan's family is from Uruguay, South America."

The stare-down and handshake continued.

"Where you from?" Juan said.

Dustin didn't flinch. "Right where you're standing."

Frankie and Sophia were smiling as they watched the standoff.

A few more seconds passed and Juan spoke again, this time to Sophia, although he didn't look away from Dustin. "*Tu hesposo es un terco.*"

Sophia laughed. "*Tu no tienes ningun idea.*" She leaned over to Dustin and explained. "He said, 'Your husband is stubborn,' and I said, 'You have no idea.'"

Juan aimed his next words at Dustin. "How long have you guys been married?"

"Sixteen years," Dustin said.

Juan shook his head. "You married a Mexican and you

still don't speak Spanish."

Dustin smiled ever so slightly. "She's only ever taught me one line and said it's all I would ever need to know. *Yo soy blanco*."

Juan released his grip and pulled his hand away. "You win. But you cheated; you made me laugh."

Everyone else looked around at each other. Had they missed something? He laughed? His expression never changed.

"He laughs like he bleeds," Trevor said. "On the inside."

Everyone laughed. Well, it wasn't certain that Juan had, but clearly everyone else did.

Trevor looked at Dustin. "What did that mean, your one line of Spanish?"

Juan spoke up. "I am white."

Trevor laughed. "Yes, I can see where that should get you by."

Dustin looked at the gun on Juan's side. "You got a permit for that?"

It was clear Juan knew what he was talking about, but didn't let on. "For what?"

Dustin smiled. "That Baretta PX4 nine millimeter on your side."

Juan finally smiled. "Yes, I do. Want to see it?"

"The permit… no," Dustin said.

Juan nodded as he pulled out the gun and handed it to Dustin with the barrel facing the ground. "You shoot?"

Dustin didn't take his eyes off the gun. "Yeah. I have one just like this."

"Marine?"

Dustin nodded, still admiring the weapon.

Juan seemed to enjoy finding a fellow soldier. "Were you in Iraq?"

Dustin shook his head. "Desert Storm was before my time and I was already out before the second one. What about you?"

Juan nodded. "I got to spend a little time in Iraq, as well as Pakistan and Libya."

Dustin looked confused but didn't say anything. He certainly didn't sound like a normal soldier and figured the SEAL and merc references might well be accurate.

"Wait right here. I have something to show you." Juan turned, walked to his car, and came back carrying a case. He opened it so Dustin could see inside.

Dustin's eyes gleamed. "Holy moly. What in the world is that?"

Juan nodded toward the 9 millimeter that Dustin was still holding. "That's just for play. This is for real work. It's a custom made job from a guy in the Philippines. It's a 54 cal."

Dustin looked at the steel construction in awe. "I've never heard of a handgun larger than a 50 caliber."

Juan took the 9 millimeter and placed it back in the holster as he handed Dustin the case. Then he walked to the side of the house, about 50 feet away, took one of the red flags that had been used to mark off the sidewalk area, and tied it to a small tree about three inches in diameter. He walked back to the group. "There's nothing but woods through there, right?"

Dustin nodded as he pulled the gun from the case. He needed no further invitation. "Is it loaded?"

"Of course," Juan said.

Juan stood beside Dustin as everyone else stood behind him. Dustin spread his stance and took aim.

"You're closing one eye?" Juan said as if surprised.

Dustin didn't take his eyes off the tree. "I'm left eye dominant."

Juan raised his hand as if to say he understood as Dustin squeezed the trigger. His hands jerked back from the recoil. The bullet went through the flag and through the tree, taking a large portion of the tree with it. Then, unexpectedly, the tree fell over from the point of impact.

"Wow!" Frankie said. "Can I go next?"

Juan smiled again. "Do you shoot?"

Frankie nodded with a big grin on his face.

Dustin handed the gun back to Juan. "Yes, he does, and he's a great shot. But I think this is too much gun for you."

Frankie lowered his head.

"That must have a high grain content," Dustin said.

Juan shook his head. "Actually it's low grain. The barrel is more spiraled to add spin to the bullet, making it a little more accurate. But you still wouldn't use it for anything far away."

Dustin was impressed.

"Tre?" Juan said, holding the gun out toward him.

Trevor shook his head. "No, thank you. I am not threatened like you gentlemen. I am quite comfortable with my masculinity."

Sophia patted him on the back. "Good for you, Tre."

Juan placed the gun back in the case. "Great shooting, Dustin."

Dustin acknowledged with a nod. "Not bad I guess, to have a broken hand."

Juan shook his own hand as if to agree. "Let me get back to work. It was nice meeting you all."

As he got out of hearing range, Sophia said, "Was he really a mercenary?"

Trevor shrugged. "That is what I have been told."

Frankie looked confused. "What's a mercenary?"

"It's a soldier who fights for money instead of a country," Sophia said.

Dustin tried to make it clearer. "It's a hired gun."

Frankie's eyes were big. "You mean that guy would shoot someone for you if you paid him. That's hard to believe."

"Why is that?" Dustin said.

Frankie grinned. "Because Uncle Tre hasn't paid him to shoot you."

Everyone laughed.

Trevor led them toward the house. It was magnificent. It was huge. The exterior walls were some sort of brick that resembled stone. The inside was even more impressive with high ceilings, marble columns in the great room, and decorated with expensive furnishings. He took them out back and showed them the back yard. It was beautifully landscaped with bright green grass and colorful shrubs. There was a large rented tent and white chairs everywhere.

"It's going to be a beautiful wedding," Sophia said with a big smile. "I'm really looking forward to it."

"I hope so. It cost enough. We have a short rehearsal here in about an hour." Leading them back inside, Trevor raised his hands on both sides. "But this is where the bachelor party will be tonight," he said as he winked at Frankie.

Frankie's eyes lit up. "Can I come to that?"

"Don't even think about it," Sophia said.

"Ah come on. I'm almost 13."

Sophia looked at Trevor. "I don't think that's old enough, is it?"

Trevor shook his head. "Sorry, little fellow. You get to hang out with Granny while the women have their night on the town. She has been looking forward to spending time with you for a while."

Frankie held his arms up above his head as if he was celebrating, strictly for sarcasm of course. He loved his granny, but spending the evening with her seemed to pale in comparison to a bachelor party.

"Where is Carol?" Sophia said.

Carol Underwood had attended the same school as Dustin and Trevor. She was two years younger than Trevor and had been a cheerleader. She had gone to college, gotten married a month after she graduated, then had taken a job teaching second grade at the same little school, and had been doing that for the last ten years. Her marriage had only lasted five years and she went back to her maiden name.

Dustin wasn't particularly fond of Carol. She was a very attractive woman with a body that Mother Nature had been overly kind to, but Dustin knew that if Trevor didn't have a nice bank account, she would not have been the type of person to give him the time of day.

"She is out shopping, I imagine. Who really knows?" Trevor said. "I told her you guys should be here around now so she should be back soon."

Dustin realized he was hungry. They had eaten breakfast early then drove non-stop. "I think we're going back to Mom's for lunch."

Trevor looked hurt, as if he couldn't believe they would ever want to leave this house. "I have plenty of stuff here. What do you guys want?"

So, they stayed there as Trevor put out veggies, sandwich stuff, chips and sodas.

Carol came in while they were eating. "Hey ya'll." Her Southern charm was in full swing.

Sophia got up, gave Carol a hug, and congratulated her. Dustin nodded his agreement. It wasn't that he disliked Carol by any means, he didn't really know her. In fact, they had only met one time back on the Fourth of July, back when he and Sophia had visited in the summer and the house was only a slab of concrete at the time. But there was certainly something about her that rubbed him the wrong way. It might be that when they visited before, and they were all staying in their mom's house the same weekend, whenever they were all in the same room, she always had her back to Dustin. Even when Dustin tried to communicate with her, she would answer but still stand facing Trevor with her back to Dustin. And although she wasn't doing that now, she still never made eye contact.

After the rehearsal, Dustin, Frankie, and Sophia went

back to Mrs. Davis' house where Dustin decided to take a nap. He had hauled newspapers the night before and was ready for some more sleep. Sophia woke him at 5:00 p.m.

"Honey?" she said. "I'm leaving with Carol to go to the bachelorette party. I think you should get ready and go on to Tre's. Several cars have already gone down there. You don't want to be late."

He didn't? The truth was, Dustin was not looking forward to it at all. But he got ready, left a sulking Frankie there, and walked down to his brother's new house. There were already several people there, several people he didn't know. He didn't see Trevor, so he went into the kitchen and grabbed a beer, then to the living room, sat on the sofa, and turned on the 60 inch TV. He could hear laughter coming from other parts of the house but wasn't sure from where or why, so he concentrated on the news.

Two hours later, at least 20 more people had arrived, and Dustin still sat in the same location. He recognized a few of the faces of his brother's friends, but not enough to connect a name. No one paid him any attention and he was fine with that. He still had yet to see Trevor. His beer still had two inches in the bottom, but had long since lost its cold. Dustin wasn't a heavy drinker, however, and held on to it just to make sure no one brought him a fresh one. At the moment, he was engrossed in the story being covered on the national news.

"Hey! You made it. Where have you been?" Trevor flopped down beside Dustin. It was obvious he had consumed quite a bit more alcohol than Dustin had.

"I've been here a while," Dustin said.

Trevor looked confused. "Really? Why did you not say something? You want a beer?"

Dustin held up his bottle and Trevor nodded.

"So, what happened to that Indian girl you kept talking about after you came home?" Dustin said.

Trevor looked at Dustin as if he was trying to focus, as if that question were making his eyes blurry and not the liquor. "What does that mean? Do you not like Carol?"

Dustin tried to fake a laugh. "Yes, of course. I wasn't meaning that. I was just curious as to whatever happened to that other girl. That's all."

Trevor shrugged. "I do not honestly know. She never called me, so I do not know whatever happened to her."

There was a moment of silence as Trevor stared at the TV. "What is going on in the world?" he said, lifting his glass of bourbon and Coke toward the screen.

Dustin looked back at the screen. "The president signed the DRS bill into law."

Trevor shrugged. "I have not even been following politics lately. But since it is a Republican in office, it would have to be something retarded. What is the DRS bill?"

Dustin shrugged, also. "I don't really understand it myself. It seems pretty meaningless. It stands for Data Recording and Sharing. All I know is the main provision makes it required for all states and municipalities to report to the federal government all new laws or changes in laws and to report the outcome of every civil and criminal court case." Dustin continued to look at the screen for a few seconds and then turned to look at Trevor. Trevor's expression caught him off guard. "What?"

Trevor was just staring at the floor. Dustin couldn't help but notice that Trevor seemed to be in deep thought, as if what he had just told him was important. Dustin continued watching him. "What is it?" Dustin said.

"I think I am getting cold feet," Trevor said. "Do you think I should really get married?"

Dustin wasn't sure if Trevor was being honest. "Why shouldn't the states and towns provide the federal government with this info?"

Trevor looked confused. "Hmm? What info? I am sorry,

what is it again?"

Dustin looked at Trevor carefully. He still wasn't convinced but he decided to play his brotherly role. "Of course, you should be getting married. You're 35 years old, for Pete's sake."

Before he could study Trevor's reaction, a guy came running into the living room. "The entertainment's here."

Trevor jumped up and ran into the other room almost as if he was glad he had something to distract him from Dustin and the president's new bill. Dustin remained seated on the sofa, glad to not take part. But the party came to him. Everyone filtered into the large living room as Trevor took his place again beside Dustin. The two dancers came in and took their position right in front of Trevor. As they began their show, Dustin realized these were not Sand Mountain girls. The music was a little too high for Dustin's taste and as the clothes began to fly, he realized he might have to go to church an extra day this week.

The other guys were yelling and dancing along to the music. Suddenly, Trevor's cell phone rang.

Dustin laughed. "It's Carol. You're busted."

Trevor answered the phone and tried to hear but the noise was too loud. He got up and walked to the edge of the kitchen. "Hello? I cannot hear you. Say again."

"Hey, Tre. It's me, Radhika. Is this a bad time?"

THE WEDDING WENT GREAT and almost everyone was sitting around eating at the reception. Dustin really liked the groom's cake. It was decorated to look like a pepperoni Hot Pocket with several bites taken out of it. The photographer had already left and the cakes had been cut.

"Can I go change now?" Frankie said.

Dustin smiled at Frankie in his tuxedo and was happy Trevor had asked him to be an usher. "Just let me get one more picture." Dustin took his digital camera out of his pocket and snapped another picture of Frankie, then motioned for him to go change.

After the bride and groom left in Trevor's new truck, Dustin, Frankie, and Sophia decided to say goodbye to Mrs. Davis and head back to Montgomery.

"It was a beautiful wedding," Sophia said as she put her arm around Frankie. "And you were so handsome."

"Yes, he was," Dustin said.

Frankie smiled at his aunt and uncle for their compliments.

After they got onto I-59 and headed south, Sophia looked at her husband. "You seem very quiet. What are you thinking about?"

Dustin looked over to her. He hadn't realized he had been in such deep thought. "Just something that happened at the bachelor party last night. I was watching the news and it was about the president signing this new bill requiring states and cities to provide the federal government information on laws and court cases, and when I explained that to Trevor, he freaked out."

"What do you mean?" she said.

"I don't know. He just reacted so weird, like he couldn't believe it. Then he tried to pretend he was just worried about the wedding, but I'm certain that was just an excuse. I wanted to press him on it, but the strippers arrived and I didn't get a chance."

Frankie and Sophia both yelled at the same time. "Strippers!?"

CHAPTER

EIGHTEEN

"YOUR WIFE IS BEAUTIFUL." Radhika handed the wallet full of pictures back to Trevor. "You've done well for yourself, Tre. I'm not surprised."

The sun was bright at noon on this late fall day as they sat at a small table inside a café in Birmingham. Trevor had been honest with Carol—that he was going to meet an old friend from the company he had worked for before they met. He just didn't mention it was a female. Carol didn't seem to mind since it didn't interfere with her shopping.

Radhika was still stunning. She wore a pants suit like the day they had first met and she was still very athletic, and her eyes still melted Trevor.

"Well, look at you—a hot shot partner in a huge law firm in D.C., practicing law. So tell me, how long do you have to practice before you can actually participate?"

Radhika smiled as if she had missed Trevor's sense of humor. "I'm not a partner, but hopefully some day."

"I never asked when we were working together, but what kind of law do you practice?" Trevor said.

"When I started practicing, I wasn't sure what type of law I wanted to specialize in," Radhika said. "I eventually 'fell' into commercial real estate. I knew I wanted to do transactional work rather than litigation. I prefer for everyone to work toward a common goal and be happy at the end, not spend years scheming about how to beat the other side and then having a win/lose outcome. After my first year with the firm, the real estate guy needed help at the time. I actually think it ended up being the right fit for me—I like that my deals are 'tangible' and I can see the actual building that I helped acquire or finance. I've done everything from hotels in New York City to condos in Ft. Lauderdale to shopping centers in California. Most of my work right now is apartment projects in the Midwest. I've met tons of great people and some not-so-great ones though, and have had some incredible experiences as a result, like business trips to go Salmon fishing in Alaska or tuna fishing in Cabo, private yacht trips in Costa Rica, San Juan Islands, and New England, wine making in California. One of my friends is a woman I did a lot of deals with and she's become my travel buddy. We went on safari to Africa in Zimbabwe, Botswana, and South Africa, and are trying to plan a trip to Peru."

"Wow, you took my answer," Trevor said.

Radhika laughed.

Trevor went for the kill. "No husband?"

Radhika shook her head. "I'm married to my work."

"Lucky work," Trevor said. He was laying it on thick.

Suddenly, Radhika sighed and looked at the ground, a very sad expression upon her face. Trevor realized this wasn't just a chance reunion.

"What is it?" he said.

"Do you remember Bradley?"

A lump came to Trevor's throat. How could he forget the lifeless form in the dark basement? He still had nightmares about it. He never could understand why Bradley was trying to steal information or what anyone could possibly do with it, but whatever the reason, he didn't deserve to be gunned down. As Trevor's mind began reliving that day, he suddenly wondered why she was asking.

"Do you know what happened to him?" Radhika said.

Trevor's heart began pounding so hard that he was sure she would be able to hear it. He swore he would never tell anyone what happened, so how could she possibly know. "Why do you ask that?"

Radhika looked around as if she was afraid someone was watching them. "You remember when Bradley went home? Well, I remembered where he said he was from. It was a small town in Virginia, so I made some calls and found his parents. They told me he never made it home. He had rented a car in D.C. but he had an accident on the way home. The car apparently slid off an embankment and burst into flames. They had to use dental records to identify him because his body was burned so badly."

Trevor stared at his feet. He knew they would cover it up but had no idea how they had done it. "I did not know that. I mean, that is terrible."

"The thing is," Radhika said, "they didn't even know he was coming home and no one had been sick in their family. Remember the story that Franks told us that day? Remember how he said Bradley was going home because of a sickness in his family or something like that?"

Trevor let it soak in. He didn't know what to say. "Yes, I do remember that. I thought that was odd at the time because they had also told us that would not be grounds to break the contract. That is strange."

Radhika waited, perhaps thinking Trevor would say more but he didn't. "I'm not telling you this for answers or opinions; I just needed to tell someone. I wanted to call you so many times after we all went home but I was too scared. I was so scared when we were there, I could hardly sleep at night. You were the only bright spot in my time there."

Trevor smiled a weak smile. He thought there was something between them but never had the courage to find out. And now it was too late. But he was still glad to be able to see Radhika again. "You were my bright spot, too. They were not particularly fun people to work for, but I have to say that I surely miss those cavity searches."

They both laughed. But then Radhika got serious again.

"There's something else," she said in a tone that made the hairs on the back of Trevor's neck stand up. "Have you ever wondered what we were building, or what its purpose might be?"

"I always wondered. It never made sense to me," Trevor said.

Radhika nodded. "Me either. But the day I called you was when the president's new bill began to make me think. Why would every state, county, and town in America need to keep the government updated with new laws and trial information?"

"I had the same thoughts," Trevor said. "It seems to co-incide with the system we were building. I remember that being one of the main functions they insisted it be able to do—update itself with new laws or changes in laws from anywhere."

Radhika agreed. "And lately, I've been hearing a lot of talk in the legal community about some politicians who are go-ing to start pushing for court reforms, stating that the system is corrupt. This is all just water cooler talk right now and I haven't heard any names, but it's the kind of talk that has to be coming from somewhere. I've heard it has some federal judges on edge and that kind of news filters down to everyone else. The truth is, most transactional lawyers don't give a hoot about court reform. The totally out-of-whack jury awards are typically on 'tort' type claims, not contract claims, and criminal law is the furthest thing from our minds. But the partners in my firm are pretty worried, enough that they called a meeting just to discuss what anyone had heard."

Trevor looked confused. "I do not understand. What are you saying?"

Radhika laughed. It was a forced wry laugh. "I don't know. You're so intelligent; I was hoping you could tell me what I was saying."

Trevor smiled but it did seem strange. "And you do not

know who these politicians are?"

She shook her head.

"It is odd, though, like you say," Trevor said. "Especially after that bill you just mentioned that the president signed recently. What was it called again?"

Radhika nodded. "The DRS: Data Recording and Sharing law. You're right; it all matches what we were working on. We now have that law requiring all states, cities, and towns to submit all the new laws and court cases and now we have these rumors about the courts being corrupt. I find it hard to believe that's just coincidence."

"So do I," Trevor said.

They sat for another hour chatting about lighter subjects, which was fine with Trevor. Then the time came for Radhika to leave.

"Well, here's to your wife and new home," she said.

Trevor took his glass of sweet tea and touched her glass of water. The conversation ended on that note as Radhika had to get to the airport. Trevor drove home with mixed emotions. He was happy to see Radhika again, but a little saddened that their time for lunch had passed, and even more sad that their chance in life had passed. And he couldn't stop thinking about the rumors and thinking again about Bradley. Whatever they had built for the government was definitely more important than they ever imagined. Trevor couldn't help but worry about the Frankenstein monster they had left on the slab at the lab, waiting for lightning to strike.

CHAPTER

NINETEEN

DUSTIN AND SOPHIA walked into the hospital with two My-lar balloons, each with identical images of a teddy bear holding a heart. After getting off on the maternity floor at DeKalb County Regional Hospital, they found their way to Carol's room. As they entered, they were glad to see she was holding the babies, twin girls, each weighing in at six pounds even. Also in the room was Dustin's mom, Carol's mom and dad, and of course, Trevor, who couldn't stop smiling.

"Oh my goodness!" Sophia said with a huge smile. She rushed to the bedside leaving Dustin by the door holding the strings to the balloons.

Mrs. Davis, the proud new grandmother, couldn't stop smiling either. "Did you guys just get here?"

Dustin nodded as he walked over and tied the balloons to a gift basket, adding to the six already there. He extended his hand to Trevor. "Congratulations."

"Why thank you, brother." Trevor stuck his hand in his shirt pocket after the handshake, pulled out a cigar, and handed it to Dustin.

Dustin smiled and ran it under his nose. "Appreciate it."

Trevor laughed. "I am joking with you. Here." He pulled a bubblegum cigar out of his pocket and held it out.

Dustin chuckled as he swapped cigars. This was much better since he didn't smoke.

"Tell me, brother, are they not beautiful?" Trevor said.

Dustin followed Trevor's gaze back to the bed where Sophia was now holding one and Carol still had the other. "They're the most beautiful things I've ever seen. Let's see if I remember—Victoria Elizabeth and Rebecca Doreen?"

Both grandmothers quickly confirmed since both middle names had come from them.

"Or Vicki and Becky," Carol said.

"'Soup' would have been a more veritable name in my opinion," Trevor said.

All eyes looked at Trevor for meaning to that comment, all except Carol, who gave him a stern look.

"What?" Sophia said. "You have to explain that one."

Carol smiled. "Go ahead. I can't stop you anyway."

Trevor was happy to explain. "We got here about one o'clock in the morning and Carol was already dilated to eight centimeters so they drugged her up exhaustively, being quite painstaking in their pain killing offerings. About an hour later, one of the nurses lodged her head through the door and asked, 'Is it soup yet?' Carol, in her state of asphyxia, replied, 'It is not soup; it is babies.'"

Everyone laughed.

Sophia seemed so happy holding a baby and Dustin often wondered if she regretted just a little that she never held her own.

"So, you guys had to come in the middle of the night?" Sophia said.

Carol nodded. "Yeah, and someone forgot almost everything, like my overnight bag for example."

Trevor hung his head playfully as if in shame. "I will drive to the house, retrieve it at once, and hopefully redeem my honor." He looked around at everyone in the room. "I shall be back as soon as I can."

As he walked toward the door, Sophia said, "Dustin, why don't you go with him?"

Trevor stopped and smiled. "Sure, come on, brother."

They walked in silence out to Trevor's truck, got in and he drove away from the hospital and turned down Airport Road to head toward the mountain.

"Quite a day," Dustin said.

Trevor smiled at Dustin's words. "Indeed. Quite a day."

Dustin added, "Now I can mark that off my list of things I never thought would happen."

"Funny. That was on my list, too," Trevor said with a grin.

Dustin turned to look out the side window as they passed the tiny airport. "Seems like only six months ago I was marking another one off my list—the day you got married."

Trevor laughed. "You cannot fool a math wizard like you. You solved the big case. Carol was, in fact, pregnant when we wed. Congratulations, Sherlock."

"I hope you're planning on raising them in the church." Dustin said.

Trevor stared at his brother with a bizarre look. "I plan on raising them in our house."

"I'm talking about having them attend church," Dustin said.

"I know very well what you are talking about, brother, and it is not your concern. My girls will be provided for with everything they need: food, clothes, education, and insurance."

"It's insurance I'm talking about—for their souls."

"I suppose you would like to make sure they vote Republican as well?" Trevor said.

Dustin nodded as he smiled thinking about the possibility. "I would love that."

Trevor shook his head. "It amazes me really, that you still think you can be a Republican and a Christian."

"Of course," Dustin said. "Haven't you ever heard the term 'Christian Conservative'?"

"Yes I have, brother," Trevor said. "I have also heard of jumbo shrimp, dry rain, and original copies."

Dustin ignored the oxymoron references. "How can you believe that something as complex as life was a cosmic accident? Do you really believe man just evolved from mud?"

"Whoa there, brother," Trevor said. "That is your theory, not mine. It is your Bible that says God created man from dirt. Do not try to pass that ridiculous hyperbole off on me."

"It has always puzzled me," Dustin said, "that you can believe in Bigfoot, UFOs, and that weird Mexican dog-like creature, and not believe in God."

"It is called a Chupacabra, brother, and there have been numerous eyewitness sightings for all those things you named here. How many people have reported seeing God lately? We have documents of people claiming to see Jesus, which were forged hundreds of years after the alleged authors had died, but no eyewitness accounts of God—ever."

"You believe in wind and air and you can't see those," Dustin said. Then he tapped his chest. "You don't need to see God, you can feel him."

Trevor laughed. "So, he is like indigestion?"

"Yes, exactly." Dustin nodded with confidence. "So, what about church?"

"I shall let my daughters make their own decisions," Trevor said.

Dustin shook his head. "Children can't make their own decisions. That's what parenting is all about."

"I hear you, Deputy Fife."

"What does that mean?" Dustin said.

Trevor looked over at Dustin. "You are the Andy Griffith buff; you should know. It was always Barney, who never had children, who was always explaining to Andy how to do it."

Dustin smiled. "Good point. But I have a son. His name's Frankie."

"That explains a lot," Trevor said. "I always thought I noticed a little friction between you and Hannah. Now I know why."

They both laughed at the absurdity of Dustin being Frankie's natural father.

"That's too funny," Dustin said. "That would certainly cause friction." Suddenly, Dustin looked at Trevor. "Yes, that would cause—"

"Admit it," Trevor said. "You know absolutely squat about raising a child."

"Maybe," Dustin said as he looked again at the huge tattoo on Trevor's arm. "But I know that if you let them make their own decisions, don't be surprised when they're 11 years old and they come home one day with tattoos."

Trevor groaned. "How many of your ex-Marine buddies have tattoos? I have never heard you passing judgment on them."

"There's no such phrase as 'ex-Marine,'" Dustin said.

Trevor rolled his eyes. "Oh, that is correct. Once a jarhead, always a jarhead. Right, brother? But it still distracts from the question."

In truth, Dustin did not want to address the question. "I don't know how you can call yourself an American and not support the troops."

Trevor scoffed. "Nice dodge, brother. But really, the troops? That phrase, in itself, is a parody. That is the true camouflage. There is no such thing as 'the troops.' It is an ambiguous idea propagated by feeble minds who try desperately to justify the killing of innocent people. The only thing that exists is individual people. Some are suicidal, some are homicidal, some are pedophiles, and some simply choose military service over prison. But put this bunch of social misfits together and they form 'the troops,' a grandiloquent mirage of superiority, one to be lauded and revered."

"You're full of it," Dustin said. "In any group of people in our society you're going to find people with different personalities and character traits. What makes 'the troops' so superior, as you call them, is the fact they are willing to die to give people like you the right to your libel."

"It is slander, goofus," Trevor said. "Libel is with the written word. But you are right about one thing; any group in society will inherently boast these types of degenerates, especially that group you find in the pews next to you every Sunday."

Dustin changed course. "Probably wouldn't do any good to go to church anyway, now that you're wealthy."

Trevor looked over at Dustin as if trying to figure out his angle this time. But they were a few seconds away from his house, so he said nothing until he pulled into the circular driveway and stopped by the front entranceway. "Hold that thought, brother, I shall be right back." He left the truck running as he rushed into the house and grabbed Carol's overnight bag, which had already been packed with the things she wanted to take to the hospital. He came back out, tossed it in the back seat, and began to drive away. "Now, what in the name of Einstein are you talking about?"

Dustin looked straight ahead and remained calm. "You always said that if the Bible was true, having money would keep you out of Heaven."

Trevor shook his head. "I said eternal life, not Heaven. And I did not say it at all; Jesus said it. But according to you, having money is the true American way, so I can buy my way into Heaven."

"It's funny now that I think about it," Dustin said, beginning to enjoy this. "You always knocked the rich, yet I don't see you giving all your money away. You always said it was the government's place to take care of the poor, yet it wasn't the government that gave you all your money."

Trevor bit his lip. After all, it was indeed the government who paid him all that money.

"What? You don't remember all these conversations?"

Dustin said. "You were always the big supporter of all those socialist welfare programs."

"Oh, I remember those conversations, brother," Trevor said. "And they were always as retarded as this one. No matter how many times I explained to you, your little brain just simply could not understand. Welfare programs are a consummation of a capitalist society, not a socialist one. In a true socialist society, as you have pointed out more times than I can count, everyone is automatically taken care of. But, in a capitalist society, especially one like we have in this country, it constructs this respite between those with and those without, making programs like this necessary. Or we could, of course, simply turn our backs on the poor and handicapped and let them die off like Jesus would have wanted."

This debate continued all the way back to the hospital, into the elevator, and finally ended before returning to Carol's room, where both walked in and saw the babies again and forgot what they were talking about.

Sophia looked up and smiled. "See, I knew you two could get along."

~

FRANKIE STARED at the small images on Sophia's cell phone. "They're so tiny."

Sophia flipped through the images so they could see each of them. "I've got to transfer these to my computer so I can save them."

"I wish I could have gone with y'all," Frankie said.

Dustin sat down beside Frankie on the sofa and put his arm around him. Sadie crawled up beside him like always. "Me, too, buddy. But with only two days of school left, there wasn't any way for that to happen. You can go with us for the Fourth of July."

Sophia got up and walked over to the computer, sat down, and began transferring pictures. "I love the names, Becky and Vicki. They're perfect."

"Me too," Frankie said with a grin. Then he looked at Dustin. "Do you think Uncle Tre will be a good dad?"

Dustin was shocked at the question and actually had to ponder it before responding. "I think he will be a great dad."

Frankie seemed happy with that answer. Then he looked puzzled again. "What makes a great dad?"

Sophia turned and looked at Frankie as his question seemed to pull at her heart strings, since Frankie would never know firsthand what a great dad was.

Dustin stared at Sophia as if hoping for help with this one. Then he smiled down at Frankie. "A great dad is one that will do anything for his kids. He will always be there for them no matter what. And he will always be prepared to give them a knuckle sandwich for asking silly questions."

Frankie giggled as Dustin held his clenched fist in his face. As he leaned back against the sofa, however, his smile disappeared. "So, that's what a dad is for."

Dustin suddenly felt rotten for building up the role of a father. He thought of a way to redirect his answer. "That doesn't just go for dads. That applies to anyone who loves you. It's the same with Sophia and her mom, the same with my mom and me. It isn't just about dads." He paused for a second then added, "And it applies to you and me."

"Really?" Frankie smiled again. "You'd do anything for me?"

Dustin laughed. "You bet."

Frankie looked up at the ceiling as if trying to think up a scenario. "What if I broke my leg? Would you carry me all the way to the hospital?"

"You betcha."

"What if I was drowning in the ocean? Would you jump

in and save me?"

Dustin nodded.

"What if there were sharks in the water?"

"Even then," Dustin said.

Frankie thought some more. "What if I got put in jail? Would you break me out?"

Dustin quickly thrust his left hand into Frankie's belly, causing him to squeal from the tickling fingers. "No, you little criminal. I would leave you there until you rot."

CHAPTER

TWENTY

"STOP!"

"You stop!"

"Victoria, Rebecca, do not make me spank you." Trevor smiled at his own empty threat. He had never spanked his girls. The exchange between him and his two-and-a-half-year-old twin daughters was a common one.

Trevor tried to concentrate on his work on his laptop computer as he kept an eye on the girls who were sitting in front of the TV. Even though he still had a nice balance in his bank account, building programs was what he loved. He had thought he would enjoy a life of leisure, but that was not the case. He was only happy on the computer. Plus, he could earn a little more than his expenses and how much his wife could spend every month.

The doorbell rang. He waited for his wife to go to the door, but she never came out of the bedroom, where she spent most of her time watching her own TV.

"Are you going to get that?" Trevor yelled out.

There was no answer. She had agreed to answer the door whenever he was working, an agreement she had never kept.

Trevor went and opened the door and saw Sophia and Dustin. "Hey, guys. I did not know you were up." That wasn't true. Not only had his mother told him they were coming, he had seen them arrive. But the last time they came, they only stayed for a day and never paid him a visit. He didn't think it was right for him to go out of his way to see them when they only had to drive five more seconds to see him.

"Come in," Trevor said. "Honey, Sophia and Dustin are here."

The kids looked up from their TV as Dustin and Sophia entered. Dustin smiled. He loved his nieces, both with light blond hair, much lighter than their mother's. They were both very bright little girls, ahead of the curve in just about every way. They had been talking since before they turned two and Dustin was very impressed with them. "Oh my goodness. Look how y'all have grown. Uh oh… I feel the monster coming on." Dustin raised his arms up over his head and made a growling noise and took a step toward the girls, which caused them to shriek and run to their bedroom. Dustin followed.

Trevor invited Sophia to have a seat on the sofa and offered her a sweet tea, which she accepted.

"The kids are growing so much," she said.

As Trevor smiled and nodded, Carol came in and greeted Sophia, said it was good to see her, then returned to wherever she came from, never to be seen again.

"Her show is on," Trevor said weakly.

"Oh?" Sophia said. "What's her show?"

"The Shopping Network."

They both laughed.

Dustin came back in with one girl under each arm.

"Help, Daddy," Vicki screamed.

Trevor threw his hands up and shook his head. "I am too afraid of your uncle."

After a while, the girls went back to the TV and cartoon they had been watching as Dustin sat on the chair beside the sofa.

"So, you staying busy, Tre?" Sophia said.

Trevor smiled at Sophia because she was always nice and genuinely interested in whatever he was doing. "Pretty much. Still building programs—antivirus programs mostly."

"Why didn't you start that web business back up?" Dustin said.

Trevor just shrugged. It wasn't nearly the first time Dustin had asked that very same question in the last three years. "I enjoy building programs."

"So, what else you working on? I know you always got some ideas cooking," Sophia said.

Trevor paused for a second as if wondering whether or not to show them. His brother had never taken an interest in his inventions and probably wouldn't care to see one now. But Sophia's smiling face assured him that she was interested; she always had been. He clicked on a few links on the laptop and an image of a bicycle appeared on the screen. He handed Sophia the laptop and sat back and let them take in the image.

Dustin moved over beside Sophia and leaned over close to get a better view.

"OK," said Dustin. "The front and back wheels both have solid centers, rubber or graphite maybe, so I'm guessing they're interchangeable."

Trevor nodded but said nothing.

Sophia spoke up. "I see the pedals but there's no chain."

Trevor smiled. "That is correct, honey bunny. The bicycle has evolved over time but they all still run on chains and sprockets, the very same way they were propelled since their conception in the early 1800s."

Dustin studied the picture carefully. The framework was basically the same, but there was a small rubber wheel about four inches in diameter facing perpendicular to, and pressed up against, the rear wheel, positioned on the part of the frame running from the center of the back wheel to the place where the pedals normally were positioned. "So, this is what propels it. Is there an identical one on the other side?"

Trevor smiled. He walked over, clicked again, and it brought up an image looking down from the top of the bike, and the other small rubber wheel was visible. "The pedals move up and down instead of in a circle and run up the frame leading to the seat, so there is no wasted motion. As you shift your weight and push the pedal downward, it rotates the driveshaft inside the frame leading to the rear wheel, which turns the small wheel, which in turn spins the rear wheel forward."

"It's a beautiful design," Sophia said. "But what makes it better than bikes on the market today?"

"It's not," Dustin said. "The small wheel would propel the bike, but with it out at the edge of the rear wheel, it wouldn't go very fast."

Trevor smiled. "Now to see how it works." He reached over and clicked again and the screen was filled with an elaborate animation. He pointed to the animation as it worked. "You are right, brother. At this point, it would be easy to pedal and move slower than the first gear of a 21-speed bike. But as you shift, the wheel slides backward." The animation almost appeared like it could hear Trevor as the smaller wheels slid backward on the rear wheel. Trevor continued. "The pedals have a range of six inches and the driveshaft is one inch in diameter. So, each full trip of the pedal spins the little wheel six rotations. As the small wheels get closer to the center, it makes the rear wheel rotate more times and propels it faster. Once you reach the inside of the rear wheel, where it is only about two inches in circumference, one full motion of one pedal would still turn the smaller wheel six times, or 75 inches, which would in turn spin the rear wheel 37.5 times. One full motion of both pedals would spin the rear wheel 75 times."

Sophia looked impressed as always and Dustin lost interest as always.

"Isn't that neat?" Sophia said to Dustin.

Dustin shrugged. "I don't think it would be much different than a 21-speed bike."

"Humor me, brother. Pretend I am not me and you are

not you, and let us do some simple math," Trevor said. "Can you at least try that?"

"Ok," Dustin said. "If it's a standard 26 inch wheel, then one rotation would be 113 inches. 75 rotations would be almost 8500 inches, or about… 700 feet."

Trevor sat back and smiled.

Sophia was lost. "You have to explain that to me."

"What it means is that if you were in the highest gear, so to speak, one full thrust of both feet would move you 700 feet," Dustin said.

"Oh my goodness," Sophia said. "It would literally fly."

Trevor smiled. "Exactly."

Dustin shook his head. "No one would have the leg strength to use it. It would never be marketable. The bikes out now are still better designs."

"You are still an idiot, brother," Trevor said.

"And you are still a dreamer," Dustin said.

"I think you should market it, Tre," Sophia said. "I think it's an awesome design."

Trevor smiled at Sophia. "I have contacted some companies about building a prototype, without giving them the blueprints anyway, but I would want to get a patent first and I'm not sure I want to spend $3500."

"Is that how much it costs?"

"Pretty much, honey bunny," Trevor said. "You have to pay a patent attorney to run a patent search, and the fee for a U.S. patent right now is $3000."

"I think you should do it. Absolutely." Sophia's enthusiasm was sincere.

"I've had a prototype of one invention made. I might just pursue this one if I ever tire of building programs," Trevor said.

"Didn't you tell us that you had developed a program for the new tax laws," Dustin said, as if a window of opportunity had opened, "one that helps you do your taxes faster?"

Trevor stared at Dustin for several seconds. "You do not have to pretend to want to visit, brother. You can simply convey the truth, if you even know how."

"What would you know about truth?" Dustin said.

"Well let me enlighten you, brother. I know that you guys have only been to my house three times now, counting this visit, even though you have visited mother a scant 300 feet away numerous times. I know that no matter how successful I am, you still look down your nose at me like I am not fit to touch your Bible. How is that for truth for you?"

Dustin threw up his hands. "Maybe that's why we don't visit, because of how you're acting right now. Everything between us has to be a competition with you. It doesn't matter how much money you have, you're still so hung up on trying to prove you're better and smarter than I am. Hey, look around you. You won. OK?"

"I do not feel the need to prove anything to you," Trevor said. "I never did. You were the one always trying to prove you were better. You had the rougher life. You always worked harder. You are a good Christian, whereas I am an evil person. Do you not find that ironic? You are the so-called Christian and I am the atheist, yet you love guns and I detest them. You support war and I oppose it. You have always judged me and I have never judged you. You cuss like a sailor and I never swear. And still, as smart as you are, brother, you cannot even understand what I am saying."

Dustin motioned for Sophia to come with him. "Let's go."

Trevor laughed. "Yes, run away when the heat is on. Why can you not just admit that what I am saying is true? Why is that impossible for you?"

"We've been here more than three times, haven't we?" Sophia said. "If not, I apologize. We love you, whether we always show it or not. You're family. You always will be."

Trevor realized that Sophia was the only constant cool-headed person in this trio. She had always been the buffer between them and he knew she didn't deserve it.

"Look, I didn't come here to fight. I'm sorry, too. I did come down mainly to borrow the tax program. If you can loan it to me, fine. If not, it's no biggie if you don't want to. I just thought I would ask. I'm sorry if we haven't come to visit more often, especially since I love my nieces."

Trevor stared at his big brother. "OK, sure. I can make you a copy." He invited them to his office, which adjoined the living room.

Dustin took a seat in front of the computer and Sophia stayed in the doorway to keep an eye on the girls, but both seemed to notice the elephant in the corner.

"What did that cost?" Dustin said, pointing to the life-sized R2D2.

Trevor looked over at his latest Star Wars acquisition. "Plenty, but well worth it." He moved his hand in front of the droid replica, which made the lights come on, the head spin halfway around, and emit R2D2-type noises.

Sophia laughed. "That is so cool."

Dustin didn't think so. "A waste of money."

Trevor smiled. "Of course. But I wasted more on that." He pointed to a document in a custom frame. "That is one of the original drafts of Star Wars with handwritten notes from George Lucas."

"Oh my," Sophia said.

"Oh my indeed," Trevor said. "Did you know that in the original version, Yoda is Luke's father?"

Both Sophia and Dustin stared with open mouths. "You're kidding," Sophia said.

Trevor laughed. "Yes, I am." He pulled a thumb drive out from his desk drawer and began going through a short stack of discs on his desk. He couldn't find what he was looking for. He called out in the direction of the living room. "Kids, what are you watching?"

One of them answered. "Blue Bird Ballerina."

"Excuse me." Trevor got up and went into the living room. "I will trade you Ollie Owl Goes Over the Rainbow." It must have been an agreeable trade because Trevor came back with the Blue Bird Ballerina DVD. He opened his CD drive, placed the movie inside, and closed it. Immediately his screen displayed a menu that read:

Blue Bird Ballerina
Hidden Files

He clicked on the "Hidden Files" link and 20 names appeared. He placed the thumb drive in a USB port and opened a blank screen. Then he clicked on the link from the DVD titled "1040" and slid it over and dropped into the blank thumb drive window. It immediately read "Upload Complete." He took the thumb drive out and handed it to Dustin.

"That's incredible, Tre." Sophia was still looking at the screen. "You have files hidden on movie DVDs?"

Trevor realized why they were staring. "Yes. It is an old habit. I used to always hide my best programs on movies. That way if anyone ever broke into my office, they would not think to look there."

"That's brilliant. If I were to put that movie in my computer, I could find your files," Sophia said.

Trevor smiled. He had always loved Sophia's enthusiasm. "No, honey bunny, your computer would never see them. If you did it, it would only play the movie. Only a system I design would know to even look for it."

Dustin took the thumb drive and slid it into his pocket.

They visited for another hour, talking with Trevor and playing with the girls then said their goodbyes. Trevor was glad they had come.

CHAPTER

TWENTY-ONE

DUSTIN AND SOPHIA sat still as Hannah delivered her entire speech, most of it totally unnecessary. She explained that things had gotten serious between her and her new boyfriend, a sergeant in the Air Force. Dustin wasn't surprised. With two Air Force bases in Montgomery—Maxwell, the larger base, and Gunter, the smaller annex—it was not the first military guy she had dated. Hannah had dated so many guys, Dustin never tried to keep track. But this time was different, maybe not the actual relationship, but the events that it was about to create. Her boyfriend was getting transferred to Texas and Hannah had decided to go with him.

"Like I said, it's just that Frankie has all his school friends here and he really loves you guys," Hannah said.

Dustin nodded. He was, for the first time, listening intensely to Hannah, probably because it was the first time he had ever been interested in what she was saying. "You know he's welcome to stay here. Absolutely," he said as he kept one hand on Sadie. He looked down at the still not-so-pretty beast that had at one time been Frankie's birthday present and realized it wasn't the first time they had to take over Hannah's responsibilities. And Dustin didn't mind. He was happier with Sadie being here and he knew he would be happier with Frankie being here. He couldn't help but smile.

Hannah didn't smile. In fact, she looked like a kid who had been caught stealing. It was easy to see the guilt was eating away at her. "It's only for one year and Tom gets rotated back to Maxwell."

Dustin couldn't have been happier. He felt like he had raised Frankie anyway. Now he was 16 years old, still working with the lawn business, and spending more time at Dustin's than he did at his mom's anyway.

A few weeks later, they picked Frankie up on the day that his mom was leaving. He seemed very solemn as he put his bags on the twin bed in the small guest room, a bed he had slept in many times. Even though it was clear that Frankie loved his aunt and uncle and would probably enjoy staying with them more than he liked living with his mom and grandmother, his expression made it clear that there was something amiss, like a tiny gnawing in his mind that he had been abandoned.

It was still summer break, so Frankie had been working full time with Dustin cutting lawns. Before, Dustin had been driving to get him each morning, but now he simply had to wake him. But unlike before, when Frankie was always ready and waiting when he got to Hannah's house, Frankie was seldom ready on time anymore. Dustin had trouble getting him to get out of bed in the mornings and even when he did, Frankie wasn't very responsive and moped around all day instead of working hard like he had always done before. The last week before school started back, Dustin did not bother to try to wake him at all, but left him home, which seemed to be OK with Frankie.

The real problems came when school did start back and Frankie's less-than-caring attitude continued. Dustin and Sophia found themselves having to make him get up to go to school. When they received word from the school regarding too many absences, they became really concerned. Dustin was torn between considering disciplinary actions, something he never imagined he would have to do with Frankie, or giving him time to get over what was bothering him. For fear of making the wrong decision, he uncharacteristically did nothing at all.

"WHERE ARE YOU GOING?"

Carol barely glanced at Trevor as she passed by, Vicki and Becky on each hand. "I told you the girls need new clothes."

Trevor leaned back on the sofa as they went out the door. It was a lazy Saturday afternoon in the middle of August. It was too hot outside and he had no motivation to do anything anyway. His cell phone rang.

"Yes, hello?"

"Hey, is this a good time?" Radhika said.

Trevor sat up. Radhika had called twice in the past year just to chat, and that's how she always began, even though Trevor had told Carol about her and explained that she could call anytime she liked. "Of course. How are you?"

Her voice had a bit of urgency. "Are you watching this?"

"What?" Trevor said.

"CNN. If not, turn it on."

Trevor got up and looked around for the remote, found it and sat back down. He aimed the little black box at the TV and pressed the button that turned it on. Unsure of what channel was CNN, he pulled up the menu. There it was, channel 36. He clicked the control.

"...and there is staunch opposition to the legislation, some calling it illegal and unconstitutional; other lawmakers calling it much worse. Senator Poindexter, the senior senator from South Dakota, has started a firestorm..."

Trevor squinted as he stared at the screen. "What am I watching?"

"It's happening," Radhika said.

Those words sent quivers down Trevor's spine. "Is this about what I think it is about?"

There were several seconds of silence as Radhika was

watching on her own TV. "It'll show him again. You can't miss him. Poindexter is a good name for him because he has the most pointed face I've ever seen."

Trevor froze. "He has what? How do you mean?"

"His chin is really pointed," she said.

Trevor closed his eyes and thought back. Could it be? His question was answered almost immediately as he opened his eyes and focused on the screen.

"Senator Poindexter, Senator Poindexter. Can you explain to us the premise of proposition 1015?"

The Senator continued walking, then stopped and faced the camera. Trevor couldn't believe it. It was him. It was the guy that Agent Daniels and Agent Marks had tried so hard to hide that day when he gave his demonstration on the last day of the job in D.C.

"Let me make it very clear," Senator Poindexter began. "The proposition is about fairness and justice. We have a perfect court system in this country except for one element—the human element. There are too many innocent people serving time because they can't afford a decent lawyer and too many prosecutors who will do anything to increase their winning percentages. There are too many guilty people going free and too many American families who never find justice after a loved one has been brutally raped or murdered. That's what we're talking about here today—making the system work for a change."

The Senator abruptly walked away with half a dozen reporters chasing and calling his name.

"Lightning just struck," Trevor said in a whisper.

"I'm not sure what you mean but got the gist of it," Radhika said. "I can't believe it, Tre. They weren't wanting a computer that could predict court cases; they were wanting a computer that could actually make those decisions. My God, do you know what that means? What are we going to do?"

"Nothing," Trevor said.

"What?"

Trevor repeated the command. "We do nothing. We honor our contracts. We do not do anything; we do not say anything."

"I don't understand," Radhika said. "Why so firm?"

Trevor clarified with one simple statement. "These people are dangerous."

"Why do you say that?" Radhika said.

Trevor thought about telling her the real story behind Bradley but decided against it, and he was certain he wouldn't want to provide it over a telephone, even a cell phone. So he changed direction—somewhat. "Anyone who has power can be dangerous. I just would not want you to get in any trouble with your job."

Radhika seemed to sense there was more behind Trevor's words than he admitted, but she didn't push it. They talked for a few more minutes before hanging up.

Trevor looked around his home. He didn't care what the government was going to do; he wasn't going back to his mother's basement.

CHAPTER

TWENTY-TWO

DUSTIN SMILED as he watched his beautiful wife singing in the choir, her long black hair cascading down the front of her rose-colored robes. The service was coming to a close and he had enjoyed the sermon. The only thing that made the morning church service less than perfect was the empty spot on the pew next to him.

As it ended and the choir left to go remove their robes, Dustin shook hands with other members and guests at Calvary Baptist Church. Although it was fairly cold outside, the inside was a little warm for Dustin and his collar was always wet from perspiration by the time church was over. All of his ties were faded around the neck section from where Sophia had washed out the salt stains many times. Dustin was trying to get out the front door before someone asked the question again that he didn't want to answer anymore.

"Good to see you, Dustin," a tall heavy man said, his hand extended. "Where's Frankie?"

Dustin repeated the answer for the sixth time. "He over-slept." This was mostly true. The entire truth was Frankie simply refused to get up and go to church.

Finally, Sophia came out and they drove home from church. Frankie wasn't there. He stayed gone all day and didn't return until late that night after Dustin and Sophia had gone to bed. This had become normal as well.

The next day, however, something abnormal happened. Frankie's school called Dustin requesting a conference that very afternoon. Dustin left his crews working and went to the school for the 3:00 p.m. appointment.

Dustin sat across and stared over the desk at Mrs. Wu, the vice principle of the high school. She was in her mid-fifties, tall, slender, and a handsome Asian woman, especially for her age.

"Thanks for coming by, Mr. Davis," she said. "Let me start by saying that we think Frankie is an exceptional young man. His teachers have expressed their fondness for him. He's polite and doesn't cause trouble; however, they are concerned about his lack of enthusiasm recently and participation in their classes. It's not that he's misbehaving; it's more that he's become despondent."

Dustin thought about how to respond.

"I'm sorry," Mrs. Wu said, "That means he doesn't really show interest. He basically just mopes around now."

Dustin exhaled deeply. He was used to people assuming because he worked with his hands, he must not be intelligent enough to hold another job, or to understand three-syllable words. "I've noticed this at home, also."

"Is there something specific going on—health wise or emotional—that could be causing this?" Mrs. Wu asked.

"The thing is," Dustin said, "his mom moved to Texas several months back and he lives with me and my wife now. I think he's going through a period of depression, thinking she ran out on him."

Mrs. Wu looked over her notes. "He lives with you now? Have you provided us with that updated information?"

Dustin looked her directly in the eyes for several seconds before answering the obvious. "Did your school call me?"

She smiled and nodded. "OK, dumb question. I get a little confused trying to keep up with so many students. I do see here you are the one who signs his Progress Report. This also surprises me that you haven't contacted us."

Progress Report? Mrs. Wu was not the only one confused

and surprised. In Dustin's time, students took home report cards, but he had not even thought to ask Frankie about those. Dustin asked to see the paper she was looking at. As he scanned over the document, he noticed all the productivity lines had fallen off sharply, except for two—math and computer programming. There were notes for absences, missed work, and several notes from worried teachers. He also noticed the signature at the bottom right, the signature that was not his own.

"He excels at math and computer programming? I didn't realize that," Dustin said.

"He can excel at everything if he puts his mind to it."

"I must apologize for this, Mrs. Wu," Dustin said. "I work so much and am so used to Frankie doing well, I guess I never even paid attention to this last report." He handed it back to Mrs. Wu.

"Don't feel bad," she said. "That happens with most parents. In today's economy, it's hard enough providing kids with food, clothes, and a roof over their heads, let alone be able to address every other detail of their lives. It could be worse. These reports don't always make it home. Some students simply sign it themselves. The good news is, we do have programs in place that could very well help. We have remediation and counseling available, which can include you and your wife, and we also have student tutoring programs after school and during off periods. I can also schedule conferences with each of Frankie's teachers if you like. It's not all bad news; we have the most important thing we could ask for at this juncture—a parent, or guardian in your case, who cares about what's going on. I wish I could tell you that's not a rare thing."

Dustin said he would discuss it with his wife and with Frankie. He thanked her and got up to leave, then turned back around. "Mrs. Wu, do you have kids?"

She smiled. "One daughter. She's in college now."

"But she was 16 once. How did that go for you?" Dustin

said.

Mrs. Wu laughed. "Let me put it this way. That's the year I had to start dying my hair. I know what you're going through. It's not easy. You're torn between being too strict or too amenable."

Dustin thought about it.

"That means too submissive and easy going," she said.

Dustin smiled and turned and walked out.

That night before Dustin could talk to Frankie and Sophia about his school visit, Frankie headed to the front door.

"Where do you think you're going? It's a weeknight." Dustin cringed as his mom's words slipped out of his mouth.

"We're just going out," Frankie said as a lame explanation. "I'll be back by 11 o'clock."

Dustin followed him to the door and watched him get into the car with three other teenagers. It was already dark out as he watched the car drive away. In the five months since Hannah had been gone, Frankie had seemed to change. Maybe it was just the natural part of being a teen, but Dustin didn't like it and he certainly didn't like Frankie's new friends.

"Honey, all kids go through this," Sophia said trying to reassure her husband.

"I didn't," Dustin said.

Sophia smiled. That was true. Few people were as square as the man she married, or few kids were forced to grow up so quickly. "OK, all normal kids."

Dustin tried to smile at the joke but he couldn't help but worry. This had become pretty regular in the last two months and the gray on each side of Dustin's head had become more prominent. He sat in his recliner and tried to regain interest in whatever show he had been watching, but he had already missed too much as he and Frankie argued, so he flipped it to Fox News. "Look at these weirdoes," he said.

Sophia stopped reading her book and looked up at the

TV. "More protesting?"

"Yep," Dustin said. "These slackers need to get a job."

She didn't say anything, perhaps not wanting to instigate more things for her husband to worry about.

The two houses had passed The Fair and Just Act by the two-thirds needed, much to everyone's surprise, and it had cleared the states by the three-quarters vote needed there, which surprised people even more. It was half expected that the Supreme Court would strike down the measure, but they refused to step in. So, as of New Year's Day, an amendment to the constitution was passed making Article III, Section 2 null and void. No longer did a person have a right to trial by jury. On top of that, the government announced a no-bid contract to MerCorp, a previously unheard of tech company, to provide EVs—Electronic Verdict machines—to every federal courthouse in the country.

Several hours later, Sophia looked up from her book and realized that Dustin was still watching the news, and it was past 9:30, past his bedtime. "Is your expression due to the protestors or are you thinking about Frankie? Honey, you should go to bed."

Dustin shook his head without looking away from the screen.

"Well, I am." She put down her book and went to the bathroom to take a shower. When she came out, before going to bed, she walked back into the living room. "Why do you support this change to the constitution?" she said.

Dustin finally looked away from the TV. "I think it's the best thing Congress has done in a long time. It cuts out all the baloney. It used to be that they would march murderers into the courtroom wearing a new suit with a new haircut, making them all presentable, just to influence the jury. The entire process of selecting a jury is all based on bias."

"That statement seems wrong," Sophia said. "I thought

the goal of selecting a jury was to have a non-biased jury."

Dustin rolled his eyes. "It just doesn't work that way. If you end up with a jury of 12 people, you might have 22 to choose from. Each lawyer gets five strikes, in which they try to get rid of the ones that they think will be most biased, but that's all they get. What if there are more than six biased people in the mix. He's out of luck. Meanwhile, the other lawyer or prosecutor is trying his best to keep them. All it takes is one on the jury to have a bleeding heart and you got a hung jury and a killer walks free. I've seen it happen. Not anymore, not when every courtroom in America is set up on the new system."

"Every courtroom?" Sophia said as she stared at the TV. "I thought it was just federal courts."

Dustin shook his head. "That's just the start. They're talking about having this in every courtroom in the country within a year. Every civilian courtroom, anyway. The military has decided to stick with their system."

"What about all the judges? Are they just out of a job now?" Sophia said.

"No. A lot of judges do not preside over actual court cases, and even those that do have many other responsibilities. They've created a new position called 'Court Administrator,' which basically has the same power as a courtroom judge. They set the charge, like determining who might be charged with murder and who will be charged with manslaughter. They also have the ability to plea bargain. A lot of judges and even some high ranking attorneys have already been appointed to that position."

"That scares me a little," she said. "I don't understand it at all. And I can't understand how you can be so behind it. I wish you weren't so obsessed with it. Why don't you come on to bed? You only have a few hours to sleep before you have to get up."

"I'm going to wait up for Frankie," he said.

Sophia seemed to know there was no sense trying to get him to change his mind, so she turned to go to bed, leaving him with her last words. "Take it easy on Frankie."

Dustin muted the TV as she disappeared into the hallway. The truth was, he was more concerned with Frankie than he was the news. He didn't know what he wanted to say; he only knew he wasn't comfortable with the current situation. He felt it was time to make a big decision. As the TV flashed up different images with no sound, it lured him to sleep.

He jolted awake as the front door opened at just after 1:00 a.m., which made Sadie, who had fallen asleep in Dustin's lap, jolt awake also.

Frankie seemed surprised to see his uncle up at this time. "Are you about to go to work?" Frankie said.

"No," Dustin said rubbing his eyes and looking at the clock. "I was waiting to talk with you. I figured I could wait up until 11."

Frankie apparently picked up on the sarcasm. "I have to go to school tomorrow," he said.

"This won't take long," Dustin said. "I just want to talk. Can you spare your uncle a few minutes? Do you want something to eat?"

Frankie shook his head and took a seat on the sofa.

Dustin got up and sat beside him and Sadie followed. He looked at the floor as he tried to think of where to begin. "I know I'm not your father, but I know I act like it sometimes. I don't mean to; I really don't. I just can't figure out what's happened between us. We used to spend so much time together, but at least we weren't stuck in the same house. I know I can be a pain. And I know I'm not as fun to hang around as your friends. Heck, I wasn't even fun at your age. I just want to say that it's me, Dustin. You know? It's me."

Frankie looked at his uncle as if trying to understand what he meant.

Dustin continued. "Remember the circus, the monster truck rally, all those hours of baseball practice? I'm still the same guy and you're still the same guy. You know that, right?"

Frankie sat motionless, staring at the floor.

"Have I not always been there for you?"

Frankie nodded.

"I always will be," Dustin said. "Do you remember the pact we made when you were ten?"

Frankie looked up at his uncle with teary eyes then looked back at the floor.

"Do you remember?"

Frankie sat still for several seconds before nodding.

Dustin wanted verification. "What was our pact?"

A tear rolled down Frankie's cheek. "We promised we would always be best friends."

Tears rolled down both of Dustin's cheeks. "I've never broken that pact. You're still my best friend. I was there the day you came into this world. I fell in love with you that very day and I've never stopped loving you. I know things change and I know you're restless and need space, but that doesn't mean we have to be enemies, does it? And I know your mom leaving probably feels bad, like she left you, but you're not alone. As long as I'm breathing, you'll never be alone."

Frankie looked up at his uncle with bloodshot eyes but said nothing. Maybe he didn't know what to say.

"All I'm asking," Dustin said, "is for us to be totally honest with each other, like best friends should be. I can smell the cigarette smoke on your clothes. I don't know if it is from others smoking around you, or if you have taken it up. And I don't care. I can't support it since you're not legally old enough, but I'm not going to tell you how to live your life. I just want to be a part of your life, if even in a supportive role."

Inside the bedroom, Sophia stood at the cracked open door as tears dropped from her face.

"I guess that's all I wanted to say," Dustin said.

Frankie sat there several seconds as both of them dried

their eyes. Finally, he got up and walked toward the hallway. "I'll see you in the morning," he said.

"One more thing," Dustin said turning to face him.

Frankie stopped and turned around.

Dustin smiled. "I think it's time we started looking for you a car."

Frankie smiled and looked down at the floor. He looked back up and nodded. "Good night, Uncle Dustin."

"There's just two conditions," Dustin said, which stopped Frankie in his tracks and made him turn back around. Dustin raised his index finger. "Number one—no smoking in the car. The smell never leaves and it decreases the value."

Frankie nodded.

Dustin raised his middle finger beside the index. "And number two—from now on, I sign your Progress Reports."

CHAPTER

TWENTY-THREE

TREVOR FOLLOWED the directions on his GPS and pulled into Radhika's driveway around noon and parked his rental car behind her SUV. Her house was in a very nice subdivision with moderately priced homes. He got out of the car and immediately tried to wrap his coat tighter around him as the weather in Washington D.C. was a lot colder than Alabama. It was completely overcast and the wind was tenacious.

Radhika opened the door and smiled then invited Trevor inside. She noticed how he was trying to stay warm and laughed. "Poor southern boy."

Trevor laughed as well. "You know it. This is not normal. Why would anyone live here?"

"Come into the kitchen and I will make you some hot chocolate," she said. "We still have a couple of hours before we need to leave."

Trevor walked in and sat at the little breakfast table and took off his coat as the heat in the house began to comfort him. He looked around at Radhika's house. It was very neat with nice furniture and several actual oil paintings on the wall—no frames, just canvases.

"Did you paint those?" he said.

Radhika looked up from the stove where she was heating water and toward the paintings. "Goodness no, I can't paint. There's a little coffee shop near work where I like to go sometimes, and they display and sell works from local artists."

She took a couple of cups and emptied the contents of

two containers of instant hot chocolate mix and poured the water. She took them over to the table, set one in front of Trevor, and took the seat across from him.

Trevor took a sip. "That is good. I needed that."

Radhika smiled. "I knew you wouldn't be able to resist."

Trevor looked up. "What? The hot chocolate?"

"No, silly, the tour," Radhika said.

Trevor smiled.

The protests had continued, so, in a public relations stunt, the government had decided to offer guided tours of the federal courthouse where the electronic verdict computer was located, for a small fee of course, in hopes to garner some support. As soon as it was announced, Trevor had called Radhika.

"You are right," Trevor said. "I had to see it for myself. I am still not convinced it is a good idea. Maybe we should wear disguises."

Radhika looked at Trevor as if trying to decide if he was making a joke or being serious. "Really? Do you really think these people are dangerous? Is there something you're not telling me?"

Trevor tried to ease the mood. "No, I am just kidding around. But, of course, there is something I am not telling you, mostly because I am married and you can likely kick my butt."

Radhika smiled. Even though Trevor was married, she seemed to enjoy hearing those little innuendos proving he still had a thing for her.

They sat and chatted for a while until it was time to go. Trevor moved his car so she could drive her own vehicle. That was fine with Trevor since he wasn't quite used to heavy traffic. To him, heavy traffic was a tractor with three cars behind it waiting for a chance to pass.

She drove downtown and entered a parking structure a few blocks from the federal courthouse which was located on the corner of Third Street and Constitution Avenue. From there they walked. Trevor was indeed uneasy about this tour and it showed on his face. What if someone recognized them? But Radhika was right; it was something he had to do.

Although Trevor had seen on the news many times what was going on here, he still wasn't prepared for the image that came into view as they neared the courthouse. The scene was overwhelming. There were at least 5000 protestors and, since the police had barricaded the sidewalk nearest the courthouse, they were packed like sardines on the opposite side along every street as far as the eye could see. As they walked directly through the mob, Trevor read as many signs as he could.

"Communists at Work"
"Remember the Constitution?"
"The Death of Liberty"
"Big Brother"
"Freedom: Guilty as Charged"
"Where Will it Stop?"
"Free Speech is Next"

As it became clear that Trevor and Radhika were going into the courthouse and not there to protest, the protestors lashed out, crowding around them as much as their signs would allow, yelling and screaming threats and obscenities. Trevor grabbed Radhika by the arm and quickly led her across the street. They had to show the police officers their tour itineraries to get through the barricades.

They entered the front entrance and went through the metal detectors where they were instructed to empty their pockets into a plastic tray. The guards directed them where to wait. As they followed the guards' instructions and walked down the hall, there was already a large group of people there. They blended in with the crowd and waited. At 2:30 on the nose, a young woman appeared holding a clipboard and began explaining the tour. She was dressed in a pants suit almost identical to Radhika's.

"Welcome, everyone," she said. "We're glad you could make it. Let me go over a few things and we will get this tour started. First, make sure you stay with the group. We will take a few restroom breaks as we go throughout the facility. You're going to see the control center and actually be able to see the super computer in person. That's what makes this incredible process work, and why it has already been so successful. Then you will get to witness an actual trial and see it in action."

They followed with the crowd as the young woman continued her spiel, mostly full of the same rhetoric the politicians had used to force this idea into law. Finally, they came to a door in a hallway.

"Inside here," the woman said, "is the nerve center. You will see the most incredible computer ever made. We will need to go through single file. Stop and look at the computer then move on. Do not address the guards."

Trevor and Radhika waited as the group entered the door one-by-one until it was their turn. Trevor's anticipation was growing as he entered the room. Inside was a long room about 25 feet in length. On the left sat three armed guards. Trevor stared at them and they stared back, expressionless. He then directed his attention to the right wall. There was a long window, approximately 15 feet long and four feet high, positioned in the center of the right wall.

As he was able to move up alongside the window, he could see an identical room on the other side. In the back wall of the opposite room was a vault-like steel door. And right in the center of the floor was Frankenstein himself, the giant computer in all its glory. Trevor felt his stomach tighten and couldn't take his eyes off the monstrosity. He stared at the black metal construction, the lights along the top that he had seen before, and the 12 cooling fans on one side. It was like being reunited with a long lost friend, only it wasn't a friend at all, but a complete stranger, one you never really knew to begin with. A woman behind Trevor nudged him. He looked up and realized he had been standing in the same spot for too long and the line had progressed without him. He moved on and caught up with Radhika.

As the group reassembled in the hallway, the woman led them to a courtroom and instructed them to find a seat. Trevor and Radhika sat near the back of the room.

The woman stood in the center aisle in front of the group. "What you're about to witness is a real case." She looked down to read her notes. "The defendant in this case is charged with possession of a weapon banned by the National Firearms Act in pursuant to Title 26 of the United States Code. I will be explaining the process as the trial progresses, but I must ask all of you to refrain from talking amongst yourselves and please turn off all cell phones at this time."

Trevor noticed several people in the front left row who were staring back at the woman with looks of disgust. He concluded they must be the defendant's family. There was a lone man in a suit on the right front row. Before long, an officer led a young man in from a door near the front left of the courtroom. He was wearing the basic orange jumpsuit issued to prisoners. As the officer led him to a table in the front section, he looked despairingly toward his family. An older woman started to cry, most likely his mother.

It seemed odd to Trevor that the defendant was wearing a prison uniform instead of regular clothes. Had he not been able to afford bail?

The man in the suit got up and joined the guy at the table in the front section, no doubt the lawyer.

The Court Administrator entered from a door in the back wall and took a seat behind an expensive executive desk. He was wearing a suit but no robes. There was no large podium-style area for judges anymore and no area for juries. The CA opened the folder on his desk. "Case number 12254, The U.S. versus

Robert Finch, is called to order." The CA then took out two discs from his folder. The lawyer got up, walked to the desk, and handed him two other discs.

The tour guide explained. "The discs you see now are what store the information for the case. One disc represents the police report, evidence collected, and testimony from witnesses. The other disc represents the defense. Both the CA and the defendant's attorney have one of each and these discs must be identical or it will be rejected by the computer."

Trevor noticed the CA holding the four discs up for them to see. He couldn't believe it. This was indeed a circus and the performers were working together in perfect unison. It reminded him of the old monkey dolls holding the musical cymbals out to each side and when you turned it on, the monkey clangs the cymbals together. Trevor laughed at the absurdity, amazed at the metamorphosis the judges had forgone. First, they lost their gaudy wigs still utilized in the old country, next came the robes, and finally, their dignity. He glanced over at the defendant's family who seemed appalled that this case was being narrated in complete disregard to the plight of their situation. He felt sorry for them.

"Now," the tour guide said, "the CA will insert the discs into the system to be analyzed."

On cue, the CA stood up, walked over to the back wall, and placed the discs into the appropriate slots, two on the left side and two on the ride side, and pushed a large button below the screen. Truly, a monkey could have pulled it off as easily. An hourglass appeared on the screen and, within seconds, it stopped as a green light above the screen came on and a strip of paper printed off underneath the screen. The CA stood motionless, awaiting his next cue.

The young female tour guide smiled. "You can see how fast it is. The verdict is already in."

At that, the CA tore off the sheet and read. "In case number 12254, The U.S. versus Robert Finch, the defendant is found guilty as charged and sentenced to five years at Cumberland Federal Correctional Institution."

The CA exited the way he came in and the federal officer, who had never left the room, collected the defendant and led him away as the older woman broke down into more tears. As her family tried to comfort her, the tour guide concluded her presentation, completely oblivious to their emotional state.

"That's it, folks," she said. "Now you have witnessed the precision of the most advanced verdict system ever designed. Please exit the courtroom and take a right, which will take you back to the main entrance. Thank you and have a great day."

Trevor and Radhika returned to her SUV and began the drive back to her house. She seemed to notice that Trevor was in deep thought. "Well, what did you think?" she said.

Trevor turned to look at her. "I am not sure what I think. What do you think?"

Radhika smiled. "I don't know either. But it seems to be working. I think you did a good job designing it."

Trevor couldn't shake the bad feeling he had. "I just do not know. It was over so fast. That guy was surely guilty but it just seemed so heartless. Do you know any trial lawyers?"

She nodded. "Why?"

"What do they say? Do they think the system is fair?" he said.

Radhika nodded again. "Yes, I think so. An attorney at our firm, a guy named Lowenstein, is always bragging on the system. He told me about a trial he had last month where he really believed his client was innocent and said the police had no real evidence. But he was sure that if it went before a jury, he would have been found guilty simply because of his priors. The guy apparently had a long record of not-so-friendly crimes. Lowenstein said that even if he cleaned the guy up and put him in an expensive suit, he still would look like a thug. He had a temper and there was no way he could sit through a trial and hear the prosecutor making accusations about him without blowing up. But it went through this new system and he was found not guilty."

Trevor looked straight ahead as he considered what she was saying. She noticed his expression again.

"That's not to say I am in favor of it, mind you," she said. "I'm just saying that maybe it's going to be OK."

Trevor looked at her and nodded. "Maybe it will."

They drove on to Radhika's house in silence. Trevor did not go back inside, only hugged her, got into his rental car, and drove back to the airport.

CHAPTER

~

TWENTY-FOUR

DUSTIN LOOKED UP at the gray skies. They had been threatening rain all day, but so far so good. He watched Trevor flip the burgers on the grill as he held out his paper plate.

"Raw or crisp?" Trevor said.

Dustin smiled. Even Trevor taking over the grill in his backyard couldn't spoil his mood. Frankie's graduation was all that mattered. "You know me—"

"Yes, I do." Trevor cut him off as he slid the long spatula under the least cooked burger on the grill. "You prefer the ones so rare a good veterinarian could have them back on their feet in no time." He plopped the undercooked slab of meat on Dustin's plate.

Dustin smiled and nodded, wondering how many times he had said that in his life.

"Are you not going to let her out?" Trevor said.

Dustin followed his gaze to where Sadie stared out the back screen door. "She wouldn't come out. She doesn't like crowds. And she doesn't move about too well these days."

"Really?" Trevor said. "She is not that old."

Dustin nodded. "That's true. But the vet told me that because she didn't get the nourishment in her first year like she needed, it has caused problems. We have to keep her on constant meds. I knew the moment Hannah brought her into my house that it wasn't a good idea. That woman cannot take care of herself or her son, much less a dog."

"Who would have thought Frankie's birthday present seven years ago from someone else would have cost you so much money over the years?" Trevor said.

Dustin paused at those words. "Yes, who *would* have thought? And yet, that present didn't cost me as much as your present has from the same birthday."

"What are you talking about?"

"The Flair phone," Dustin said. "Who do you think has been paying the $150 monthly fee since the original activation?"

Trevor ignored the question. "So, what is the deal with Hannah?" Trevor said.

Dustin looked over to where Frankie was playing with Becky and Vicki. He was raising his arms up and playing the monster game, much like Dustin always did, causing them to scream and run behind their grandma for help. Sophia and Carol sat in lawn chairs and chatted. He shook his head. "I don't even know. All I've heard is that she didn't last long with the Air Force guy but found her another one over there and stayed. It's been about three years and I think she's called maybe four times. Sophia chewed her out when she said she wasn't going to be able to make it for Frankie's graduation. We offered to pay for her plane ticket but she said she couldn't leave."

Trevor returned his attention to the grill. "I feel bad for the little guy," he said. "Hannah was not much of a mother, but she was the only one he had."

Frankie came running to the grill and up to Dustin. "I got to get going."

"Going?" Trevor said. "This is your party. What do you mean 'going'?"

Frankie avoided the question. "Thanks for the graduation gift, Uncle Tre."

He wasn't getting off that easily as Trevor gave him a hard stare.

"He's going to Panama City Beach with some friends," Dustin said, knowing how Trevor hated for people to ignore questions.

Trevor directed his stare at Dustin. "And you are letting him?"

Dustin shrugged. "He's 18 years old. He's an adult. I don't *let* him do anything."

Trevor shook his head in an exaggerated motion. "Please tell me you have talked with this young man about the birds and the bees. You do have protection, do you not?"

"The birds and the bees?" Frankie said and laughed. "You better believe I have protection." He reached around and pulled his wallet from his back pocket, much to the shock of both uncles. But then he pulled out a box of Benadryl. "I'm always protected from the bees."

Trevor and Dustin both laughed so hard that all five females stopped and stared, obviously wandering what they had missed.

"I have to go." Frankie turned and headed for the back door.

"Are you driving?" Trevor said.

Frankie gave him a thumbs-up and then disappeared into the house.

"So, that clunker you bought him is still running?"

Dustin was still smiling at Frankie's joke. "Yeah, believe it or not."

It was actually not a clunker. Dustin had surprised Frankie and Sophia by paying cash for a 2018 Toyota Graphite Hybrid. Frankie only had to pay for the insurance, which wasn't cheap by any means, and his own gas, which also wasn't cheap.

Trevor chuckled. "I am still surprised you bought a hybrid. You—Mr. There-Is-No-Such-Thing-As-Global-Warming."

Dustin didn't swing at the low pitch. They had had this argument many times.

"You still think one million scientists from 120 different countries who speak 50 different languages got together in a secret meeting just to invent a global conspiracy to trick all conservatives in the world. Amazing. And yet you still do not believe that there is more to the JFK shooting," Trevor said.

Second pitch and Dustin still didn't swing.

"When you have to swim to work every day, you still will not admit it." After the third pitch and no swing, Trevor changed subjects. "Well heck," Trevor said, "if you can keep that antique truck of yours going this long, I guess you can keep his piece of junk on the road."

Dustin laughed. "You need glasses, old man. My old 2002 Ram has been gone for over a year."

Trevor froze, shifted his eyes back and forth, and then stepped back to peer around the side of the house. There in the driveway was an old red Dodge Ram pickup. He looked back at Dustin and turned his hands upside down to signify his confusion.

As Dustin watched the grease drip off the spatula onto the ground, he explained. "It finally konked out on me. That's a new truck. Well, a newer truck. It's a 2006."

Trevor's mouth dropped open. "Oh my. You are full of surprises. That is practically brand new."

Dustin chuckled and turned to go back to join the ladies.

"So, what is Frankie going to do now that he is out of school?"

Dustin turned back around as Carol came back to get another grilled delight. "He's going to go to AUM in the fall. He got a partial scholarship."

Trevor nodded as if to approve. "Still do not know if I would have let him go to Panama City Beach though."

"Well, look at it this way," Dustin said, "It could have been worse. He could have wanted to go to the protestor's camp in D.C."

Everyone knew what he meant. Although the Electronic Verdict machines had now been placed in every courtroom in

America, every federal, state, county, and municipal courtroom in the entire nation, the protests had continued and had turned into a huge movement. The parks in Washington D.C. were now covered with tents and protestors.

Carol grabbed a hotdog off the grill and turned to walk back to her chair. "Well, Tre and his girlfriend can show him how to do it from experience."

Dustin's smile vanished as his eyes followed Carol all the way back to her seat as she sat down, completely oblivious to the hornet's nest she had just kicked.

Trevor's eyes also followed her, his look conveying that he did not believe she would say something like that in front of his brother. And it wasn't even accurate. A few months back, he had told Carol he was going to Washington D.C. to join the protestors, but he had lied. It was when he and Radhika had gone through the tour.

"Is she kidding?" Dustin said.

Trevor cringed. "About which part, brother?"

Dustin persisted. "I don't care about the girlfriend. Tell me you haven't been up there as part of this ridiculous protest."

"Every red-blooded American should be up there right now in defiance of this tyranny," Trevor said as he continued to work the grill. Dustin's silence made him look up.

"You hypocrite," Dustin finally said. "It was you who was always bitching about the system being flawed because of one aspect—human errors. Do you not even remember that? It was you who complained about judges not recusing themselves, about overzealous prosecutors, about people on juries not going by the evidence but by their emotions. I can't believe you."

Dustin's voice had everyone in the yard staring at them again.

"Honey, calm down," Sophia pleaded from across the yard.

"The fact is," Dustin continued without acknowledging

Sophia's request, "the system is working perfectly. There is no longer a backlog in the courts. There are no frivolous and endless appeals. Now you have to have new evidence to be granted an appeal because you can't rely on a different judge, better lawyer, or more sympathetic jury to overturn a previous verdict. And most importantly, murder, rape, assault, and all violent crimes are down over 50% across the entire nation. All crimes are way down because justice is finally working. Criminals are too afraid to commit crimes."

The louder Dustin got, the calmer Trevor stayed. "Fear is not a substitute for justice," Trevor said. "In Iran, the penalty for stealing is having your hand cut off. The penalty for adultery is death. As a result, they have the lowest stats on theft and extramarital affairs in the civilized world. By your logic, that makes their system more perfect than ours."

"Don't you dare compare that crazy part of the world to us," Dustin said. "I've had a lot of friends serve in Iraq and they can attest to how backward that whole region is."

"Au contraire mon frère. Perhaps your friends could tell you about the statue of Hammurabi, which still stands in your Green Zone in Baghdad. Of course, like you, they are probably too ignorant to know its importance."

"And what is its importance?" Dustin said.

Trevor flipped the burgers. "He was the ruler of the Babylon Empire almost 1800 years before your Jesus walked the earth, and his laws, known as Hammurabi's Code, were the first written laws ever recorded and our laws and courts today are based on those stone tablets, which now reside in the Louvre in France. In other words, that backward area you call it was the very building block for our perfect system you used to rave about. I might have complained about the old system, but you embraced it, so I am not the only hypocrite here."

Dustin had had enough. He turned to walk away then stopped and looked back at Trevor. "The old system was out of whack. I witnessed it first-hand. And you of all people know how bad it was. Or do I have to remind you of the Traylor affair?" Huffing as he strolled across the yard, Dustin returned to take the seat by his mom.

Mrs. Davis stared at her oldest son as he sat back down. She didn't have to ask what it was about; everyone could hear Dustin clearly from across the yard. The neighbors didn't have to ask what it was about.

"What's the Traylor affair?" Carol said.

Dustin shook his head.

"It happened ten years ago when Trevor was in the valley at a video store," Mrs. Davis said. "Trevor was picking out a DVD for the night and this guy, William Traylor, came into the store." She looked back at Dustin. "Didn't he go to school with you?"

"Just for a spell," Dustin said. "He dropped out in the tenth grade."

"Tell Carol the rest," Mrs. Davis said, possibly since she couldn't remember the details.

Dustin picked up the story. "William's a troublemaker. He's been in and out of jail many times—theft, assault, marijuana possession, public drunkenness, you name it, always in a fight with someone. He's a short guy, about my height, a few inches shorter than Trevor, lean, wiry, with more tattoos than you can count, and long, straight blond hair that usually comes past his shoulders."

"Oh, I remember this," Sophia said.

Dustin looked up at his wife. He knew she would remember once he started telling the details. "Anyway, it was never clear if he had been drinking that night or was simply showing off for his girlfriend, but he ended up in a heated discussion with Trevor, who, being Trevor, most likely insulted him repeatedly. William punched Trevor in the face and challenged him to a fight. It would have been interesting to see the outcome since

Trevor was clearly bigger and stronger, but William was as mean as a snake—and dirty. But Trevor didn't take the challenge, he did the right thing. He drove to the police station with his new black eye to press battery charges. They told him they didn't do that and he would have to go to the magistrate."

"What is that?" Carol said.

"A magistrate is like a judge in small towns," Dustin said, "usually appointed to that post. The magistrate was out of the office so Trevor filed his request with the secretary. After a week, he hadn't heard from them and William had not been arrested. When he called, the secretary explained that the magistrate had reviewed the case and decided a warrant was not in order."

"What? Why?" said Carol.

Dustin continued. "We weren't sure at first but we finally discovered that this magistrate also had a private practice, which is normal for small town magistrates, and one of his clients was—you guessed it—William Traylor. He was representing him in a custody case where the ex-wife was claiming that William was too violent. Gee, can you imagine? Needless to say, his client being arrested for battery would not have helped his case."

"We sent letters to everyone," Mrs. Davis said, "but nobody did anything."

"So, what finally happened?" Carol said.

"It got worse for a while," Mrs. Davis said. "That guy seemed to find Trevor everywhere and each time he caught him out and about, he taunted and challenged him, calling him a coward among other names. This happened several times when I was with him. It was horrible. There seemed to be no end but one day it just stopped. We saw William in the grocery store one day and William saw us, but to my surprise, he quickly looked away and left the building. We never knew why but that was the end of it. He never messed with Trevor again."

Carol looked shocked. "You think his lawyer finally set him straight?"

"That's what I think," Mrs. Davis said.

Dustin looked at his wife. He knew that Sophia knew why. He had to tell her back then why he had to suddenly go to north Alabama alone. Dustin drove straight to the auto repair shop where William worked. There were four other employees in the shop at the time, including the owner, and everyone stayed out of the way as Dustin made a beeline for William who was standing in front of a car with the hood raised, his eyes opened wide. Dustin walked up and poked him one time in the chest, the impact of which left a golf ball-size bruise that lasted a month, and said only one sentence. "You mess with my brother; you mess with me."

That was what ended it. Dustin knew Trevor was a pain in the ass, but he was *his* pain in the ass.

Trevor had been listening to them rehash the story and his distraction had left some of the meaty treats black on one side.

Sophia got up and walked over to him. "I don't understand, Tre," she said. "I've heard you say that many times, too, that humans were the problem with an otherwise perfect system."

Trevor smiled at Sophia. "I know, honey bunny. You are right. But it was just an embellishment, just a romantic notion like saying we should do away with taxes, which of course we could never do. I only meant that we need to reform the system so that human error is not brazen and flagrant. I never meant we should remove humans from the most important decision in a person's life. This is something I would not even expect to see in a communist country, let alone the most democratically free country in the world."

Sophia nodded. "I agree with you. But there is some good news."

"What is that?" Trevor said.

She pointed to the grill. "I like mine well done."

CHAPTER

TWENTY-FIVE

DUSTIN SAT WITH HIS ARM around Sophia, wishing he could cry, for no other reason than making Sophia feel better. But he had never cried at a funeral, not even his dad's, and it was not something he could even make himself do. The weather was nice and warm, without a cloud in the sky, as they sat underneath the green canopy next to the gravesite where they were about to lower Maria Garza, Sophia's mother. Frankie made up the only other person under the canopy; a handkerchief in one hand, as he had no problem crying over his grandmother's death. Trevor and Mrs. Davis had come down for the wake to pay their respects, but had not stayed for the funeral. Carol and the girls had not made the trip.

It had happened suddenly without warning. At the last minute, she had called Sophia and told her not to come pick her up for Frankie's birthday party, his nineteenth, because she wasn't feeling well. Later that day, Sophia became worried when she called to check on her several times, but no one answered. When they went to her house, they found her in bed not breathing. She was pronounced dead at the hospital.

Most of their family were still in Mexico, or spread out all over the country, so the three of them made up the entire lot of family representatives. There were about ten other friends of Mrs. Garza's there as well, who now stood behind the seats and watched the proceeding. She was being buried beside her late husband, Francesco, Sophia's dad, whom Frankie was named after.

Hannah had missed the wake but arrived the morning of the funeral and now stood in the crowd of friends. Dustin didn't know why she wasn't under the canopy with the rest of the family, nor did he care. Perhaps, since this was her first time back since she had left four years ago for her one-year stint in Texas, she felt like she didn't deserve to be with the rest of them.

When she had shown up at Dustin and Sophia's house that morning, Frankie would not look at her, much less speak to her. It had been over a year since her last phone call, and he simply pretended she didn't exist, much like she had done with him.

Frankie was about to complete his first year of college at AUM and had straight A's so far. Dustin was very proud of him. He had grown out of his rebellious phase and appeared to be a very responsible young man. Only once had he done something to make Dustin fall back into the parental mode and lecture him. A few months earlier, Frankie had sneaked out of the house at 2:00 in the morning to visit his girlfriend. It wasn't that he had to sneak out; he just didn't want Dustin to know where he was going at that hour since his girlfriend was still in high school, and more importantly at the time, was still 17 years old. Dustin had warned Frankie about being careful since he was 18 and she was still 17, but young love is hard to contain. When her parents caught him sneaking in her window, however, that's when it hit the fan.

What made it worse for Dustin was that he was asleep in the living room when it happened. He had finally quit the contract job with the newspaper, or rather it had quit him when the newspaper decided they could hire employees to do the same job for much less than the contractors made, so he didn't have to get up at strange hours like he had for so many years. But he had gained a little weight over the years, and hardly ever visited the gym anymore, and his snoring had progressed to the point where Sophia couldn't get any sleep, so Dustin had begun sleeping in the living room on the sofa. And he was always a light sleeper, which made him even more bothered that Frankie had been able to sneak out at all.

After it was over, Dustin and Frankie walked to the truck as Sophia went to speak with Hannah. Dustin watched as they stood by Hannah's car, or at the least the one she was driving, and conversed for several minutes before hugging. Sophia walked back toward them while Hannah stayed standing outside the vehicle. Dustin knew what that meant.

Sophia's eyes were totally red as she walked up to Frankie. She tried to convey Hannah's wishes, but couldn't speak at the moment.

Dustin helped her. "Is she going back today?"

Sophia had her head down with a tissue wiping her eyes. All she could do was nod.

Dustin looked at Frankie. "Maybe you should—"

Frankie's glare cut him off.

Dustin tried a different approach. "Everyone is hurting right now. You might regret not taking this opportunity."

Frankie stared in the direction of his mom for almost a full minute then slowly walked over to where she stood. Dustin watched as they stood and talked for several minutes. Several times Hannah reached up one arm, as if hoping Frankie would take the cue and embrace her. He never did. Finally, he turned and walked back.

"We're going to have lunch somewhere," Frankie said, trying to maintain his composure.

Sophia started to cry again as Dustin nodded his understanding. "We'll see you at home later then, OK?" Dustin said.

Frankie walked back, got into the car, and they drove away.

Dustin and Sophia went home. A few hours later, when Frankie hadn't returned, Dustin looked outside and noticed his car was gone. He guessed he needed some alone time.

Frankie didn't return until three days later on a Friday. He was still wearing his clothes from the funeral. He changed and left again, not coming back until Sunday night. Dustin left him alone, even though he was worried about him. By Monday, everything seemed to go back to normal. Frankie had begun going to classes again and working with Dustin on the lawn service on Mondays and Wednesdays, since he only had one class those days and it was an evening class.

Thursday at 5:30 p.m., Dustin came home with the truck, pulling the lawn service trailer. He backed into his driveway, parking the trailer beside the house as always. As he exited the truck, two police cars pulled up and parked on the edge of the road in front of his house, then a third car, a black sedan. Four police officers got out and walked toward the house. Two walked right past Dustin and headed for the back.

"What the hell's going on?" Dustin said.

The officers ignored him and the ones on the front porch started knocking on the door.

Dustin walked up to the steps. "I asked you what the hell you're doing."

The officers turned to look at him and then looked past him toward the black car. Dustin turned to see a man in a dark blue suit get of that car and walk toward him. The man was tall and broad, bald, and had a gun on one side and a badge hanging from his belt on the other.

"I'm Detective Dillard," the man said, extending his hand.

Dustin ignored the offer. "What's going on? This is my house."

The detective withdrew his hand. "We're looking for Francesco Garza. Do you know him?"

"That's my nephew," Dustin said. "But you guys must have the wrong guy. What do you want with him?"

"We just need to ask him some questions. Does he live here?" the detective said.

Dustin looked at the two police officers on the porch with their guns drawn and he knew there were two more in the rear of the house. "Yes, he lives here, but he's in college right now."

"And you are?"

"Dustin Davis. I'm his uncle."

The detective nodded. "Do you mind if we look inside?"

Dustin reached into his pocket and took out his keys and held the front door key up for the detective. He took it from Dustin and held it out as one of the officers came down and took it from him. The officer opened the front door and went inside.

"Are you going to tell me what this is about?" Dustin said.

"We just need to ask him some questions," the detective repeated.

The officers came out of the house and holstered their firearms. "There's no one here."

"Where is your nephew right now?" Detective Dillard said.

"I told you already, he's in school. He doesn't get home until around seven o'clock tonight. If you want, I'll bring him down to the station as soon as he gets home."

The detective nodded. "I appreciate that. Where does he go to school?"

"AUM," Dustin said.

"What class is he in now? Do you know?"

Dustin thought. "Uh, he has a chemistry lab right now."

"Do you know where he was last night around 2:30 in the morning?" Dillard said.

Dustin nodded. "Here asleep."

The detective looked at Dustin for a second. "OK. I'm going to have an officer here take a statement from you." He motioned to one of the officers who came down and pulled out a notepad.

As Dustin began to answer the officer's questions, the detective walked away and pulled out his cell phone. Dustin watched him closely as he spoke, wondering who he was calling.

After the call ended, he walked back over.

"OK, Mr. Davis. Thank you for your time." He motioned for the officers and they radioed the ones in the back of the house.

As they all started toward their cars, Dustin said, "Do you still want me to bring him down when he gets in?"

"Yes," the detective said. "That would be great."

Dustin watched as they got into their cars and drove away. He took out his phone and sent a text to Frankie and Sophia.

Sophia was already on her way home when she received the text. When she got there, Dustin explained what had happened. Her expression was of shock.

At 7:30, Frankie still wasn't home. Dustin was getting very worried. At 8:15, his cell phone rang.

"Hello?" Dustin said.

"Uncle Dustin."

"Frankie, where are you?"

"I'm at the police station," he said. "The campus police picked me up at class today and brought me here."

Dustin's face turned red as he realized the detective had lied to him. "We're on our way."

They drove to the police station, went inside, and told them why they were there. After waiting for several minutes, Detective Dillard came and got them then led them to his office. As they all took a seat, Dustin vented.

"You lying jerk. You called the university and had him picked up."

The detective ignored the insult. "We had a warrant for him. That's my job."

Dustin pressed for information but the detective said he couldn't tell them anything. He explained that the Court Administrator would have to set bail and that would be sometime the next morning. They left with their hearts broken that he had to spend the night there. They didn't even get a chance to see him so they could explain that. Dustin was angry with the whole chain of events and it showed.

When they got back home, Sophia looked up a bail bondsman and called. They informed her that bail has to be set before they can bail him out, and wouldn't know the bail until the CA set it. They were both exhausted and finally went to bed.

The bondsman called the next morning at eight o'clock. Dustin had already left three messages on his voicemail. "OK, the CA has set the bail," he said, "and it's not pretty. It's 75,000."

Dustin couldn't believe it. If only they owned their home they could simply sign for it. So many times they had considered it was time to build or buy a new home, and so many times they had just not taken the first steps, but continued to save for that special day.

Dustin pulled back the receiver and stared at it. He looked at Sophia with the same stare. "Holy shit."

When he got off the phone and told Sophia what the bail was, her face dropped. "Maybe we should call Tre."

Dustin looked at her like she was crazy. What did Trevor have to do with any of this? He didn't respond at all but grabbed his wallet, cell phone, keys, and checkbook, and walked out the front door. Sophia followed. They went down to the bondsman's office and wrote out a check for $7,500 dollars, 10% of the total. Between his mom's therapy, which Trevor had never paid half like he promised, the car they had purchased for Frankie, and now this, their dream house was getting further away. But Dustin was not even thinking about this; he just wanted to get Frankie out of there.

An hour later, he was finally released. No one talked at all on the drive home. When they got there, Sophia said she was going to fix breakfast for everyone. Like the car trip, no one talked as they sat and ate. Finally, Dustin broke the stillness.

"What did they say?" he said.

Frankie looked tired and angry. "They arrested me for

armed robbery. They think I robbed a convenience store."

Sophia and Dustin were absolutely stunned.

"That's crazy," Dustin said.

Frankie just nodded.

Sophia got up and put her arms around Frankie. "Honey, have you called your mom?"

He shook his head.

Sophia leaned down. "Don't you think you should?"

"I can't. She lost her phone. Or she doesn't have any minutes or something. She told me she would have to contact me when she got a new one."

Dustin shook his head. "We're going to fix this. Don't worry."

CHAPTER

~

TWENTY-SIX

AFTER DISCUSSING it all weekend, they decided they couldn't leave it in the hands of a court-appointed attorney, and did some research to find a reputable law office in Montgomery that handled such cases.

"Come in and grab a seat." Nolan Blevins was standing behind his desk and motioning to the two seats in front of his desk as the receptionist led them into his office. His coat was on the back of his chair and his long sleeves were rolled up to the elbows, for even though it was a newer office complex, the temperature in the office was not quite comfortable. He was a broad but slender man, 60 years old, with entirely white hair—not gray—but white. It was styled with gel and longer than Dustin thought a professional man should wear it, especially given the age, and that, along with his adolescent smile and bronze skin, which testified of many hours on the golf course, made him appear much younger. He wore a large gold wedding band on the ring finger of his left hand along with a gold Rolex on his left wrist, and a larger gold Harvard class ring on the ring finger of his right hand.

Dustin looked him over carefully. In contrast, Dustin had always appeared older than he was and he detested men wearing jewelry. He didn't even wear his inexpensive wedding band, mainly because he had bent it too many times working on cars, plumbing, or whatever project he was too cheap to contract out. Finally, Sophia had just retired it to her jewelry chest. And watches did not work on Dustin's body. His dad had told him when he was just a kid that the Davis men couldn't wear watches because of the chemical makeup of their bodies, but Dustin, even at that young age, brushed it off as hyperbole. But as he became a man and every watch he ever owned, from cheap digitals to expensive windups, only lasted for about three months and even watch repair shops couldn't make them work again, he realized his dad was telling the truth.

Dustin and Frankie took the two seats and Sophia stood behind Frankie's chair, her hands resting on the back. Mr. Blevins took his seat as well and opened the manila folder on his desk. Dustin looked around the office with its lavish furnishings. There were several diplomas hanging on the wall behind the attorney in expensive frames.

Mr. Blevins looked up at Frankie. "And I suppose you're Mr. Garza?"

Frankie nodded.

"What do you like to be called?" he said.

"Frankie."

"OK, that's what we'll do. I have the file from the CA's office so let me go over that first. It says here the Gasco convenient store on the 2300 block of Atlanta Highway was robbed at gunpoint around two-thirty a.m. on the morning of Thursday, April 26th. An undisclosed amount of cash was taken and you are being charged with that crime. The charge is aggravated robbery, which is a capital offense in the state of Alabama, and carries a 20 year to life sentence if convicted."

Dustin looked back at Sophia as if to make sure she had just heard what he had heard.

"Here's what they have in the way of evidence," Mr. Blevins said. "The clerk on duty said it was a Latino, tall and thin, late teens, driving a black Toyota Graphite. They also have a video of the event." He thumbed through the folder, pulled out several photos, and handed them to Frankie. "Here are some still shots."

Frankie looked at the photos and then to Dustin with a weird look on his face. Dustin reached for the photos, assuming the guy in the picture to be a good likeness, but was also shocked. The photos were so grainy and distorted you could hardly make them out.

Dustin handed the photos to Sophia and looked at the attorney. "Is the video like this?"

Mr. Blevins nodded. "I assume so. Does that look like it could resemble your nephew?"

"Oh yeah." Dustin's voice was dripping with sarcasm. "It looks like it could resemble Elvis Presley, too."

Mr. Blevins didn't smile. "Now I think it would be best to speak with Frankie alone."

Sophia handed the photos back to Mr. Blevins. "Why is that?" she said.

"Because the attorney/client privilege only applies to me. If Frankie says something that could incriminate him and you guys hear it, the CA could make you testify at a deposition and it could be used against him," the attorney said.

Dustin looked hard at Frankie. "Do you want us to leave? If there's anything you need to tell Mr. Blevins that we might not need to hear, let me know."

Frankie looked at Dustin as if he couldn't believe he would ask. "I have nothing to hide, Uncle Dustin. You guys don't need to leave. I haven't done anything."

Mr. Blevins shrugged. "OK, let's get started. First, have you ever been to that convenience store?"

"Yes," Frankie said. "I get gas there all the time." Then he said, "Hey, most of them should know me there. Did the clerk say he recognized the robber?"

Mr. Blevins looked at Frankie with a bit of surprise. It wasn't clear if it was because what Frankie said struck him as something an innocent person would say, or if he was surprised because it was an intelligent question. "No, he didn't, but he's new. It was only his second day of work."

"Can't we have him meet Frankie so he can say it wasn't him?" Sophia said.

"Bad idea," Mr. Blevins said bluntly.

Dustin thought it sounded pretty good. "Why is that a bad idea?"

Mr. Blevins looked at them as if trying to decide how best to explain. "When I was in law school, one of my classes was in this large auditorium-style classroom. One day, as the professor was writing on the chalkboard, a man suddenly rushed in with a gun, robbed the professor of his wallet, and ran out. We were all in shock, not believing what had just happened. Then the professor calmly informed us we had all just been eyewitnesses to a crime—a fake crime. Then he asked us all to write down the physical traits of the robber. There were at least 40 students in that class and he read off at least 40 different descriptions. I didn't even get the guy's hair color right. This exercise was to prove a point: that even though eyewitness testimony is con-sidered the strongest testimony in a court of law, it is in fact the least reliable. To put it bluntly, people are often times trau-matized, at least temporarily, during a stressful event, and their mind plays tricks on them. What if we take Frankie to this guy and the guy's mind convinces him that Frankie looks exactly like the guy who pointed a gun at him. What then?"

Dustin and Sophia didn't answer, but they got the point.

Mr. Blevins said, "The police haven't even asked for a lineup, so let's be thankful." Everyone nodded so he continued. "Let's look at our defense. Where were you at the time of the robbery?"

"I was in bed asleep," Frankie said.

Mr. Blevins looked at Frankie a few seconds as if waiting to see if he was going to elaborate. Seeing Frankie was not, he said, "And you live with your aunt and uncle here. Is that cor-rect?"

Frankie nodded.

"I sleep on the sofa," Dustin said. "And I'm a light sleeper, so I would have known if he had tried to sneak out in the middle of the night."

Both Frankie and Sophia kept their eyes on Mr. Blevins, afraid to look at Dustin as if it would be like they were questioning that statement. Even though what Dustin said was mostly true, they knew it had, in fact, already happened once.

"Do you own a gun?" Mr. Blevins said.

"No, sir," Frankie said.

"Have you ever fired a pistol?"

Frankie looked over at Dustin. "Yes, we used to go to the firing range all the time."

Mr. Blevins looked at Dustin. "Do you own a gun?"

"Yes, I do. I have a 12 gauge shotgun and a 9 millimeter." Then Dustin thought to ask another question. "What type of gun was used in the robbery?"

Mr. Blevins shook his head. "They don't know. The clerk had no idea and the video doesn't show it well enough. But you do drive a black Toyota Graphite, correct?"

"It's midnight blue," Frankie said.

The slight color difference was ignored, meaning it was too close to prove anything. "Do you have any priors at all?" he said.

"No, sir," Frankie said.

"Nothing?"

Frankie thought. "No... Well, I had a speeding ticket once."

Mr. Blevins seemed to think for a second if that was important. "Where? And how fast were you going?"

"Sixty-five on Atlanta Highway."

Mr. Blevins kept reading. "It says here you go to college and are doing well there. And you have a job working for D&S Lawn Service. How long have you been doing that?"

"Since I was seven," Frankie said.

Mr. Blevins looked up and smiled.

Dustin clarified. "That's my business."

"Ah," Mr. Blevins said as he acknowledged. "You have no record at all, no drugs, no fights, no bad reports at high school or college?"

Frankie shook his head.

"I see you're a member of Calvary Baptist Church. Do you attend regularly?" he said.

"I try."

Mr. Blevins sat back in his chair and looked at the three of them, his eyes moving from one to the other and holding that stare for several seconds. "OK, let's get to brass tacks. You have no record, no priors, and that's a great thing. You're a clean-cut college kid who works and goes to church. I'm sure you can produce a lot of character witnesses. In other words, you're an upstanding member of society with a bright future. These are all great things and gives us a lot of bargaining power."

Bargaining power? Dustin leaned forward in his chair. "What do you mean, 'bargaining power'?"

The lawyer looked at Dustin. "I mean it gives me a lot to take to the CA and make a bargain."

Dustin leaned closer. "You mean plea bargain?"

Mr. Blevins made a face as if that was an odd question. "Of course."

"This is crazy," Dustin said a little louder than he intended. "We gave you a $2000 retainer so you could tell my nephew to admit to something he didn't do? He's not going to admit to something he didn't do. If he was going to plead guilty, why would we need you?"

Mr. Blevins remained calm. He seemed to realize he wasn't dealing with people who were in and out of trouble like was the case with his normal clients. "I don't think you understand. You don't want this to go to trial. No one wants to go to trial anymore. It's a whole new ballgame now that it's all electronic. Why do you think the system is not backlogged anymore?"

Dustin couldn't believe what he was hearing. "I thought it was because trials took hardly any time now. Instead of lasting weeks, they're over in a matter of minutes. And there aren't as many appeals now. Isn't that the reason?"

Mr. Blevins shook his head. "That's a small part of it. The real reason is that nobody wants to face Judgment."

Dustin recognized the name from the news. It was what people had started calling the Electronic Verdict machines. They had even started promoting a new reality TV show to begin in the fall titled Judgment, supposedly to replace the void left by all the regular court shows that no longer were broadcast.

"What happens if he pleads guilty?" Sophia said.

Mr. Blevins leaned forward and placed his hands on each side of the folder. "Well, having no priors and going to college and having a regular job is our ace in the hole. I'm pretty sure I can get the CA to accept a plea bargain and reduce the charge to a lesser included offense, say simple robbery, which carries a seven year sentence, of which Frankie would only have to serve three."

"Three years… in prison?" Dustin said. "For something he didn't do?"

Frankie didn't say anything, only looked confused.

Mr. Blevins waited for it to sink in before speaking. "Believe me, if you decide to face Judgment, it could end up being a lot worse."

Frankie finally spoke. "And I suppose it will cost a lot more for a defense?"

The attorney nodded. He noticed their indecisiveness and excused himself while they could talk it over.

"I can't let you guys spend more than you already have," Frankie said after Mr. Blevins exited the room. His eyes conveyed his sincerity.

Dustin was still upset at the entire turn of events, but spoke calmly. "You have no reason to feel guilty, Frankie. You didn't do anything."

"That doesn't seem to matter," Frankie said.

"I don't care. I'm not letting you spend three years in prison for something you didn't do. Right?" Dustin turned to Sophia for support, but she said nothing. "Listen guys, we're going to figure this out. Let me talk to this guy alone."

Sophia and Frankie left and asked Mr. Blevins to go back in.

"I just want to get this straight," Dustin said after Mr. Blevins retook his seat. "You're telling me that with absolutely no hard evidence, no gun, no money, no nothing, and a blurry video, that my nephew could really lose if this went to court."

"That's what I'm telling you," he said.

Dustin could feel the blood building behind his cheeks again. "This is insane. I thought this new system was working."

Mr. Blevins looked at Dustin for a second. "Define working. If you mean making people too afraid to go to court, then yes, it's working. If you mean more accurately dispensing justice, I don't know about that. Things have changed so much. Before, this probably would have gone before a grand jury and they almost always agreed that there was enough evidence to arrest someone. Now, they don't even bother with grand juries. I don't think it would have made it to trial in the old days but the charges might not have even been dropped either. If it had gone to court, a good lawyer could have probably swayed the jury. Now it doesn't matter how good the lawyer is; you can't sway the machine. Now a lawyer is considered good by how well he can bargain with the CA. You have to realize, I'm sure most of my clients are probably guilty, so getting a deal is great for them. I believe Frankie is innocent; I really do. But I have to be honest with you about his chances and his choices."

Dustin began to believe Mr. Blevins. "When does he have

to plead?"

"A week from today."

"Let's say he pleads not guilty," Dustin said, "how long before he would go to trial?"

Mr. Blevins looked long and hard at Dustin. "OK. If he decides to plead not guilty, seeing as how he has no priors and a settled home life, I'm sure the CA will agree that he's not a flight risk and would allow for the maximum 120 days."

Dustin bit his lower lip. "So, that gives us four months. And in that time, Frankie can still change his plea and make a bargain, right?"

Mr. Blevins cocked his head sideways as he considered it. "Yes. The thing is, most defendants, if they wish to plead not guilty, they don't bother with an arraignment. They just send them straight from jail to trial. In the last two years, I've never gone before the CA to plead not guilty."

Dustin got up and extended his hand. "I just want some time to do some research." They shook hands and Dustin turned to walk out then paused. Turning back around, he said, "Something just came to me. I remember one of the reasons they repeated over and over to push this idea of the Electronic Verdict machines was that there were too many corrupt judges and they had too much power. But, if what you say is true and most everyone goes running to the CA just to avoid the system, and these guys are all former judges, then it seems like they now have more power than ever before. These computerized verdict machines have insured that more decisions than ever before are made by humans. Does that sound right?"

Mr. Blevins looked impressed. "I'd say you hit it right on the nose."

Dustin shook his head at the irony. "So, these guys are now literally judge, jury, and executioner. Why are they called Court Administrators?"

The attorney smiled. "Because 'God' was already taken."

CHAPTER

TWENTY-SEVEN

TREVOR SAT at his mother's dining table and listened intensely as she explained everything she could remember from Sophia's phone conversation. "This is ridiculous, Mother. You and I both know Frankie isn't capable of something like that."

His mother nodded as she stared through water-filled eyes.

Trevor tried to offer comfort. "They say they have a good lawyer, so he will do the right thing and prove Frankie's innocence. I am certain they will see the error and drop the charges soon."

His mother smiled as Trevor got up and kissed her on the forehead before walking out.

As Trevor walked back to his house, however, he couldn't help but worry. If what his mother had conveyed was accurate, and Dustin was encouraging Frankie to plead not guilty and go to court, that meant Frankie would go before Trevor's very own creation. Trevor had only seen it in action one time but that was years ago when he and Radhika had gone on the tour and it seemed to work perfectly then. But still, the nagging feeling of guilt tugged at Trevor's conscience. When he got back into his house, he called the only person he could to ask for advice.

"He's going to face Judgment?" Radhika said.

"It appears so," Trevor said. "You told me years ago that one of the partners in your firm liked the system. Is that still the case?"

There was a pause before Radhika answered. "I don't

think so. He doesn't even handle criminal cases anymore, only injury and liability cases. He lost a big case a year ago and was very upset about it and hasn't taken on another case like it. He said it was because there was more money in liability, but it makes me wonder."

"That is odd," Trevor said. "Do you think you could find out more information?"

"Sure," Radhika said. "I have to be in Birmingham next week on Thursday and Friday to close a deal. Why don't I come up to your house on Saturday and I can let you know what I find out, if anything, and it will give me a chance to meet your family."

Trevor liked that idea. "Sounds like a plan."

~

DUSTIN, FRANKIE, AND MR. BLEVINS sat in the court-room waiting for Frankie's arraignment. Lawyers and their clients were called up one at a time to go before the Court Administrator, who sat behind an expensive executive desk in the front section. The only other objects in the front area were a single conference-style table and several chairs on the side of the courtroom, opposite the CA, just inside the enclosed area. There was a black canvas hanging over the back wall.

There were only seven cases and they went in alphabetical order, which meant there were four before Frankie.

The CA opened the first folder. "Matthew Thomas Collins."

A lawyer stood up and walked to the front, his client walking ahead of him. He motioned for his client, a man who appeared to be Dustin's age, to stand at the table. They both stood and waited.

The CA thumbed through the documents in the folder. "Mr. Collins, you have been charged with the distribution of child pornography. How do you plead?"

The lawyer answered. "Sir, on behalf of my client and in accordance with your agreement, I am authorized to plead guilty."

The lawyer walked up and handed the CA a single sheet of paper. The CA looked at the document and pulled one out of the folder and held them side-by-side as if making sure they were identical. He then nodded to the lawyer who returned to his place beside his client.

The CA looked at the man charged. "You understand that by pleading guilty you are waiving your rights to change your plea?"

"Yes, Your Honor," the man said.

The attorney nudged his client.

"I'm sorry. I meant yes, sir."

"Very well. You are hereby guilty of possession of illegal images and sentenced to five years probation. Your attorney will be provided with the terms of this probation, and you will report to a probation officer once a month until this sentence is served."

That was it. The lawyer and client seemed satisfied. Why wouldn't they be? This was the deal the CA had already made with them before today. They left the enclosed area and walked out of the courtroom.

It suddenly dawned on Dustin that there was not even a stenographer present. They were no longer needed. Everything was already written down.

The next three cases proceeded in the same manner. Then he called Frankie.

"Francesco Fidel Garza."

Nolan Blevins and Frankie got up, walked into the front section, and stood at the table.

The CA looked through the file with a puzzled look on his face. Then he looked up at the two men at the table with a scornful gaze. "Francesco, you are charged with armed robbery. How do you plead?"

Mr. Blevins cleared his throat. "Sir, on behalf of my client, we plead not guilty."

The CA stared at them for several seconds as if not believing what he had just heard. "Very well. It will be entered." He took a pen and began to write on the top page in the file.

"Sir," Mr. Blevins said, "We request the maximum time before going to trial."

"On what grounds?" the CA said.

"We need time to properly prepare evidence for this case. And, if you'll notice, my client has no priors and is an upstanding college student and member of society," Mr. Blevins said.

The CA read over the file a little closer. Then he reached into the top drawer of his desk and pulled out a calendar and scanned over it. "Very well. The court date will be set four months from today on August the 11th, 2026."

"Thank you, sir." Mr. Blevins motioned for Frankie to leave the front area as he followed.

Dustin got up and walked out with them.

As they got outside, Mr. Blevins shook Frankie's hand. "We'll stay in touch." Then he shook Dustin's hand. "I hope you know what you're doing.

~

"THANK YOU," Radhika said as Carol handed her a glass of water.

"You're welcome." Carol took her seat again by Trevor on the other side of the large dining table. "I'm glad to finally meet you. Trevor speaks really highly of you."

Radhika smiled. "He speaks highly of you, too." She looked around the large dining room. "You guys have such a beautiful home. I hate the girls couldn't be here. I so wanted to meet them."

Carol nodded. "I wish they could have met you as well. But my mom and dad have been planning this trip to take them to Lake Winnie for months."

"What's that?" Radhika said.

"Lake Winnepesaukah," Trevor said. "It is an amusement park in Rossville, Georgia, up close to Chattanooga. It is really a neat place. Mother used to take me and Dustin there when we were younger."

Radhika smiled as she took a sip of water. "So, tell me about your nephew. Are you 100% sure he's innocent?"

Trevor nodded.

"Absolutely," Carol said. "If you knew Frankie, you wouldn't even ask. The girls love him. He's a great kid."

Radhika looked down at the table before beginning. "Well unfortunately, I haven't been able to find out much. All of the attorneys I knew that handled criminal cases in the past have all given it up."

"Why is that?" Trevor said.

"For one thing," Radhika said, "there just isn't as much work as there used to be. You have to realize that almost all criminal activity is down 50%. So right away, there are half as many cases. Plus, since hardly any cases actually go to court now and are settled with the CA beforehand, lawyers who do handle criminal cases can handle more now than ever. So, for the most part, it's a simple matter of supply and demand."

Trevor searched Radhika's face for expression. "But there is more to it than that, is there not? What do they say about the system? Are they afraid to go in front of Judgment?"

Radhika exhaled deeply. "That seems to be the situation. All I have heard so far is basic gossip and innuendoes. But there certainly seems to be a consensus that facing Judgment is not a pleasant thing."

Carol was confused. "But that's just for people who are

guilty, right?"

Radhika shrugged.

Trevor didn't like the sound of it.

"That's crazy," Carol said. "What kind of morons built this thing?"

Trevor and Radhika's eyes met and they quickly looked away.

"I'm going to try to find out more once I get back to Washington," Radhika said. "I'll do everything I can to help."

Carol smiled and looked at her husband. "You were right. She is wonderful."

They sat and chatted about other things for a while. Then Carol took Radhika on a tour of the house before she had to leave.

CHAPTER

~

TWENTY-EIGHT

FOR THE SECOND TIME, Dustin sat in the observer's section of the courtroom in Montgomery, this time for actual trial cases. He had to see the system at work for himself. He looked around and noticed the place was crowded. He wasn't sure why since there were only five cases scheduled all day. When he had decided to witness a case first hand, he was surprised that they only held court on Tuesdays and Thursdays, and this week both only had a total of nine cases between them.

He had spent 15 hours a day in front of the computer ever since they left the lawyer's office. Sophia had taken over the lawn business completely. Dustin now had three supervisors, one for each crew who could take the trailers home with them, and Sophia worked on the accounts and paperwork. Without the gym or newspaper jobs, Dustin threw himself entirely into this case. He wasn't about to advise his five-feet-eleven, 155 pound nephew to choose three years in a maximum security prison filled with the worst society had to offer, not without exhausting every avenue.

A door opened and an officer led five men, all seemed young and all were dressed in orange jumpsuits with numbers across the chest and the initials ADOC on the back, to a bench in the front left half of the courtroom, just behind the short partition with its ornate wooden gate that led to the front section. No more expensive suits were needed for defendants. Inside that front area was the same conference-style table with four chairs, all facing the back wall. Near the back wall was the small but expensive executive desk. It was nothing like courtrooms used to be set up. But the most obvious difference, the thing that commanded the most attention, was the back wall itself. The black canvas was gone and there was the Electronic Verdict machine; there was Judgment in the flesh. It almost looked like an ATM machine to Dustin. It had a small screen in the center top, and several slots and CPU connectors beneath the screen. A large black button protruded out underneath the screen with a paper slot under that. A large green light adorned the top.

The CA entered through a back door to no fanfare or announcement. He was a short man, in his late sixties Dustin was guessing, with short white hair and a neatly trimmed beard and mustache. Just like at the arraignment, this CA also wore no robes, just a simple suit. No one stood up as he entered and that's when Dustin noticed there was not even a bailiff, but the officer had stayed after showing the defendants where to sit. The CA wasted no time. He sat at the desk, opened the first file on top of the stack, and called out a name.

One of the men on the front row stood up, as did a man in a suit from the right pew adjacent to that one. It was his attorney. He met him in the middle and they both entered the small gate. The young defendant sat down but the attorney opened his briefcase and took out two small computer discs, walked up to the CA, and handed them to him, then returned to take the seat beside his client. The CA stood and inserted the two discs on the right side of the machine, in two separate disc slots. He then took out two discs from his file and inserted them in the left side.

Dustin had read up on the procedure and knew it well. One of the discs represented the evidence as supplied by the police department, and the second represented the defense. Both the CA and attorney had identical discs, and they had to match for Judgment to do its job.

The Court Administrator pushed the center button, an

oversized black monstrosity positioned right beneath the screen. An hourglass appeared on the screen and began to spin. It only made one half turn and disappeared as a green light came on above the screen and a slot just below the giant button spit out a printed tear sheet about five inches wide. The CA tore it off and read.

"Case number 1515, the city of Montgomery versus Darren Michael Jones, the defendant is found guilty and is sentenced to five years to be served at Kilby Correctional facility."

That was it. It was over. Dustin heard a couple begin to cry somewhere on the other side of the room of spectators. The attorney had the young man stand as he stood alongside him with his hand on his shoulder and a "Gee, I'm sorry" look on his face. The young man had a bewildered look on his face as the officer led him to the same door they had entered, and passed him along to another officer waiting outside the door.

The following four cases all progressed in the same fashion, each being found guilty by the ATM machine in the wall. When the last case was over, the CA simply turned and exited the same way he had entered. Dustin looked at his watch—all five cases in less than an hour.

He drove back home with his mind racing. If Mr. Blevins was right, and these men were really guilty, surely they would have jumped at the chance for a deal. Why would they face Judgment unless they were truly innocent? And if they were really innocent then Frankie was really in trouble.

Later that day, Dustin told Sophia and Frankie that he had only watched one case to see how it worked. He didn't want to scare them with the truth. But now things seemed more urgent as Dustin went back to the internet to try to figure out what else to do. He needed to know what the statistics were to understand what their own chances would be to go to trial.

Several days passed as he continued to stay glued to the computer. He was up before Sophia went to work and there in the same position when she came home, and most nights, even there when she went to bed. It had been over a week since the courtroom visit and he was getting frustrated. It was a Saturday and Dustin would not stop even for the weekend.

"Honey, can't you relax and take a break?" Sophia said, "Let's go out and eat tonight."

There was no reply.

She walked over and looked over Dustin's shoulder. "Is there anything I can do to help?"

Dustin leaned his head back and peered up at her. "I don't know if there's anything anyone can do to help. I've tried contacting the courts to get copies of cases, but they denied it. I filed a motion through the Freedom of Information Act, but that only pertains to the federal government. Local governments don't have to share a thing. I was so embarrassed that I didn't even know that. But I need that information so we can determine how serious it is."

Sophia patted him on the shoulders. "I'll make us some lunch." She turned to go into the kitchen. Suddenly, she hurried back to Dustin. "Hey, wait a minute."

Dustin spun around in the chair. He was ready for any idea.

Sophia stared upward as if searching her memory. "You say only the federal government has to share information, right?"

Dustin nodded.

"And you say you need copies of local cases to study?" she said.

Dustin wasn't sure where she was going, but he was glad she seemed optimistic about it. "It doesn't have to be from this area; it can be from any city. The main thing I need to see are similar cases. Why?"

"What was that law you used to talk about back when they first started this thing?" she said. "You know, you said it didn't make sense to you. It had the initials like a doctor."

Dustin was completely confused. The initials of a doctor? Dr? His eyes suddenly lit up. "Oh my God. You're right. DRS—The Data Recording Sharing law. All cities and towns have to provide the federal government with all new laws and the outcome of all court cases. That means the federal government has all the information I need, and that means the Freedom of Information Act applies. You're a genius."

Sophia smiled as Dustin turned back around to the computer. "A kiss would have been nice, but I'm happy that I remembered something that could help."

It was helpful, and if nothing else, it gave Dustin a boost of adrenaline and some direction that he desperately needed.

Several days later, Dustin sat at the table waiting for Sophia to say something. He had petitioned the US government to obtain copies of court cases. It had taken three emails from Mr. Blevins, two times filing the Freedom of Information Act, and over one hundred phone calls for Dustin to succeed. The problem wasn't that the government was not finally cooperating, it was that they refused to provide the files for specific types of cases, and Dustin learned the hard way that the "Freedom" in the Freedom of Information Act only referred to citizens being free to obtain information; it didn't mean the information itself was free. They only agreed to deliver 500 discs at a time, which contained the information of 50 cases each, at the low cost of one dollar per case.

Sophia had been helping Dustin every chance she got. Frankie, likewise, spent every free moment around school and work to help. It had taken almost a month to get this far and they knew time was running out. But the thought of spending $25,000 more made Dustin and Sophia have a conference.

"What do you want me to say? We have to do this," Sophia said.

Dustin smiled at his wife. "You know this will take most of the rest of our savings. Between Frankie's car, the bail, and

Mom's therapy, which Trevor never sent us the check for, this will just about tap us out."

Sophia shook her head and shrugged her shoulders. "What else can we do?"

"Die in this house it looks like," Dustin said as an attempt at levity.

But the decision was made and the discs were ordered.

CHAPTER

TWENTY-NINE

DUSTIN SAT AND STARED at the plain unmarked box he had just opened, the box that had cost him 25 grand. Nothing but a simple mailing sticker adorned the outside. It resembled a box in which a telescope might be shipped. But inside were 500 discs with 25,000 court files.

Sadie sat by Dustin's feet and sniffed the box.

"Crazy, huh, girl?" Dustin said as Sadie looked up at him.

He slid the first one out and placed it in his CD drive. It immediately displayed a list of 50 cases in numerical order of their assigned numbers. He clicked on the first one and it displayed a spreadsheet of the first case. It was a court case involving a domestic dispute. He didn't bother to open the details but rather went back to the menu and clicked on the second. It had to do with a civil case where two brothers were suing over a will. Third case: a custody battle. Fourth case: murder. Fifth: DUI. Sixth: a violation of the noise ordinance in Indiana.

He leaned back in his chair in disbelief. This was ridiculous. Then he had a thought. He picked up the phone and dialed.

"Hello?" Carol said.

"Hey, Carol. This is Dustin. Is Trevor there?"

A few seconds passed. "Hello?" Trevor said.

"Hey Trevor, it's me Dustin. I need your help."

There was silence on the other end of the phone. Finally, Trevor said, "You are asking me for help? Do my ears deceive me?"

"Yeah, I'm asking you for help," Dustin said. He told

Trevor about the entire thing, some of which their mother had already explained to Trevor who had questioned her several times to learn what was going on. But when Dustin told him about Judgment and how long it had taken him to get the government to turn over the court files, Trevor dropped his head. Dustin got to the point. "I have all these court files but they're not listed in any order. I just need the ones involving cases similar to Frankie's."

"For what possible reason?" Trevor said.

Dustin was a little taken aback by the question. "We're trying to determine what course of action to take and time is running out. I think the system is flawed and if I can prove it, maybe I can keep Frankie from serving time for a crime he didn't commit. That's the reason."

Trevor didn't say anything. Everything he had now in life seemed to dangle from that secrecy clause in the government contract. And it wasn't just losing his money. Trevor had learned the hard way about the kind of people they were dealing with. Ever since he had returned home, often he still woke up in the middle of the night with cold sweats after having the same nightmare—he was back in that basement trying hard to hide. Only in his dreams, he never made it out. He could only sit up in bed after he jolted awake and stare into the darkness because he could never get back to sleep after that.

Dustin wondered if he had hung up. "Are you there?"

"Yes, I am still here," Trevor said. "I am just not sure what you want me to do. Was it not you who said this system was perfect? Is that not what you kept saying?"

Dustin couldn't believe what he was hearing. "I didn't call you to have an argument. I need you to write a program that will scan these discs for the appropriate cases. That's all I'm asking."

"I would not know how to do that," Trevor said.

Dustin held the phone to his head in shock, which started to manifest itself into anger. He had never heard Trevor say he couldn't do something, especially when it came to programming. "What the hell's the matter with you? This is Frankie we're talking about. You remember him, don't you?"

"I know who we are talking about, brother," Trevor said. "I love Frankie. I would do anything for him. I just do not know how to do what you are asking. If you need money—"

Dustin hung up, his face red and pulse racing. Trevor had never been there for him, why did he think he would now? He clicked on the seventh case and continued this all day.

Later that night, about 2:00 a.m., Sophia awoke and realized Dustin wasn't snoring. She walked into the living room and saw the light from the computer and desk light. She walked over and put her hands on Dustin's shoulders. He kept studying the screen without looking up.

"Honey, it's late," she said.

"OK, check this out," Dustin said. He pointed to a notebook under the desk light. "I started just going through and looking for L's."

Sophia leaned over to see the scribbling on the notebook. "What am I looking at? What does 'L's' mean?"

"Latinos," Dustin said. "The files are in no order at all. They are not in chronological order or categorized by area. I have to just search through until I see a relevant case. Here's what I have discovered. Going back three years ago, when Judgment was first introduced, there were a lot more cases then, and the case outcomes all matched the evidence. If there was strong evidence against the defendant, they were found guilty. If the evidence was weak, they were exonerated. It's pretty consistent. But as time progresses and the cases get more recent, there becomes fewer cases and the percentage of guilty verdicts increases—a lot, regardless of the evidence. In the last year, in every criminal case involving a Latino, they have been found guilty, some with hardly any evidence at all. The system is supposed to base verdicts on precedence, and it's supposed to be able to learn, so I'm wondering if it's taking the person's race into account as well. I mean, come on, every Latino in the world can't be guilty."

Sophia looked again at the notebook. "Every case in the last year from anywhere in the country involving a Latino ended with a guilty verdict?"

Dustin nodded.

"What about the B's?" she said.

"What do you mean?"

Sophia still stared at the notebook. "Maybe it's not just Latinos but all minorities."

Dustin's eyes had huge bags under them as he looked at her as if wondering why he hadn't thought about it. For the next hour, while Sophia looked on, he searched for cases involving black defendants. And likewise, as the cases became more recent, the percentage of guilty increased and all within the last year were found guilty.

"Oh my goodness," Sophia said. "The machine is racist? Is that what you're saying?"

Dustin nodded. "I think so. This means we have something to show. If we can prove to them that the machine is biased, maybe we can get someone to listen."

Then Sophia had a thought. "What about the W's?"

Dustin yawned. "I'm sorry. The what?"

"The W's," she said again.

Dustin was so tired it took a minute to sink in and he laughed. "Oh, you mean the C's." He began to search for cases involving Caucasians. An hour later, he and Sophia both stared at the notebook. It was the exact same pattern.

Sophia was the first to say it. "The system isn't prejudice against minorities or Latinos; it's prejudice against humans."

Dustin finally turned off the computer and went to sleep. He was exhausted but now at least he had a plan, and more importantly, he had proof. Even though it was after four o'clock when he finally went to bed, he was up at seven the next morning, ready to implement his plan.

He opened his Word file and drafted a letter.

> To Whom It May Concern,
>
> I am drafting this letter and sending copies to every congressman and senator in the country. I am also sending a copy to the White House, the Justice Department, CNN, Fox News, as well as MerCorp headquarters. The reason for this letter is to inform you that the Electronic Verdict machines are faulty. I have proof of this and it will be attached to this letter. You will see that not once in the last year has one single defendant been exonerated. If you will notice on the examples I'm including with this letter, some of the cases had no evidence at all, only conjuncture and coincidence. Although I believed this was a good idea in the beginning, I know now that removing human decision-making was a mistake. In the name of justice, I know you will review this information and agree with me that action needs to be taken immediately, at least until measures can be made to insure that American citizens are protected under their constitutional rights, and the Fair and Just Act lives up to its name.
>
> Thank you,
> Dustin Davis

And true to his word, Dustin mailed copies to every place he said he would. He mailed it to 435 members of the House of Representatives, 100 senators, all the major news services he could think of, the White House, the Justice Department, and to MerCorp, the private company that manufactured the Electronic Verdict machines. It took him two days. After that, he doubled up and emailed the same information to the email addresses of each one as well.

When it was over, Dustin slept for 20 straight hours. With two months to go before Frankie's court date, he finally felt he was making progress.

~

TREVOR SAT IN HIS OFFICE as guilt and shame consumed him. He began getting sick to his stomach as he thought of not trying to help Frankie. The entire situation had him very upset. He had not heard back from Radhika since she was at his house, so he decided to give her a call.

"Hello?" she said.

"Hello Radhika. It is Tre. Are you busy?"

"No, not at all," she said. "I just got back in town. I do have some news."

This made Trevor feel a little better, even though he didn't know if the news was bad or good. "Great."

Radhika started to speak but Trevor cut her off.

"Let us not get into it over the phone. I just thought we could have lunch. I can be up there tomorrow if you are available and have time to grab a salad," Trevor said.

Radhika agreed. She shifted around a phone meeting to clear room for a two-hour lunch.

Trevor flew up the next morning and took a cab to her house. He had picked up two deluxe salads from her favorite organic food store and brought them with him.

As they sat at her small metal and glass breakfast table, Trevor told her what was going on with Dustin. "I know he is desperate and he cannot understand why I cannot help. I still cannot believe this is happening. The entire time we were working on this project, I never considered it would ever hit close to home."

"I know you really believe he's innocent," Radhika said, "which means I believe he's innocent, but something tells me that going to trial could end horribly for him."

Trevor's heart sank. "What did you find out?"

Radhika got up and placed her empty Styrofoam container in the trash. When she sat back down, she looked at Trevor with stern eyes. "I have been speaking to a lot of attorneys who handle courtroom cases, though according to them, not near as many as they used to. Like I said before, it mostly seems to all take place behind the scenes with lawyers making deals as fast as they can. From what I understand, facing Judgment is not something you want to do if you can help it. I've heard horror stories. Lawyers think they have a strong case and their clients walk out of the courtroom with serious sentences. And then they can no longer do anything to change it."

Trevor looked down at his half-eaten salad. "That is what I was afraid of. Have you not heard any positive stories? Years ago when you and I first watched the court case, everything seemed to be working fine. What has happened? I mean, surely to goodness someone has figured out a way to make this system work to their advantage."

Radhika shrugged. "I have meetings all this week with trial lawyers who have agreed to share actual documents with me—not the names but details. From what I gather from speaking to them on the phone, they're ready to throw in the towel. One guy told me that whenever he cannot make a client decide to cop a plea, he threatens to drop the case. He said it might be unethical, but he doesn't want them going to prison with long sentences when it can be avoided. I will let you know what I can find out. I know time is of the essence. But how are we supposed to communicate? I know you don't want to talk over the phone about this and emails are even more risky."

Trevor nodded. "That is true. That does pose a dilemma, one I had not considered," he said.

They both sat there in silence as Trevor took a few more bites. As he was thinking of Frankie and his brother, he got an idea. "I think I have the solution," Trevor said with a smile. "Goodwill."

Radhika tilted her head down and peered over her small-framed glasses. "Good will toward men?"

Trevor laughed. "No, my brother is always shopping at the Goodwill and I think we can find our answer there. When is the last time you used a fax machine?"

She smiled. "I'm not even sure what they look like."

Trevor laid out the plan. They would each buy a used fax machine and keep them in their home offices. Whenever one of them needed to convey a message to the other, they would send a text to read: "How are you?" If the other was home, they would send a text back saying "Great and you?" That would mean they have turned on their fax and are awaiting the trans-mission. If the return text read "Busy," it meant they were away from their home and could not receive a fax but would send another text when they were able.

Radhika giggled as Trevor finished.

"What in the world is so funny?" he said.

"Nothing," she said. "It just makes us sound like spies."

CHAPTER

THIRTY

"I DON'T KNOW what else to do, Mom," Dustin said.

Mrs. Davis shook her head. "It just seems so drastic."

Dustin held the phone close to his head as he sat on the edge of the bed, his eyes staring at the floor. "I know. But it's been two weeks since I sent the letters and emails and I haven't gotten one email in return or one phone call or anything. I don't understand it."

"But, Dustin, I thought all the protestors had finally left Washington," his mom said.

Dustin nodded, as if his mom could see him. "Exactly. That's why I figure that one lone idiot out there might get some attention. I'm going to stand out in front of our nation's capitol building waving a sign that says 'Judgment is Corrupt: I have Proof' and I'm going to take a thousand copies of the proof of Judgment's flaws and pass them out to everyone who walks by. It has to get someone's attention. It has to."

After Dustin finished conversing with his mom, he sat there on the bed and stared at the stack of paperwork he had accumulated. It proved unequivocally that the Electronic Verdict machines were sending innocent people to prison. How could this not be vital information? How could everyone in the government ignore such a revelation? Dustin couldn't understand it. He didn't want a medal, applause, or even a pat on the back for being the whistle-blower and bringing to light such an injustice. He wanted one thing—to keep his innocent nephew out of prison. He was going to make sure he was heard. He was going to open people's eyes even if he had to grab their eyelids and force them open.

～

RADHIKA HAD BEEN DOING a lot of research and speaking with as many trial lawyers as she could. Sticking to Trevor's system, she had faxed him a lot of material regarding the concerns being talked about in legal circles. She even had a chance to speak with a retired CA to get a firsthand account of a variety of cases. Tonight she was sending him a list of actual case documents she had received from several trial lawyers that showed beyond a shadow of a doubt that the EV machines were consistently disregarding evidence from the defense.

Trevor sat in his office and watched the sheets one-by-one feed through the antiquated fax machine and spit out the fuzzy printed copies. It was about 8:00 p.m. on a Friday and Radhika had gotten home from work and sent the coded text that she had a fax to send. The cover letter explained that Radhika had been speaking to every trial lawyer she could find and was sending the data from ten cases in which the lawyer had been certain of their client's innocence and confident in their case. All ten had ended with a guilty verdict.

Trevor took the stack of papers over to his desk and studied each once closely. All were criminal cases involving defendants with few or no priors at all. The names were blackened out, as was the age, race, and any information regarding the people involved, but the information he needed was still there. Each case had the shortened version of the police file including evidence, most of the time being flimsy at best. Trevor shook his head. This was not the system he had designed. Something was wrong. Trevor had studied enough cases between his old website business and running tests with the program he designed for the government to know that something was amiss. He could look at the cases and know what his program would predict, and none of these would have been guilty verdicts. Had his system failed or had they altered it in some way? It angered him to think they had intentionally manipulated his creation.

After he had examined all of the reports, which took over an hour, he then noticed the last page and it scared him. The smudgy ink from the fax displayed Radhika's handwriting and read: "Have meeting at 10:00 with executive from MerCorp."

Trevor shook his head as if trying to convey his thoughts on that idea. He quickly scribbled on a piece of paper. His note read: "No, that is not necessary. You have done all you need to do. Thanks." He placed the paper in the fax and dialed Radhika's home number but it never connected, simply continued to ring. He took his cell phone and texted. "How are you?"

He strolled around his office as he waited on the return text. It never came. He looked at the clock—9:15. That meant 10:15 in Washington. He didn't know what to do but he didn't feel comfortable with her meeting with anyone from MerCorp. And why had they agreed to a meeting so late at night? He sent another text. "Lunch plans no good. Please cancel plans."

He paced around the office again, waiting… waiting…. There was no return text. Finally at 10:15, 11:15 Washington time, his phone rang.

"Hey, are you OK?" Trevor said.

"Yes," Radhika said. "I'm sorry to use the phones but I just got your messages."

"No, it is all right," he said. "This is fine. I was so worried about you. I did not see your note until you were already in your meeting. I did not want you to go to MerCorp. I just do not know if they will be receptive to that kind of information." Trevor began to feel guilty that he never explained how he knew they were dangerous.

There was a second of silence before Radhika answered. "I think you're right. I'm a little stressed out right now."

"Why? What happened?" he said.

Radhika took a deep breath and tried to calm down. "I met with this lady and explained the problems I had discovered with the cases. She seemed really interested and kept saying she was glad I had come to them so they could make sure everything was working like it should. She was overly nice but also seemed timid. She kept looking up at this security camera in the ceiling and that was freaking me out a little. Then she just started talking about nonsense, asking me about the weather and other dumb stuff. It seemed like she was stalling, trying to keep me there. I just got up and told her I had to leave. She tried to get me to stay by asking me to go over the documents with her again. I just left. It was really weird."

Trevor was breathing heavy himself as she recounted the story. "I am just glad you are OK."

"Oh my God!" Radhika said.

The hairs on the back of Trevor's neck stood up. "What? What is it?"

Radhika's voice was beginning to crack. "I think I'm being paranoid."

"Why? What happened?" he said.

Radhika was trying to compose herself. "I just met a car and it was driving very slowly. The driver's window was down and I swear it looked like one of those agents from years ago. I'm just losing it, that's all."

Trevor didn't know what to do or say. "Just get home as fast as you can."

"Oh no, they're turning around," she said.

Trevor sat at his desk. His knees were shaking and he couldn't think standing up.

Radhika's voice continued to quiver. "They're coming up behind me."

Trevor was panicking. "Where are you right now?"

"Uh, let me see. I'm not far from MerCorp, south of town.

I'm below Fort Hunt and I just turned onto George Washington Memorial Parkway. I'm right beside the river. Hold on, I've got to get your thing from my purse—"

Suddenly, Trevor heard a loud noise like a collision and Radhika scream. "Radhika?! Radhika?!" He pressed his ear to the phone and listened hard. He could hear Radhika still screaming and then another louder collision—then nothing. The line went dead. Trevor got up and started to leave the office, then sat back down. He didn't know what to do. He took his cell phone and dialed the area code to Radhika's phone followed by 911.

"911. What's your emergency?"

"Is this the Washington area?" Trevor said.

"Yes, it is. What is your emergency?"

Trevor lied and told them a friend had just called saying they had been in a car accident and explained where they were when they called. The 911 operator said she would dispatch an officer to that location. Trevor waited in his office for several more hours, his cell phone in his hand as his time was divided between sitting and pacing the floor. His phone never rang. He stayed up all night. The next morning he continued trying to call Radhika's house and cell phone. Nothing.

The weekend passed with the same results. Nothing. Finally, after two sleepless nights, Monday morning came and he tried her office phone. It went straight to voicemail. He then called the main number to her law firm.

"Rodgers, Murdock & Lowenstein. How can I direct your call?"

Trevor cleared his throat. "Yes, I would like to speak to Radhika Kaur please."

There was silence on the other end. Finally, the receptionist spoke. "Are you a friend or a client?"

"I am a friend. Can I please speak with her?" Trevor said.

More silence, then... "I'm sorry to be the one to inform you, but Radhika was involved in a car accident Friday night.

They think she went to sleep at the wheel. They pulled her car from the river on Saturday. That's all they found. I'm so sorry to be the one to tell you."

Trevor felt like he had been kicked in the gut by a mule. He suddenly felt dizzy. Images of Bradley lying on that cold basement floor flashed in his mind, as did the story Radhika had told him about the car accident.

"May I ask who this is?" the receptionist said.

Trevor hung up the phone, tears streaming down his cheeks. He bent over thinking he was going to pass out. Luckily, he bent over right above the waste basket as his insides erupted without warning.

CHAPTER

THIRTY-ONE

TREVOR SAT AND STARED at his computer screen. He was sick of computers. He was sick to his stomach because of what was happening with Frankie and, because of what had happened to Radhika, he was too afraid to help. He was sick of life. He did not even get up when Carol called him for breakfast an hour ago, which she had ordered even though it was almost noon.

The doorbell rang.

"I'll get it," Carol called out, who had been sitting in the living room watching cartoons with the girls.

Finally. This was the first time she had actually volunteered to get the front door, except the times she knew it was UPS delivering something she had purchased from the Shopping Network. A minute later, she appeared in the front door of his office.

"It's for you, Tre," she said.

Trevor was in no mood for visitors. "Who is it?"

Carol tilted her head to one side and then the other, as if she knew but was trying to remember. "I don't know. They're wearing suits. Maybe it's the IRS."

Yet another jab at Trevor's creative tax filing. He always did his own taxes, although he could certainly afford to hire an accountant, but he didn't think they would be inventive enough.

"Can you at least find out what they want?" he said.

Carol crunched up her face, making wrinkles on each side of her nose. This was what she did when she didn't want to do something. "No. They look kind of scary. One has this big scar across his nose."

Trevor froze. He stared right through Carol. He quickly jumped out of his seat and walked up to Carol so fast it made her take a step backward. "Listen to me," Trevor said in a tone he had never used with Carol before. "Do not ask questions. Get the girls, go out the garage entrance, and drive to your mother's house. Do it now. I will call you later and let you know when you can come home."

Carol's bottom lip began to quiver. She turned and told the girls to come with her. Trevor followed and watched as they disappeared out the kitchen door and into the garage. He noticed his hands were shaking, so he took a deep breath and tried to calm himself. As if in a trance now, he went to the front door.

There were the two agents like before, the tall dark haired agent and the short light haired agent. Daniels and Marks were standing right at the door when Trevor opened it, both smiling. Daniels was carrying a small white bag.

Marks leaned forward with a devious look on his face. "Remember us?"

Trevor scanned over the duo with a disgusted look on his face. Remembering those same words from years ago, he said, "Is that the extent of your greetings?"

Daniels chuckled. "He does remember us. How have you been, Tre? Can we come in?"

Trevor smiled. "Mi Casa Su Casa." He motioned for them to come in and led them to his office. He pointed to the two seats in front of his computer and then sat behind his desk. He felt more comfortable having something between them—anything between them.

Marks took the far seat as Daniels sat in the one closest to the door. Trevor realized he had never seen them any other way—Marks was always to Daniels' right. Daniels looked around at all the Star Wars stuff, focusing several seconds on the R2D2 statue, and smiled. He set the white bag on the desk with a grin. "We brought you some Hot Pockets."

Trevor ignored the bag. "I cannot believe you guys have not retired. The government must keep you supplied with 12-year-old boys."

Marks' smile disappeared.

Daniels laughed. "Boy, I sure have missed your sense of humor."

"What do you want?" Trevor said.

"I like that," Daniels said, looking over at Marks and pointing to Trevor. "Always right to the point. I like that." Then his smile likewise disappeared. "Have you forgotten the secrecy clause of your contract?"

Trevor didn't answer. He knew that by defending himself it would only make him look guilty. And he knew that they knew he had not violated that clause.

Marks leaned a bit forward in his chair. "Your brother's making trouble."

Trevor stared at Marks. "Yes, the man has a tendency to do that."

"He's making a lot of people nervous," Daniels said. "It seems he don't think too highly of your little creation."

Trevor stared at Daniels, then to Marks, then back to Daniels. "He does not care one little bit about Judgment, or how well it works or does not work. All he cares about is his nephew. If you want him to go away, it is real easy. His nephew has been falsely charged with a crime and all he wants is to keep him out of prison. So, if you want this to go away, make the charges go away."

Daniels and Marks looked at each other.

Trevor couldn't believe these men were sitting here in his office and he wanted them as far away from him as possible, but he did recognize an opportunity here and wasn't going to let it pass. "You are the great and powerful agents. I know you can make anything happen. This is an easy one for you and it solves everyone's problems."

Daniels shook his head. "We don't make deals with criminals."

Trevor laughed. "You are the only criminals I know. Frankie is innocent. So, why do you not get on your little phones, call your bosses, and explain to the people who do the thinking for you just how easy this solution is?"

Daniels shook his head again. "No, no, no. You don't understand. See, we've been promoted. We get paid from the neck up now. We run this show. Now let me tell you what you're going to do. You're going to convince your brother to stay away from Washington. He's planning to visit tomorrow and wave his little picket signs out by the United States Capitol. You're going to stop him. We don't care how, but we're making it your responsibility to make sure he doesn't do that."

Trevor did not even know of Dustin's plans, and wondered for a second how they did. "What about Frankie?" he said.

"He pays for his crime," Daniels said.

Trevor stared at Daniels with disdain. It was obvious he didn't like that answer.

Daniels tried to ease his tone. "The CA will make a deal for him and he can do a little time like all good criminals do, and then get on with his life."

Trevor was already dreading his next question. "And what if I cannot change my brother's mind? He is very stubborn."

Daniels smiled again. "Oh, we're betting that you can. You don't want him showing up in Washington tomorrow."

That was not an answer. "What happens if I cannot change his mind?" Trevor repeated.

Marks put the index finger of his right hand and pressed it right up against the scar across the top of his nose, right between the eyes. "Then we'll change his mind for him. And the best way to change a person's mind is to put a hole in it."

Trevor knew the answer but needed to hear them say it.

"I cannot believe you guys are still the dumbest guys I have ever met. I give you an easy way out and you have to take the hard way."

Marks stood up and leaned across the desk. "And afterward, we come back here."

Trevor stared into Marks' eyes for several seconds, then looked over at Daniels who simply shrugged as if to say that was how it was and there was nothing he could do about it.

"Well, gentlemen," Trevor said, getting out of his chair, "this has been real fun. I love reunions. We should try to get together much more often."

Marks stood up straight as Daniels got up as well. "I guess that's our cue," Daniels said.

Trevor walked out the door of his office. "Let me show you guys to the door."

All three walked quietly to the door. Trevor opened the front door and the two agents walked out. Before Daniels got all the way out, he turned back to Trevor. He looked all around the inside of the home and then said, "It's a really nice place you have here, Tre. I know you'll do the right thing."

Trevor said nothing. He stood in the doorway and watched the two men get back into their car and drive away. Only when the car was past his mother's house and completely out of sight did he close the door and walk back inside. His hands began to shake again. He couldn't believe what had just happened. He hated those guys. He hated Judgment. He hated the government. And he hated that Dustin had brought these men back into his life.

He went back to his office and sat down and took a deep breath. What to do? What to do? He was upset with Dustin and his obsessive compulsive nature. Why couldn't he just do what everyone else does? Why couldn't he just take his lumps and go on with life? He stared at his computer as if it was the culprit, as if it was to blame for everything. He knew what he had to do but he hated it. He took out his cell phone and dialed.

"Hello?"

"It is Tre. I am ready to help you."

Dustin was expressionless. "You made it clear there was nothing you could do."

Trevor ignored the shot. "I need you to come up here today. I need you to leave right away."

"I can't do that. I'm leaving in the morning," Dustin said.

Trevor grimaced, realizing Daniels was right. "This is the only chance you have. You have to trust me. It will make sense once I have explained it to you. I am the only one, brother, who can save Frankie."

Dustin paused then said, "Explain it to me now."

"No," Trevor said. "I cannot tell you this over a phone. But I promise you, I can fix everything. Either you can trust me or not trust me. It is your call." Trevor hung up the phone. He imagined his brother calling his wife to ask her for advice. That's the best thing that could happen, since Sophia had always trusted Trevor. When he thought about it, he might have very well washed his hands of his brother years ago, save for her. She had always been the voice of reason and the buffer in their relationship. Now, Trevor knew that bond would help him successfully complete the scheme he was going to attempt to pull off.

He didn't have much time. Turning on the computer, he began searching for airline tickets. When he found what he was looking for, he took out his credit card and typed in the information. When that was over, he opened the rolodex file on his computer and started scanning through the names until he found the one he was looking for—the contact number for Juan Carlos Lemos, the former Navy Seal and merc who had installed his security system. This would be the tricky part. How do you ask someone for something like this? He had no choice; the gears were already in motion. He took a deep breath and dialed his cell phone

"Hey, this is Tre Davis," he said. "You installed my security system several years ago. You said if I ever needed anything, to give you a call. Well, I need something and you are the only person I know that can possibly help. If it is not something you can do, maybe you know someone else. I'm willing to pay whatever it takes."

CHAPTER

~

THIRTY-TWO

TREVOR OPENED THE DOOR and saw Dustin standing there. Knowing he had driven non-stop, he said, "Go ahead, use the bathroom, and then I will meet you in my office."

Dustin did just that then walked in and sat in the same chair Daniels had occupied earlier in the day. "This better be good."

Trevor stared at his older brother who looked older than he actually was. He couldn't believe how Dustin had aged in the last year, or maybe just the last two months since this all happened. He seemed to Trevor to look very tired and the bags under his eyes resembled oysters. Trevor almost felt sorry for him. He pulled a device out of his desk. It was a yellow electronic wand of some kind, about a foot long and two inches wide and two inches thick. It kind of resembled what they use at the airports to scan for weapons. Trevor walked around the desk. "Stand up," he said.

Dustin didn't budge. "You gotta be kidding me. Do you think I'm armed?"

"Do not be melodramatic. I got this from Juan Carlos. This is a bug scanner. I have to make sure you are clean before we can talk. And this device here," Trevor patted a black box on his desk, which was about the size of a toaster, "is called a signal jammer and it blocks all radio and microwave signals, just in case I miss something with this."

Dustin still didn't move. "Look, I don't know where this is going but I don't have time. I don't care if you think the same guys who killed JFK are after you, or if you think the guys who killed Hoffa are after you, but please don't drag me into your delusions."

"Look," Trevor said, "I have just spent the last hour going over every square inch of my house. I am risking my life to help you, so if you do not want to play by the rules, you can get back in your piece of crap truck and get the heck out of here."

Dustin looked at Trevor as if trying to ascertain if he was being serious then reluctantly stood up. Trevor took the device and slowly made his way all over Dustin's body, making him raise his arms and even lift his shoes so he could scan every conceivable place. Satisfied, he sat back down behind his desk.

Dustin just stared at him as if he was crazy. "Can I sit back down now?"

As he sat back down without waiting for confirmation, Trevor began. "What I am about to tell you cannot ever be repeated, even to Sophia. Do you understand?"

Dustin nodded in a lackluster way, which seemed to aggravate Trevor.

"I am not playing games here, brother," Trevor said. "I need your word that what I am about to tell you does not leave this room. And, since what I am about to tell you can get me killed, I would appreciate just a miniscule of maturity. Is that too much to ask?"

Dustin nodded. "OK, I'm sorry. You have my word that what you're about to tell me will not ever leave this room. I promise to not even tell Sophia. Satisfied?"

Apparently that did satisfy Trevor. "I created Judgment."

"What are you talking about?" Dustin said.

Trevor looked all around the office, including the ceiling. "Remember where all this came from?"

Dustin shook his head as if not understanding the question.

"Remember the job I took all those years ago," Trevor

said, "the job with the gaming company that paid me all that money to program a new game for them?"

Dustin nodded. "OK. Yeah. What about it?"

"It was all a lie," Trevor said.

"I don't understand what you're trying to say," Dustin said, "or what it has to do with Frankie. Get to the point."

Trevor held up his hand telling Dustin to be patient and to watch his tone. "It was all a lie. I was contracted by the U.S. government to build a super program, one based on the program from my website that could supposedly predict court cases. I had no idea what they wanted with it until all the talk about the Electronic Verdict machines began."

Dustin watched his brother intensely as he told him everything, from the first visit of the secret agents, the conditions under which they worked, and even about what happened to Bradley. The only thing he couldn't bring himself to tell him was about Radhika, mainly because the guilt was still too strong.

When Trevor finished, he looked down and shook his head. "I have never told anyone this. I could not. And if they find out I spoke of it now, I will lose everything, and I am not just talking about the house and money; I mean everything."

"And that's why all the secrecy?" Dustin said.

Trevor nodded.

"And that's why you had to take down the website?"

Trevor nodded.

"So, what does that all mean?" Dustin said.

Trevor stared at Dustin without even blinking. "It means you cannot go to Washington like you are planning and start a one-man protest rally."

"Mom told you about that?" Dustin said.

Trevor shook his head. "You do not understand. This is not about justice; it never was. It is all about money. That is all everything is always about. MerCorp is secretly owned by the same politicians who pushed the laws through congress. They now provide their service to every state, city, and small town in America, Canada, and Great Britain—for a hefty fee, of course. The cities do not mind because crime has dropped so much. It saves them a ton of money each year. In ten years MerCorp will supply the courtrooms for 50 more countries. You get it? It is a trillion dollar industry. You think they care if the system is working or not working? You think they care that one broken-down hillbilly from the state of Alabama does not want his nephew to go to prison? Do you think they are listening to you shout out that the king is naked?"

Dustin's muscles went from tense to relaxed as he almost appeared to collapse in his chair as his head dropped as well. It was the image of total defeat. He seemed to have to force his tired eyes up to look again at Trevor. "What can we do?"

Trevor's words were sharp and clear. "We can destroy the whole freaking thing."

"How?" Dustin said.

Trevor leaned forward. "I am going to tell you exactly how to do it, but you have to trust me."

Dustin nodded.

Trevor continued. "I have chartered you a small flight from Montgomery to D.C. for Monday morning."

Dustin shook his head. "I'm already going to Washington tomorrow. I'm already booked. I'm arriving at Washington National Airport at three p.m."

"Not anymore." Trevor took out a small brown envelope and handed it to Dustin. "Small flights do not have to report their passengers. I already have it set it for you. You are going to fly into Dulles Airport at noon on Monday. From there you will take a cab to downtown D.C. Tell the driver to take you to the corner of Third Street and Constitution Avenue. That is where you will find the main federal court building where Judgment is kept. I have included plenty of money for everything you might need."

"I thought Judgment was in every courthouse," Dustin said.

Trevor shook his head. "No, there is only one computer. There is nothing more than an information-input-device in each courthouse. All the data is sent instantly to this super computer where the calculations are made and sent directly back to the other courthouses where it prints off the verdicts."

Dustin opened the envelope and saw a stack of cash, twenties and hundreds. Also in the envelope were two keys. He pulled them out and held them up to examine them. He looked at Trevor for clarification.

Trevor took a deep breath. "I am going to tell you exactly what to do, and you must do it exactly like I tell you."

"Should I write this down?" Dustin said.

Trevor looked at his brother like he was learning impaired. How could he be so dumb to be as intelligent as he was? "That is a great idea, brother. That would be great information for someone to find on you. Why do you not just get it printed on a t-shirt? 'Here is how I am going to destroy federal property.'"

"OK, I got it," Dustin said. "Excuse me if I'm just a little distracted."

Trevor got back to the plan. "When you get out of the cab, go into the courthouse. They have cases Monday beginning at one p.m. You will look just like another spectator. Put these two keys on your key chain. You will notice one has a blunt end. That one can be used as a flathead screwdriver."

Dustin looked at the key as Trevor continued.

"You will have to go through a metal detector at the entrance. Everyone puts their keys into a little tray which is slid around the detectors. No one will think to look at these keys. Once inside, proceed down the hall to where everyone else will be going. Go inside, take a seat, and wait for the first case to begin. Then, leave the courtroom and go back into the hall. Turn to your right and at the end of the hall are the bathrooms. There should not be anyone in the halls at this time and you are not visible to the guards from here. If no one is around, take the door just before the bathroom. That is the stairs and it is marked clearly. If there is someone in the hall, go in the bathroom for a while, come back out and try again. Take the stairs down one flight to the lower level. Once you come out of the stairwell, take a right and the very first door on the right is your destination. That is what the other key is for."

"What's in there?" Dustin said.

"It is called a junction room," Trevor said. "It is where all the phone lines, internet lines, and power cables are connected. It is like your utility room at home. It stays locked but never guarded. Open the door with that key, go inside, and close the door behind you. On the wall you will notice three utility boxes built into the wall. Go to the middle one, take the other key, and remove the screws and the front cover. Inside you will see a lot of wires. All of them are white or gray in color, except the one you are looking for. It is a red wire with a black stripe down each side. You might have to loosen the screws where it is connected. But either way, rip it away from its terminal then place the cover back on and exit the building. Take a cab back to the same airport and the pilot will be waiting for you. You will be long gone before they realize anything."

Dustin stared. "What does that wire do?"

"It supplies the power to 12 large fans mounted on the side of the super computer," Trevor said. "That is what keeps it from overheating. They have guards stationed outside the room where Judgment sits, so there is no way to get in there. They have a million safeguards on the actual programs, so there is nothing you can do there. But they are too stupid to realize the real vulnerability."

"That doesn't seem right," Dustin said. "They would figure it out right away, surely."

Trevor shook his head. "It will only take 15 minutes for

the computer to overheat and fry the entire thing: motherboard, memory, and one electronic verdict program. Even if they remember what electrical company they used when they set it up, by the time they get there and figure out what has happened, it will be too late. With the system down, they will be forced to put everything on hold until they can set up the old court system. Cases with flimsy or no evidence, like Frankie's, will be dismissed."

"I don't know if I can do that," Dustin said, "but what choice do I have?"

"Exactly," Trevor said. "Now I need you to repeat it for me. I want to make sure you have it. Say 'this is how I am going to destroy Judgment,' and talk me through it."

Dustin frowned at Trevor. "I got it. I'm not a little kid."

Trevor persisted. "I need you to say it, say it all. There is zero room for error here and I want to make sure you do not go in there with the written instructions in your pocket."

Dustin leaned back in his chair and shook his head. "Fine. Here's how I'm going to destroy Judgment. I'm going to go to the federal courthouse in Washington D.C. on the corner of Third Street and Constitution Avenue. I'm going to pretend I'm a spectator and take a seat inside the courtroom. After the first case begins, I'm going to get up and go to the bathroom at the end of the hall. If no one is around, I'm going to take the stairs to the lower level. When I exit the stairs, I'm going to go right to the first door on the right. I'm going to enter that room and go to the second control panel. I'm going to remove the cover and disconnect the red wire with the black stripe and then replace the cover. That will shut down the cooling fans and cause Judgment to overheat, hence destroying it."

Trevor nodded. "Perfect. Say it again."

After Dustin said it for the second time, their business was over and Trevor walked him to the door. "Good luck."

Dustin turned to smile at his brother. Before Trevor even

realized what was happening, Dustin threw his arms around him. Trevor almost choked up. It was the first time Dustin had hugged him since he was a small boy. As he hugged him back, a single tear rolled down his cheek. He watched as Dustin walked to his truck wiping his own eyes, got in, and drove away.

Trevor went back into his office and turned off the signal jammer and called Carol. "Hey, honey. It is OK for you guys to come home now. In fact, you need to come home with the girls as quickly as possible. We have a lot to do." Trevor hung up and walked out into the large living room and slowly looked all around the walls and ceiling. "You are a beautiful home," he said.

He dialed his cell phone again. "This is Tre. I need you to be here as soon as you can. I need your help." Trevor listened for a few seconds but apparently didn't like what he heard. "I do not care. Are you my lawyer or not? If you would like to remain so, I suggest you be here within thirty minutes."

CHAPTER

THIRTY-THREE

DUSTIN ARRIVED AT DULLES AIRPORT at noon on Monday. He had already contacted a cab company and the driver was waiting for him. Forty-five minutes later he stepped out at the corner of Third and Constitution. He looked at the federal courthouse with awe. The architecture was beautiful. The entrance section was a large circular design full of windows. Dustin walked into the front doors and looked around at the elaborate furnishings. He then noticed the guards at the metal detectors and swallowed hard. He strolled casually toward them and got in line.

A security guard slid an empty plastic tray across to him as he reached the metal frame of a doorway with no walls around it. Dustin placed his wallet and keys in the tray then walked through the detectors. As he came out on the other side, he calmly reached down and grabbed the keys and began to walk away.

"Hey," the guard called out.

Dustin froze then turned around, his heart pounding.

The guard walked right up to him. "You want this?" He held up Dustin's wallet.

Dustin smiled and breathed a sigh of relief. "Yeah, thanks. Might need that." He turned to follow the crowd as the guard resumed his position. He walked by what looked like a round farm silo made of beautiful wood. There were windows made into the design at different levels and it extended to the cathedral ceiling made of glass at the point just above the structure. He continued down the hall, entered the courtroom, and took a seat near the rear. It was still 15 minutes before the scheduled start of the first case so he sat quietly, thinking of what he had to do.

As the room began to fill, seven defendants in orange jumpsuits, similar to those in Montgomery, were led to the front left bench, just like Dustin had witnessed before. He scanned to the right at the seven men in suits occupying the other front pew and knew they had to be the attorneys.

Finally, the CA made his appearance and took his seat. Dustin got up and walked out into the hallway. There was not a soul around so he proceeded directly to the stairs, pushed open the door, and went inside. He looked upward to make sure no one was in the stairwell then quickly walked the steps down to the lower level. He cautiously opened the door and peeked into that hallway. There was no one there. He walked over to the first door on the right and took his keys from his pocket. He found the one Trevor had provided for him and tried to slide it into the lock. It didn't fit. Dustin leaned forward and looked at the lock and then the key. He tried again, this time a little more forcefully.

"FREEZE!"

Dustin jumped. He stood up and turned his head around to try to see. There were four men in completely black unmarked uniforms, wearing body protection, pointing four nine millimeter pistols directly at him. One of them moved in and shoved him up against the door.

"Spread 'em," he said.

Dustin spread his legs as the officer checked him for weapons. He couldn't believe what was happening.

The officer stepped back and told him to put his hands behind his back. Then, he put cuffs on and read him his rights. He asked Dustin if he understood the rights he had just been read. Dustin hadn't even heard them but nodded, his mind still reeling.

A short drive in the back of an unmarked car and they

arrived at the First District police station in downtown D.C. A female police officer took his keys and his wallet, which still had over $200 in cash.

"You'll get your personals back when you leave," she said, "but the money will be applied to your account."

Dustin had no idea what she meant, and the truth was, he didn't care.

He was put into a holding cell with five other guys. The cell appeared be large enough to accommodate 50 people. Dustin laughed as he realized just how effective Judgment really was. He imagined this cell was normally packed back in the old days, but not anymore. Now, as he had bragged about many times before, Judgment was making people too afraid to commit crimes. He had never believed in karma but it starts to ring true when it slaps you in the face.

Dustin realized he had to pee but his hands were still cuffed. They had originally cuffed his hands behind him but soon realized that the thickness of his chest, back, and arms made it very uncomfortable for him, so they had repositioned the cuffs in the front. But why was he still wearing them? No one else in the holding cell was cuffed, and they looked at him as if he was dangerous. He wasn't dangerous; he just had to go to the bathroom. He managed to get the same female officer's attention.

"Ma'am, I have to use the bathroom."

She took her key and removed the cuffs.

"I do get a phone call, right?" Dustin said.

She walked away without answering. Dustin walked through the less-than-crowded cell to the open commode and did his business then sat back down and waited. About an hour later, they brought lunch. For some reason, Dustin was given a diabetic dinner, which smelled worse than anything he had eaten in his four years in the Marines.

Two hours later, they came and got him and took him

for processing, where he was fingerprinted, photographed, and given an orange jumpsuit and rubber sandals. He was then given a pin number for the phones, which worked like a credit card, his $200 already applied to the nonrefundable account. It was a good thing since the calls were very expensive. No wonder other guys weren't rushing to the phones.

After the embarrassing call to Sophia, Dustin was led to a regular cell, which already housed a younger inmate.

"Hey, what you in for?" his young cellmate said.

Dustin stared at the young man. He reminded him of Frankie: tall, slim, and about the same age, only white with blond hair. But he was not in a socializing mood and simply sat on the bottom bunk.

"Just being friendly," the cellmate said.

"For being an idiot," Dustin said.

The boy laughed. "Yeah, that's what we all in for. But what exactly?"

Dustin had to think. He knew why he was arrested but no one had ever told him what the charge was. No one had ever questioned him, not even in the car ride over. Not one 'what do you think you were doing?' type question. That seemed weird. After he didn't answer, the young man seemed to get the drift and didn't speak again.

Dustin looked around at the gloomy room as if the reality still hadn't sunk home. The walls were white at one time, but were covered with so much graffiti that it was hard to tell anymore. In the back of the cell was a three-feet-high partition, which partially concealed a metal toilet. Dustin laughed at the irony. In trying to keep Frankie out of places like this, he now found himself here. He began to think about the earlier events. What had gone wrong? How did the officers get there so fast? And as he sat there in the dimly lit cell, the only light coming from limited bulbs in the hallway, he suddenly thought of an even more important question: Why hadn't they questioned him? It didn't make sense. The arresting officers in black had not asked him what he was doing. No one here at the precinct had questioned him either. Dustin had never been arrested, but he was smart enough to know the procedure. You don't just throw someone in a holding cell without at least minimal interrogation. He couldn't figure it out and was too tired to try. It wasn't so much a physical exhaustion as a mental and emotional one. He had failed; that's all that mattered. That was the bottom line. All the time and money he had spent was for nothing. He had not helped his nephew one iota. He didn't want to think about it anymore. He fell back on the cot and went to sleep.

A few hours later, his cellmate nudged him. "Hey, dude, they here for you."

Dustin sat up and noticed an officer at the door to the cell turning the keys in the lock.

"Come on, Davis. You got visitors," the officer said.

Dustin walked out the door as the officer cuffed him in front again and nudged him forward. Stopping at a metal door, the officer opened the door and motioned for Dustin to go inside.

"You got twenty minutes," the officer said as he closed the door behind him.

Dustin walked over to the table wearing cuffs and the jumpsuit. Sophia began to cry. Dustin was surprised to see Mr. Blevins with her, but was glad he was here.

Mr. Blevins spoke first. "Why?"

Dustin was almost ashamed, but it was a valid question. "I listened to my brother."

Mr. Blevins and Sophia both looked confused by that answer.

"You should have come to me," Mr. Blevins said.

Sophia tried to stop crying so she could speak. "I don't even know what's going on. What does Tre have to do with anything? I thought you were coming up here to protest and get someone's attention."

Dustin didn't have an excuse. He didn't even know what to say.

Mr. Blevins stared at Dustin with sympathetic eyes. "I've sent an email and put in a call to the CA's office. I should hear from them soon. I know you've heard all of this before, but the good news is you don't have any priors so I think we can make a good deal with the CA."

Dustin looked at Mr. Blevins and nodded. "You're my lawyer now as well as Frankie's?"

Mr. Blevins smiled and nodded. "I guess so."

"Yeah, let's do that," Dustin said. "Let's make a deal. I'm sorry I didn't listen to you before. You tell me what to do and I'll do it." Dustin's eyes were dull and void, like a horse that had been broken. There was no longer any spirit.

"Have they told you anything, or questioned you?" Mr. Blevins asked.

Dustin shook his head. "No. They haven't ask me one question."

Mr. Blevins looked at Sophia and then back to Dustin. "That doesn't make any sense. When I let them know I was here, I expected them to lead me to an interrogation room and bring you in there as well so they could question you in my presence. They never let an attorney see his client before they question him because he can coach them as to what to say."

That worried Dustin even more.

"It's going to be all right," Mr. Blevins said. "Everything will work out. Like I said, we can make a deal. The bad thing is, of course, that it was a federal building. But the fact that you weren't successful in whatever it was you were doing— that helps. And the fact that you were trying to break into the jani-tor's closet—that helps, too."

Those words sank in as Dustin looked up at Mr. Blevins with a new awareness. "What did you just say?"

Mr. Blevins looked puzzled as if he wasn't sure what part he was talking about.

"I was trying to break into what room?" Dustin said.

Mr. Blevins raised his eyebrows as he adjusted his glasses and looked at the file. "Yes, the room you were trying to get into is like a stock room where they keep mops, buckets, brooms, and stuff like that."

Dustin dropped his head and began to laugh. Sophia squeezed his hands. Finally, Dustin looked back up, still laughing. "It's OK, Honey. I'm not having a breakdown."

"What is funny?" Mr. Blevins said.

"My brother. My brother is what's funny. Me listening to him and trusting him is an even bigger joke."

A cell phone rang and Mr. Blevins pulled it from his pocket. "It's the CA's office." He stood up and walked away a few feet and answered it.

Dustin looked at Sophia. She was so beautiful. He had forgotten how beautiful she was. He wasn't sure who he had failed more: his nephew or his wife. "I'm going to make this all up to you. When this is over, we're building a new house and I'm going to make sure you're happy."

Sophia's tears started falling again. "I've always been happy."

Dustin started to tell her how much he loved her but Mr. Blevins' voice suddenly grabbed his attention.

"WHAT?" Mr. Blevins walked back and forth. His other words were not quite loud enough for Sophia and Dustin to understand, but there was no mistaking the tone and demeanor. When he hung up the phone, he stood there without moving for several seconds as he could only stare back in their direction. Slowly he walked over, took his seat again, and set his briefcase on the table and pulled out his laptop.

"What's going on?" Dustin said.

Mr. Blevins started punching keys on his computer without looking up.

"What's wrong?" Dustin said.

Mr. Blevins stopped typing and looked Dustin in the eye. "The CA's not making any deal for you."

Sophia grabbed the lawyer around the arm. "Why?"

"He sent an email," Mr. Blevins explained. "Let me find it."

Dustin and Sophia kept watching him as he opened the email and read.

Mr. Blevins stared at the screen. "He's saying that you're now being charged with domestic terrorism and there will be no plea bargain. You're going to face Judgment in one week's time. If convicted, you're facing life without parole."

"IF?" Dustin laughed again. "If I'm convicted? There is no if."

Sophia started crying again. She had a hard time forming words. "You said it was going to be OK. How do we go from OK to domestic terrorism? How can they do that? They can't just make up stuff, can they?"

Mr. Blevins' next word made both of them pause. "They say they have a confession. He sent me a video." He moved the laptop to the side between him and Dustin and faced it so they could all watch as he opened the file. A video began to play as soon as the file opened.

Dustin couldn't believe what he saw. It was him sitting in his brother's office. As the sound came on, he heard his own words again.

Here's how I'm going to destroy Judgment. I'm going to go to the federal courthouse in Washington D.C. on the corner of Third Street and Constitution Avenue. I'm going to pretend I'm a spectator and take a seat inside the courtroom. After the first case begins, I'm going to get up and go to the bathroom at the end of the hall. If no one is around, I'm going to take the stairs to the lower level. When I exit the stairs, I'm going to go right to the first door on the right. I'm going to enter that room and go to the second control panel. I'm going to remove the cover and disconnect the red wire with the black stripe and then replace the cover. That will shut down the cooling fans and cause Judgment to overheat, hence destroying it."

When the video was over, Mr. Blevins and Sophia slowly turned to look at Dustin, who was strangely calm. "I need to know everything," Mr. Blevins said. "I need to know everything that has transpired so I can start building your defense."

Dustin reached back over and took Sophia's hands in his. "I love you."

"Dustin, talk to me," Mr. Blevins said.

Dustin finally looked over at his lawyer. "What's your I.Q., Mr. Blevins? Do you know?"

"No, but what's that have to do with anything?" he said.

Dustin smiled. "But you consider yourself a smart person, don't you?"

Mr. Blevins shrugged. "Sure."

Dustin shook his head. "You're not. Not compared to my brother. If you were to add up the intelligence at this table, it wouldn't come close to Trevor's."

"I don't understand," Sophia said through the tears. "What's going on?"

"Trevor set me up," Dustin said.

Neither Sophia nor Mr. Blevins understood what that meant.

Dustin looked at Sophia. "He set me up to save his own hide, or worse, his money. He doesn't care about me or Frankie. He never has. He planned this whole thing to get me out of the way."

"We still have to prepare a defense. I'm not giving up," Mr. Blevins said.

Dustin looked at Mr. Blevins and smiled. "You're a good man, Nolan. I'm sorry for being such a pain in the ass. I should have listened to you from the beginning."

"What do we do now?" Sophia said.

"I'm going to tell you what to do," Dustin said, "and I expect you to do it. Both of you go back to Montgomery and take care of my nephew. You sit him down and explain things to him. Then, Mr. Blevins, you meet with that CA and make the best deal you can make. Throw yourself on the mercy of the courts. You tell Frankie to be strong and it will be over before he knows it."

The officer that led Dustin to the room stuck his head back in. "Time's up."

Dustin got up and walked away.

"What about you?" Sophia said as the tears continued to stream down her face.

Dustin turned as he was walking out the door. "Take care of my nephew."

CHAPTER

THIRTY-FOUR

"WHAT'S GOING TO HAPPEN to Uncle Dustin?" Frankie said.

Sophia shook her head. She stared down at the open bills on the table and started crying again. It was early morning and she was trying to get their payments caught up before leaving later in the day to go visit Dustin.

"I'm sorry," Frankie said as he put his arm around her.

She dried her eyes and began writing checks again.

"Are you mad at me for this whole thing?" he said.

Sophia looked up at her nephew. "No. Please don't think that. It's not your fault. I'm mad at the world, I guess."

"Are you mad at Uncle Tre?"

Sophia started crying again. She still didn't understand what was happening and she had tried several times to call Tre. Finally, Mrs. Davis had told her he was gone—for good. She didn't know what to do anymore.

The phone rang and she answered it. After only a few seconds, she hung up. "That was Mr. Blevins. He said he has some news but wants us to come down there. I sure hope it is good news."

Frankie nodded as they got up and left right away. Fifteen minutes later they sat in Nolan Blevins' office once again.

Mr. Blevins took a deep breath and delivered the news, which was not good by any stretch of the imagination. Frankie couldn't believe what he had just heard.

Sophia sat and stared at the wall. She couldn't even make

eye contact with anyone.

"When are you going up there?" Mr. Blevins said.

The tears started rolling down her cheeks. She wasn't sure how much a person could cry. Did the body produce an endless supply of tears? She tried to regain her composure. "Today. I have to be at the airport in a couple of hours."

The attorney shook his head and sighed. "I'm sorry. I don't know what to say. I have no idea why this is happening."

Sophia finally looked Mr. Blevins in the eyes. "What do I tell Dustin? What do I tell my husband?"

Mr. Blevins looked down as if searching for the answer. After several seconds, he looked back up and directly at Sophia. "You tell him the truth."

DUSTIN WAS ALMOST in a trance, like he was once in the waiting room of a dentist's office when he had an abscessed tooth and was waiting on his appointment to undergo a root canal. The waiting and anticipation were the worst part, so he blocked it out of his mind, thinking about anything and everything to thwart the images of the horror that awaited him.

That had become Dustin's state of mind. After five days, it had already become routine for him. He sat and stared at the wall most of the day. Other than going to the showers, he never left his cell, not to go to the recreation room or anything. Meals were served three times daily on a paper plate with a plastic fork. Dustin had memorized every scratch on the walls and relived every moment from his life that he could remember, even times from the pig days and the beatings he used to get from his old man. Sometimes feelings of injustice crept into his thoughts and he allowed himself to be the victim, but merely for a second. His thoughts would quickly turn to guilt for having brought this whole thing upon himself, or for having treated his brother so poorly over the years. Maybe he was a jerk like Trevor always claimed. Maybe he had always judged Trevor when he should have simply loved him. Even those thoughts were fleeting as his emotions quickly evolved into anger. Forget judging, forget forgiveness, he wanted retribution. It was always these thoughts that dominated and he went to sleep every night with those feelings giving him focus. He hoped Trevor would be foolish enough to visit him some year down the road. After all, he was going to spend the rest of his life in prison for domestic terrorism, what was one little murder charge on top of that?

At 4:00 p.m., an officer came to his cell door. "You got a visitor."

Dustin was led back to the same room and saw Sophia sitting there again. He went and hugged her for a full minute, then sat at the table across from her.

"I love you," she said with bloodshot eyes.

"I love you, too." Dustin smiled and took her hand in his. She looked as tired as he did. He noticed the gray patch in the center of her hairline above her forehead. For years she had been so adamant about dying that little spot as soon as it was barely visible. He tried not to stare at it but it saddened him to know that things like this didn't matter to her anymore. He looked around the room. "Where's Nolan?"

"He's back home preparing your defense," she said. "He said to be strong and he'll see you on Monday."

He nodded. "I hear they're having a special court session just for me that day. I guess I should feel honored."

Sophia didn't smile. "I don't know what to do. I tried contacting Tre but your mom said he left the country with Carol and the girls."

"Really?" Dustin said. "Maybe we'll see him again someday."

She nodded. "He bought plane tickets that very morning before you met with him. They flew to Miami and no one knows where from there. His lawyer told your mom that he most likely chartered a private plane and there's no telling where they went."

Dustin scoffed. "Just as well. I don't really want to ever see him again."

Sophia started to cry again. "I don't understand what's happening. I don't even know what Tre has to do with all of this, but I can't believe he would betray us like this. I know you two have always argued, but deep down I always thought he was a good person. I just don't know what to do."

"I have an idea for what you can do," Dustin said.

Sophia dried her eyes again and stared at her husband. "What?"

"Burn his house down."

Sophia dropped her head and stared at her lap. Dustin at first thought it was because of his comment then realized something else was wrong.

"What is it? What are you not telling me?" he said.

She looked up again. "Frankie."

Panic shot through Dustin's mind. "What about him? What has happened? Is he OK?"

She nodded and then shook her head. "He's fine, but the CA…"

Dustin was not in a state of mind for more bad news. Had Mr. Blevins not been able to make a good bargain? A thousand thoughts ran through Dustin's mind. "Just tell me," he said.

Tears were running down her face again. "The CA in Montgomery has refused any plea bargain at all. Frankie is going to have to face Judgment as well."

Dustin let go of her hand and sat back in his chair. He wanted to ask why but it was obvious. They were going to hurt him anyway they could. His own eyes dropped as the reality of what she had just told him sank in. Frankie was going to face Judgment. That meant Frankie was going to be found guilty of a crime he didn't commit. That meant his best friend, whom he loved with all his heart, would spend 20 years to life in prison and he was powerless to do anything about it because he was also going to spend life in prison, a totally different prison in a totally different state. He looked at his wife and suddenly realized she was the real victim here. How could she deal with the two men in her life being gone forever? How could she have a life divided between trying to earn a living with no money left in the bank all while trying to manage visiting hours for two different prisons?

"This is all my fault," he said.

Sophia shook her head. "No, that's not true, Dustin. Don't say that. I'm not giving up. I'll make people listen."

"NO!" Dustin yelled, making Sophia jump and the officer stick his head in to check on them. "I'm sorry. I didn't mean to yell. But I can't handle any more bad news and it would kill me if you got into trouble, too. We can't beat this system. Go back to Montgomery and get on with your life."

Sophia stared at her husband. "What are you saying? Is this the speech where you tell me to forget about you, forget about the last 22 years, just remarry and be happy? Is that it?"

Dustin shrugged. He didn't actually know what he was saying. He changed the subject. "How's Mom doing?"

"She's very upset," Sophia said. "She doesn't understand what's going on with both her sons. All she knows is they are both gone and people are telling her that neither are ever coming back."

Dustin felt so badly for his mom. Then he looked at Sophia almost dreading the next question. "How's Sadie?"

Sophia began to cry again.

Dustin reached over and squeezed her hands again. "We might have to think about putting her down."

"What?" Sophia said. "Are you serious?"

"She's always in pain and can't even get onto the sofa anymore. I have to carry her everywhere. What has she been doing the last fews days that I've been gone?"

Sophia dropped her head but didn't answer.

Dustin pressed her. "Tell me."

Sophia dried her eyes. "She's pitiful. She just lies around and won't eat. I have to bring water to her."

Dustin's eyes dropped. "OK. Let's be realistic for a few minutes. OK?"

She nodded.

"We both know I'm not getting out of this. We need to say it out loud. I'm going to be sent to a federal prison for life. We have to prepare for what you should do, which includes deciding what to do with Sadie. I'm sure they will have visiting days or however it works, so I want you to come sparingly. We can no longer afford for you to come all the time. You can bring Mom when you come. That's going to be our life from now on."

Dustin could see her trying hard to fight back the tears. He knew she was trying to be strong for him, for Frankie, for her mother-in-law, and mostly for herself, and he loved her for it. He continued. "We need to figure out what to do with the lawn business. It has a lot of settled accounts, so you can keep it up as long as you like. You do everything anyway. Or you could sell it for a nice profit and get a regular job. What do you think?"

Sophia shook her head. "I like what I do. It pays well and I would prefer to keep it going, at least until I'm old and senile."

Dustin smiled. "Well, the good news is you're halfway there. You're already senile."

Despite the unbearable circumstances, Sophia offered a weak smile. "What do I do if I hear from Tre again?"

Dustin's smile disappeared.

Sophia pressed him. "What do I do about Tre?"

The officer came back in and told him it was time to go. Dustin got up as the officer led him to the door.

"What do I do?" Sophia asked again.

"Burn his house down," Dustin said.

CHAPTER

THIRTY-FIVE

DUSTIN SAT AND STARED at the wall. He hadn't slept all night and now it was only hours away from his court date.

Dustin's cellmate seemed to sense he was in a sad state of mind. "Hey, dude, it's a lot better once you get to the prison. I mean, you'll probably have your own room and can make calls and write letters anytime you want. They have an exercise yard, a library, and a nice activity room."

Dustin tried to smile at his young acquaintance. He still didn't even know his name and felt weird asking after an entire week. "You've been in prison before?"

"Oh yeah. This will be my second stretch. I did a year before," he said.

Dustin looked at him earnestly. "What's it like? I mean, is it as bad as they say? You know, with having to watch your back and being raped and all?"

The kid laughed. "No, man. You been watching too much TV. It ain't like that at all. Most the time people mind they own business. You know? Besides, you a big dude. Ain't nobody gonna mess with you."

Dustin turned back to the wall. "It wasn't me I was worried about."

The time passed and a federal officer showed up to get Dustin, who was cuffed and led to a processing area. From there he was driven to the federal courthouse, the very site of his crime. He was to be the only trial this day, a special session, and instead of being taken around to the side door, it became clear that he was going to be taken in through the spectator entrance.

As they paused before entering the courtroom, Dustin stared down the straight and narrow passage leading through the flock of onlookers tightly packed into the wooden pews of the federal courthouse. Straight and narrow certainly defined Dustin and how he walked through life. You would be hard pressed to find a soul who more laboriously obeyed the rules. But in the flash of an eye, he had veered too far off the road. Maybe life was not a road at all, but like this gathering suggested it could simply be a precarious trail, a worn path through a dense jungle abounding with perils on either side. Or could life be more like a tightrope, rigid and barely flexible, biding its time anticipating that first miscalculated step to upend the journey and turn one's life upside-down? Such was the case with Dustin.

He scanned from wall-to-wall at the array of strange faces of people he didn't know, people who were there just to witness his demise. Then he spotted Sophia and Frankie and was comforted at the only two smiling faces in a sea of indifference. His comfort quickly dissipated, however, as the reality of the surreal came crashing down, and he knew that whatever fate awaited him, also awaited Frankie, whom he had loved like a son from the day he was born. The heaviest burden on his heart right now was not that he was surely doomed to be thrown in prison, but that he had failed to save Frankie from the same fate.

The courtroom was much larger than any he had ever seen. The ceilings were 20 feet high and the beautiful trim work had been created with intricate wood inlays, which had been meticulously polished. People sitting on both sides of the room twisted their bodies to fully rotate their heads to the rear, much like a wedding ceremony where everyone tried to watch the bride walk down the aisle. It almost resembled the sanctuary of a church and reminded Dustin of the day he was baptized. As he stared down the center to the front section, however, he knew it was not salvation awaiting him.

Although there was no smoking in the entire building, the air was thick and musky, almost toxic. Along with the tight prison wear, it was hard to breathe. Dustin looked down at his feet to keep from getting dizzy and the sight of his prison-issued shoes against the carpet gave him balance. The orange sleeves went all the way to the handcuffs on his wrists. He was starting to feel nauseated and hoped he wouldn't have to stand in one place for long.

As if on cue, the federal officer nudged Dustin down the aisle between the mob of observers, through the short wooden gate that separated spectators and participants, and to a chair that rested in the center of the front section. Nolan Blevins sat in the chair next to him and tried to offer a weak smile. Dustin tried to return the smile, although in the back of his mind where demons whisper, he already knew the outcome of this day. Only Dustin and Mr. Blevins occupied the enclosed area.

He stared at the front wall with its built-in computer. Every button, light, and control seemed to emanate with heartless evil, devoid of compassion or mercy. He knew too well that many defendants had faced Judgment in the past three years, most with nowhere near the evidence that now stood stacked against him, and walked away with life in prison.

He closed his eyes and thought back to the events that had brought him here. How could this be his destiny? The whole scenario was so full of irony that he could only shake his head as he prepared to put his life on the line and be judged by this system and this machine.

The CA entered through his door and took a seat at the desk. He opened the file and read. "Case number 12232, The U.S. versus Dustin Robert Davis." He then motioned to Mr. Blevins who got up, walked over, and handed him three discs. One was the police report, one was their defense, and one was the DVD of the recording of Dustin in Trevor's office, the DVD that his brother had so conveniently provided to the police to make sure the nails were driven firmly into his coffin.

Everything Trevor had told him that day was a setup. He knew Dustin's love for Frankie made him easy bait, and he threw him to the wolves. Dustin shook his head, laughing inside at all the metaphors that came to his mind when thinking of his traitorous brother. He wondered if Trevor even knew he had managed to screw Frankie in the process—wondered if he even cared.

The CA took all six discs and placed them in the appropriate slots. The hourglass appeared in the window and began to spin. It was almost over. Seconds later it was still spinning. Dustin stared at the rotating image on the little screen. Something seemed wrong and even the CA turned to look at the screen. It had never taken this long before.

Dustin began to reflect over his life and his brother. He still couldn't believe Trevor would betray him this way. They may have argued about everything but they were still family. It just didn't fit. As he looked up at the screen and saw the hourglass was still spinning, his eyes suddenly shifted to the side as his memory began to wander. He turned to look back at Frankie and Sophia who both looked at him with pitiful eyes. He remembered how well Trevor got along with both of them.

Dustin looked back up at the screen and a huge smile came across his face. He turned to look again at Sophia and Frankie and began to laugh. The CA was already uncomfortable with how long it was taking for Judgment to make a decision, and Dustin's laughter did not seem to go over well with him at all.

Mr. Blevins took his pen and wrote on the legal pad on the table and slid it over in front of Dustin. It read: "What?"

Dustin took the pen and wrote: "My brother is the smartest SOB on earth."

Finally, the hourglass disappeared and the light above the screen came on, signifying the verdict was ready. The little slip of paper printed off beneath the screen and the CA tore it off and looked at it. He looked at it like it was in a foreign language. He looked up as if he wasn't sure what to do. Finally he read: "In case number 12232, The U.S. versus Dustin Robert Davis, the defendant is found... not guilty."

The courtroom erupted with cheers and applause. The CA stared at the cheering crowd in confusion then directed the federal officer to remove the cuffs. The federal officer also looked puzzled. The CA quickly turned and left the room.

Dustin was hugging Mr. Blevins, who was still in shock, as Sophia and Frankie made their way through the still ecstatic crowd. Sophia threw her arms around Dustin and held him close. Dustin reached back and grabbed Frankie and pulled him in as well.

"It's going to be OK." Dustin pulled away to make sure Frankie heard him. "It's going to be OK."

Tears of joy and disbelief were streaming down Sophia's face. "I don't understand. How?"

Dustin beamed with pride. "It was Tre! It was Tre!"

They made their way through the crowd and out through the main entrance of the courthouse. Outside, the sidewalks were filled with cameras and reporters. Dustin held his hands up to block the sun. He hadn't even considered the importance of his trial. Reporters with large microphones tried to push their way up to him. Some yelled out questions from afar. Mr. Blevins tactfully blocked everyone and led them around the side to where his car was parked. As Dustin and Sophia slid into the back seat, he and Frankie got into the front.

Some reporters still hung around outside the car, hoping for an interview. Mr. Blevins turned to face the backseat. "You have to tell me what happened in there."

Dustin looked at Sophia, Frankie then Mr. Blevins as all eyes were on him. He took his fist and gently tapped the side panel on the car door beside him. "Back door."

There was nothing but blank stares.

Dustin laughed. "Back door." He looked at Sophia. "Remember, Tre always installs a back door into every system he designs. Only he knows about it and he can go in and make changes to any program."

"How?" Mr. Blevins said.

"The DVD." Dustin turned to look again at Sophia.

"Oh my gosh," Sophia said. "That's right. Tre said he always hides his best programs on movie DVDs."

Dustin nodded. "He wasn't setting me up; he was using me, using me to get to them." He looked at Mr. Blevins.

"Your brother really is that smart?" Mr. Blevins said.

"Yep," Dustin said, putting his arm around Sophia. "Let's go home."

Before Mr. Blevins could start his car, his cell phone rang. "Hello?"

Dustin and Sophia noticed the intense look on Mr. Blevins' face and watched with interest. What could it be now?

He hung up the phone and turned again to the backseat. "That was Trevor's lawyer."

"Did they find him?" Dustin said, hoping he would be able to thank his brother.

Mr. Blevins shook his head. "No. He doesn't seem to think they'll ever find them. But he called to inform me that before Trevor left the country, he signed his house, car, and all his belongings over to you guys. And he opened a bank account for you in the sum of a quarter million dollars."

Dustin laughed out loud. "That's my brother."

Frankie was staring at his uncle as the tear stains were still clearly visible. "I'm moving with you guys, right?"

Dustin nodded and smiled. Then he thought of something and looked at his wife. "You didn't burn the house down, did you?"

CHAPTER

THIRTY-SIX

TREVOR SAT IN HIS CHAIR with his bare feet in the sand and shifted his eyes between the laptop sitting on his legs and Vicki and Becky trying to build a sand castle. Unlike what he had led everyone to believe, they had not left the country, but had in fact, under an assumed name, purchased a small house on a very secluded beach a few miles above Hollywood, Florida. It was a place where no one could find them... or so he thought.

Two figures appeared from the side of the house, 200 feet away, and began walking slowly in his direction. One of them was shorter with light hair, and the taller one had dark hair. It was obvious they were walking quietly as not to alert him or the little girls.

Trevor had an earpiece to listen privately to the computer, so he never heard them come up behind him. The shorter one with light hair reached around and grabbed him in a choke hold. Trevor didn't flinch. He simply reached up, grabbed the person by the wrist, and kissed their forearm.

The person leaned down and kissed him on the cheek. "Anything good on the news?" Carol asked.

"Same old, same old," Trevor said.

"Look who I found at the front door."

Trevor turned around and smiled. "You found it."

The dark haired person nodded. "You gave good directions. Good thing, too. This is really hidden."

Carol smiled. "Have you met the girls?"

"No, I haven't. I've only seen pictures."

Carol called for the girls to come over. "Vicki, Becky, I want you to meet someone. This is Radhika."

"Hello, Miss Radka," they both said then turned to run back to their sand construction.

"You were right, Tre. You have some beautiful kids," Radhika said.

Trevor looked confused. "I am sorry. You must have me confused with someone else." He took out his wallet and opened it to show his ID. "My name is Matthew—Matthew Jackson. This is my wife, Virginia."

Carol laughed. "You can call me Ginger."

Radhika looked at the very authentic-looking ID. "Sorry. Nice to meet you, Matthew and Ginger."

Carol took Radhika by the arm. "Do you swim?"

Radhika smiled a really big smile. "Oh yes, I swim."

"Great. Come on, let's go put our suits on and hit the waves," Carol said.

Trevor watched them run back to the house. He turned his attention back to the computer and clicked the play button on the news video he was just watching.

"Authorities are still baffled. For the last two days, every trial in every courtroom in the country, and indeed, every country using the Electronic Verdict machines, has ended with a surprising result. When the evidence is entered, each one has printed the same message: 'System Failure.' A spokesperson for MerCorp called it a temporary glitch and has assured the government that they are working night and day until it is back up and running. Top computer experts have been called in and they are confident they can correct it."

Trevor laughed. "Want to bet?"

"Meanwhile, authorities have instructed all local courts to go through and throw out any cases that do not have hard evidence and it's rumored that talks are underway to reinstate judges and reactivate the jury process just in case."

Trevor closed that video and opened another.

"Police are still puzzled over the two bodies found in an abandoned warehouse in downtown Washington D.C. The men have been identified as Sean Patrick Daniels and Carl Fredrick Marks. Both men worked for Homeland Security, but at this time it is unclear exactly which department. Both were found with their hands tied behind their backs and a single bullet wound to the head. A police spokesperson said it was an execution style shooting and they are not ruling out a professional hit. Powder marks suggest they were shot at point-blank range and ballistic reports indicate the ammunition used were odd size bullets for a handgun, larger than 50 caliber. No other information has been made public."

Trevor turned off the computer and took the earpiece from his ear. "Carl Marks? That is too funny. I still like Scarface better."

Carol and Radhika returned wearing their bathing suits carrying a bag with towels and personal items. Trevor couldn't take his eyes off the both of them.

"What are you grinning at?" Carol said.

Trevor turned to look out over the ocean, which was almost perfectly calm and a beautiful bluish-green, then at his six-year-old twin daughters, then at his wife and friend. "What did I ever do to deserve to be surrounded by such beauty?" he said.

"Nothing," both women said and started laughing.

"Come on," said Carol and headed toward the water.

Radhika followed then stopped and walked back to her bag. She kneeled down and took out a long, shiny, cylinder-shaped object with a black rubber piece coming from the center, and handed it to Trevor. "This needs to be refilled." She turned to walk back toward the water where Carol was already splashing around.

Trevor looked at the object in his hand, laughed, and then called out. "It worked, though, did it not?"

Radhika turned around and gave him a thumbs-up. "Yes, it worked perfectly. But I still think SCUMBA is a stupid name."

The End